I0601619

Alexander H. Japp

Some Heresies Dealt With

Alexander H. Japp

Some Heresies Dealt With

ISBN/EAN: 9783337027568

Printed in Europe, USA, Canada, Australia, Japan

Cover: Foto ©Andreas Hilbeck / pixelio.de

More available books at **www.hansebooks.com**

SOME HERESIES

DEALT WITH

BY

ALEXANDER H. JAPP, LL.D., F.R.S.E.

Author of

"LIFE OF DE QUINCEY," "THOREAU: A STUDY," &C., &C.

LONDON

THOMAS BURLEIGH

1899

BRADBURY, AGNEW, & CO. LD., PRINTERS,
LONDON AND TONBRIDGE.

To HERBERT SPENCER, Esq.

Dear Sir,

On July 4th, 1896, you wrote to me, after having glanced at the second of the essays in this volume, as follows : " If, when the article has been revised and type-written, you send it to Mr. Percy W. Bunting, of ' The Contemporary Review,' you may say that I think it is worthy of his attention." Mr. Bunting, notwithstanding my having clipped and pruned it severely, did not think it fit for general reading (though nothing in it is, in my idea, nearly so objectionable as much in a book that every one reads, and is expected, and told that it is his duty to read), so I have restored it to its first condition (which I do hope may not be worse than its last), with a few additional passages ; and now, as the only poor return I can make to you for your appreciation of my little effort, and your great kindness to me—a stranger to you—in regard to it, I dedicate to you this little volume, which contains only a few trifles besides one other longer essay, which Mr. Bunting also declined, though, no doubt, for different reasons than led him to reject the second one, despite your kind recommendation of it.

With profound respect and gratitude,

I remain, Dear Sir,

Yours faithfully,

ALEXANDER H. JAPP.

CONTENTS.

ERRATA.

1. P. 13, 3rd line from bottom of text, Hebrew initial letter should
   be ‏ע‏ (*ayin*), not ‏צ‏ (*sadhe*).

2. In one or two cases, *waw* has been used instead of final *nun*.

3. P. 199, line 7 from top, Stracher should be Strachey.

SOME HERESIES DEALT WITH.

HEBREW "PASSINGS-OVER"
HARMLESS RITES.

MR. ANDREW LANG in the "Contemporary Review" for August, 1896, had an interesting article in which he presented some new and curious facts, suggesting survivals of the ancient and very widespread observance of "passing through the fire," or, more properly, " passing over to the god through the fire." Some of these instances were clearly coloured by later knowledge of herbs and chemicals, or it may be magic and spiritualism ; and, though Mr. Lang dexterously wove his materials together, it may be questioned whether he did not fail to draw the proper inference, and, in vulgar phrase, just a little " put the cart before the horse." He argued from them that probably all the Hebrew " passings through the fire " were of the same or very similar character—I fear rather forgetting some of his own deliverances in "Custom and Myth," as well as in " Myth, Ritual, and Religion "[1]—and actually wound up his article by saying, " At present I think it highly probable that the Jewish ' passing through the fire ' was a *harmless rite*," forgetting the

---

[1] " Myth, Ritual, and Religion," *passim.*

law that all merely ceremonial observances had once a real and serious basis—formulated neatly by Grimm when he says that all superstitions were once parts of serious religion and worship, and all merely formal rites had once a practical bearing, in which he was followed by Nilsson.   As an instance of what is here meant, most anthropologists and sociologists now agree that the practice of throwing shoes, slippers, &c., after the newly-married bridegroom is a survival from the very ancient marriage by capture, as is the custom in some places of actually advancing a party to the house of the bride's father with firearms, &c., which they make a great noise in discharging, while they pretend to carry the bride away as if by force amid cries and missiles thrown after them by the party of the bride's father.   So also with the Parsee ritual, where the bull of the old sacrifice is represented only by a hair of the tail ; or the baked clay offerings to ancestors of Prof. Petrie's New Race, in which meat, fruits, and flowers were well simulated in clay, &c. ; so also with the baked clay votive figures found in tombs in Cyprus and elsewhere.

Now, in his desire to carry out his idea, Mr. Lang even goes so far as to lay it down that *probably* all the " passings through the fire " of the Hebrews were, like these survivals, " harmless rites." I think it could be demonstrated from the Hebrew language itself (with which Mr. Lang confesses himself unacquainted or unfamiliar) that such was very far from being the case. It is quite true that Mr. Lang makes a kind of easy survey of what certain Biblical critics have thought about the " passing through the fire," balances them off, and finds 'tis about even weight ;

so that the way along this line is thus open for him practically to confute himself, and directly to contradict his main positions in " Custom and Myth " and " Myth, Ritual, and Religion." But for any practical purpose in that matter independent study of the Hebrew Scriptures is essential, because the amount of special pleading and dodgery, as the late Mr. Myers, of Keswick, well said in his " Catholic Thoughts," " not only to make Hebraism better than it was, but actually to Christianise it "—to find in it exactly what was sought in order to meet self-interested preconceptions—is more than surprising, is indeed sad and perplexing beyond words, and makes one almost despair of truth and of conscience. So the weighing up and balancing of such authorities does not amount to much, even though done by Mr. Andrew Lang.

Supplementary proofs of my position can be found very near home—in Scotland, in Ireland, and in the Isle of Man, if not in some parts of England. I shall deal with the Hebrew part first.

I.

And, to carry out this programme, let us look in due order first at the Law, and then at the Prophets, and finally at the Poetical Books.

I. Our Authorised Translation is apt to be misleading on some of these points. Look at Exodus xiii. 12. There the Hebrew is וְהַעֲבַרְתָּ כָל־פֶּטֶר רֶחֶם לַיְהֹוָה, which is not " Thou shalt set apart," but " Thou shalt pass-over to Jahwé," &c. If this was originally a merely " harmless rite," what about all the machinery of redeeming ?—a machinery, by the way, which soon came to be complicated by devices of priests and Levites to gain greater revenue to the sanctuary. But it is evident that this redeeming was an after-thought, for Sir John Lubbock has well referred to Lev. xxvii. 28 and 29, where it is written :

"No devoted thing, that a man shall devote unto the Lord of all that he hath, *both of man and beast*, and of the field of his possession, shall be sold or redeemed : every devoted thing is most holy to the Lord.

"None devoted, which shall be devoted of men, shall be redeemed, but shall surely be put to death."

And Sir John rightly drew the conclusion from this (*see* "Origin of Civilisation") that there *were* human sacrifices and *passings-over* to Jahwé among the Hebrews.

It is true that at Exod. xiii. 2 a different word is used, which is perhaps rightly enough translated "sanctify." It is קַדֶּשׁ, but in the light of other things it can only indicate one fact : "*Sacrifice* unto me all the firstborn, whatsoever openeth the womb among the children of Israel, of man and of beast : it is mine."

At Lev. xviii. 21, we read (and surely Moses or another must have been an arrant fool to legislate against what had no existence, according to Mr. Andrew Lang, who quotes this passage with a turn to it) :

"Thou shalt not let any of thy seed pass through the fire to Moloch"; and, strangely enough, in ordinary reference Bibles, a reference is given to 1 Kings xi. 7 : "Then did Solomon build an high place for Chemosh [literally from כמש, to burn—that

is, the burner], the abomination of Moab, . . .
and for Molech, the abomination of the children of
Ammon. And likewise did he for all his strange
wives, which burned incense and sacrificed to their
gods."

Now did Solomon do this with those clear words
from Leviticus and Deuteronomy before him? Let
Mr. Andrew Lang and the Editor of the "Contemporary" answer that—it has a very direct bearing on
our chief point.

Here is another fine specimen of the way in which
the Hebrews in their own book are said to have
followed the strange gods and the strange customs :

"The Sepharvites *burnt their children in fire* to
Adrammelech and Anammelech, the gods of Sephar-
vaim. So they feared Jahwé, and made unto themselves of the lowest of them priests of the high places,
which sacrificed for them in the houses of the high
places."[1]

The word for burnt here is burnt—that is, שָׂרַף—
undoubtedly burnt.

The idea of ransom or redeeming was at the best
a mere expedient—the claim and the right of the
god remained as a matter of principle. When a
Jewish father offered a lamb instead of his son, his
thoughts, if he thought at all, must have led to his
picturing his god as an exactor of blood, of life ; and
substitution, redemption, and ransom after all tell
inevitably of something that went before, as the ram
Abraham offered told of Isaac.[2] But listen to what

---

[1] 2 Kings xvii. 31, 32. Read also vv. 15-17.

[2] I lay no weight here on what Von Bohlen, Ewerbeck, and
Ghillany have said of substitutionary elements in circumcision
and its correspondent substitute, though they were scholars and

Keil—even Keil—has said about the way the priests turned the redeeming business to their own profit :

"The firstlings of unclean animals are to be redeemed according to the valuation of the priest, with the addition of a fifth of the value, and, if this be not done, then it is to be sold according to the valuation. Hereby the earlier law which ordered that an ass should be redeemed with a lamb or else killed (Exod. xiii. 13, xxxiv. 20) is modified in favour of the income of the sanctuary.

"The devoted human being shall be put to death. According to the sound of v. 28 (Lev. xxvii.), it stood free for any Israelite to devote, not only out of his cattle and fields, but even out of human beings that belonged to him, such as slaves or children. הֶחֱרִים, 'devote,' signifies to dedicate to Jehovah in an irredeemable manner, as חֵרֶם, which word denotes what is removed from the use and abuse of men, and given over to God in an irrevocable and irredeemable manner, so that *human beings were killed*, while cattle and other things fell for ever to the sanctuary or were also destroyed for the honour of Jehovah. The last, without doubt, happened only in the case of property of idolaters ; at least, it is only commanded for the complete punishment of idolatrous towns (Deut. xiii. 13). Hence, however, it follows that the vow to 'devote' could only be suspended over persons who obstinately resisted that sanctification of the life to which they were pledged, and that it did not stand free for any one according

thoughtful writers. And to see how real a matter this redeeming of the firstborn was, one has only to read the last section (vv. 44–51) of the iii. chap. of Numbers.

to his pleasure to ' devote ' a person.   Otherwise the
practice might have been misused."[1]

It is a very remarkable fact that both this Hebrew
word חרם and the Greek word *anathema*—'ανάγθημα
and 'ανάθεμα—do not originally mean to curse, to
execrate, but to devote, to give up, to set up, *to offer
in sacrifice*.   Both forms of the Greek word are from
'ανάτίθημι, to lay up, to set up as a votive gift.   The
Hebrew word חרם more especially illustrates this.
It is closely related indeed to the word חרם, high
or devoted ; the idea of being lifted up is essential to
it.   What inference can possibly be drawn from this?
Nothing less than this, that the idea of devoting, or
lifting up in sacrifice—that is, passing through the fire
to the god—by degrees became the very process by
which the displeasure of the god was shown.   " The
lifting up, the devoting, the hanging up in the sun "
before Jahwé as curse, as punishment, was simply the
same process, only with a perverted motive, as the
hanging up in the sun or the passing through the fire
of those who had been devoted to him.   And the question arises—a question I would fain have Mr. Lang to
answer—how far does this really imply that here we
have, as is universally found, when you trace honestly
and independently far enough backward, that gods
uniformly are developed out of demons rejoicing in
such sacrifices, whether they are expiatory as being
devoted to the god, or signs of his displeasure and
cruelty, really two sides of the same character—where
the actual facts beautifully correspond with the
developments of language ?   In the one case you have
a cruel death to expiate the god's anger, or to appease

[1] ii. p. 69.

it, or keep it away ; in the other, you have it expressed
a craving satisfaction in pain, death, punishment.
"Anathema maranatha " (אֲתָא מָרַי) may mean either
blessing from the Lord or cursing from the Lord,
as you care to read it, wherever it appears. It may
well be said of others besides the *manes* or gods of
the Romans that the people, ascribing to them a
love of blood, duly ministered to this love of blood,
and they did it from both sides at once, signified above.

We are clearly told that Ahaz and Manasseh
"burned their sons in the fire," and that the great
majority of the Hebrew monarchs followed the evil
example of their fathers. Solomon, said by some
divines—Dr. Fairbairn for one—to share with David
the honour of exhibiting monotheism at its best and
loftiest, anew set up the fires of Tophet in the valley
of Hinnom—Ge-Hennom, that is, Gehenna—and
Tophet comes from תּוּף, to burn. Jehu, we read,
served the Lord and destroyed Baal and the priests
of Baal by a stratagem, and yet he sacrificed to the
golden calves (bulls) that were in Dan and Bethel,
and we know all too well what that worship implied
—the offering up of the firstborn. Here we have
the dreadful observance on the part of an enemy of
Baal and of the priests of Baal. The explanation,
perhaps, is that there were two Baals: the Syrian
Baal, with which in too many points the earlier
Jahwé was identified ; and the Tyrian Baal—points
which have been ably dealt with by Dr. Oort in his
reply to Professor Dozy, mainly about the religion of
the Simeonites who settled at Mecca. He points
out that while Elijah put to death 450 priests of the
Tyrian Baal, he left untroubled the 400 priests of the

Syrian Baal who, we read, sat or ate at Jezebel's table.

Another point. There are the very best grounds for holding that the account of Abraham's intended sacrifice of Isaac in Gen. xxii. was written in David's age, and written for a purpose—written with a view, indeed, of discouraging the practice, but yet *commending* it, as emanating from a holy and divine impulse, and certainly not condemning it,[1] just as Mr. Farnell proves that the divine and human in sacrifice are involved in each other.

This is a most important matter, as proving by another class of evidence that even in the time of David human sacrifices and "passings through the fire" were common, so as to call for this kind at once of indirect justification, apology, and commendation of substitution.

II.

The point, whether or not there were passings-over to Jahwé or Baal in the time of the Prophets, is not left by any means to inference. Ezekiel is full of it —the horror of it seems literally to have possessed him. His book is red with blood as, according to him, the land was—of human blood, of the blood of children sacrificed—*passed through the fire*. Read the 9th, 16th, 18th, 20th, 23rd, 32nd, and 36th chapters, more especially the 13th to 18th verses of the last-named chapter. The translators have done their level best to hide the enormities of it; but the truth, the dreadful truth, they could not hide. Turn to chapter xvi. 20, 21 : " Thou hast taken thy sons and

[1] Colenso, Pent. v. 178.

thy daughters, . . . and these hast thou sacrificed
unto them to be devoured [devour].   Thou hast *slain*
my children, and delivered them to cause them to
pass through the fire for them."

Again, take this : " Because men say of thee that,
thou art a man-eater (אתי אָדָם אֹכְלֹת), and hast made
thy people childless, I will no more bear the reproach
of thee among the nations [heathen]" (xxxvi. 13, 14).

And here, most assuredly, we have the funniest
perversion for a purpose ever effected by translation
on any book.   The translators in first clause translated by us above insert the word " land "—" Thou
land "—where in the original there is not the least
suggestion of land in any form, and in some editions
with marginal references a reference is given to
Numbers xiii. 32, where the spies report on the land
as eating up men (!).   But a change of subject is
indicated in the Hebrew here by the space or sign of
new paragraph, which is more marked indeed than
it is even at verse 16, of which the Authorised Version
translators take no notice.   In truth, the change
from apostrophising the land to addressing the people
begins at verse 13, and not at verse 16, as the Authorised Version would fain make out, and the connection of ideas with verse 17 is clear : "When the
house of Israel abode in their own land, they defiled
it by their own way and by their doings : their way
was before my face as the uncleanness of a woman
removed.   Wherefore I poured my fury upon them,
for the *blood that they had shed upon the land* (it was in
this sense that the land figuratively ate men), *and for
their idols with which they had polluted it.*   Therefore
I scattered them among the heathen."   As though

the land was blighted and barren because of the curse brought on it by their uncleanness and idolatry. The word for "idols" here, by-the-bye, is גִּלּוּלִים, the essential idea of which is something round—that is, rounded stone, or pole or pillar, as here. To our mind there is no suggestion in the Hebrew to justify the reference to Numbers, as is surely proved by the words : לָכֵן אָדָם לֹא־תֹאכְלִי עוֹד וְגוֹיַךְ לֹא תְכַשְּׁלִי־עוֹד, which is most literally : "Thou shalt not eat men any more, nor be any more cannibal to thy corpses [or bodies]." [1]

The Revised Translation, sad to say, here follows and perpetuates the blunders of the Authorised Version, which is not to be wondered at in a body of men that could change "Unstable as water, thou shalt not excel" to "Thou shalt not attain to any

---

[1] In unpointed Hebrew the plurals of the words גוים and גויה would be very like each other, though גוים could hardly be mistaken for גויך, and certainly גְּוִים (bodies), which is identical, pointed, with גּוֹיִם (peoples, nations, bodies corporate), might very easily be confounded, while in various forms of the words afterwards mistakes might, in pointing, very easily have arisen, not to speak of mistakes in translation—in part, at all events, dictated by preconceptions. (Myers' idea of consciously Christianising Mosaism largely to blame; see "Catholic Thoughts.")

We have a case in which both words occur at Psa. cx. :—

ידין בגוים מלא גויות מחץ ראש על־ארץ רבה,

which Dr. Perowne thus translates :

"He shall judge among the nations,
He hath filled (them) with corpses,
He hath smitten through heads over wide lands."

Bishop Perowne says on מָלֵא ב : "The second accusative is understood, אָדָם, 'He hath filled them [the nations] with corpses,'" the verb being transitive, as often. Others make of מָלֵא an adjective governing גְּוִיּוֹת : "it (the field of battle or the land) is full of corpses."

excellency." They make uncalled-for alterations, and spoil the English ; where very serious altera-tions were wanted they simply let them slide, or trim and half-do, as very notably in the cases of the שעירים and קדשים.

And once more : " They have committed adultery, and blood is on their hands : with their idols they have committed adultery, and have also caused their sons whom they bare unto me to be passed *through the fire and given them for food* " (xxiii. 37).

That looks like "harmless rite," don't it ?—" given them for food "—eating human flesh, even though sacrificially ? *Given them for food !* plainly set down. Does Mr. Andrew Lang regard that as part of a harmless rite, eh, or does he boldly delete that ? Did not Pliny observe with regard to early Italian or Sicilian human sacrifices, that the difference is but small between sacrificing human beings and eating them ? and is this not likely to be true of the custom generally in East as well as in West?

Before you have got over the first twenty verses of Isaiah you find he is on the same key, denouncing thus : " Your hands are full of blood " (i. 15) ; and the second Isaiah or another passes on to the very same thought : at chapter lix. 3, " Your hands are defiled with blood, and your fingers with iniquity." And again, showing clearly what so affected him (lvii. 5), " Enflaming yourselves with idols under every green tree, *slaying the children* in the valleys under the clifts of the rocks."

Jeremiah is quite as definite. He cries out : "They have built the high places of Baal, *to burn their sons with fire, for burnt offerings* unto Baal, which I commanded them not " (xix. 5). Here, be it noticed, they are not burnt in the fire, so that any cover could be given to a mere ceremonial passing or leaping through it, but "burned with fire,"[1] and *for burnt offerings*. If there is any loophole here for Mr. Lang to crawl through, we can't see it. And, besides, what else can mean that prophecy of Jeremiah vii. 31-3: "They have built the high places of Tophet, which is in the valley of the sons of Hinnom, to burn their sons and their daughters in the fire; which I commanded them not. . . . Therefore, behold, the days come when it shall no more be called Tophet, nor the valley of the son of Hinnom, but the *valley of slaughter* "?

The word for burn here is burn, שָׂרַף, and surely Jeremiah knew what that word meant, as well as what he meant to say: so at other parts in Jeremiah and elsewhere; so also at xix. 5, just quoted, and there the word for burnt offerings is burnt offerings = עֹלוֹת. It is exactly the same word, though with the modified spelling, which is used at Judges xi. 31, with reference to the sacrifice of

---

[1] " It is plain from Jer. vii. 31, that the children were really burnt. Such sacrifices were offered to Baal and Molech (Jer. xix. 5, xxxii. 35), and were probably of Canaanite and Ammonite origin. But they were engrafted on the worship of Jahwé, as appears from Micah vi. 7, Jer. xix. 5, Ezek. xx. 25, 26. It is interesting to observe that, according to a view common among scholars, the traces of human sacrifice among the Greeks, *e.g.*, in the Tauropolia at Halæ, in Attica, may have been due to Canaanite, *i.e.*, Phœnician influence." *See* Addis's Hexateuch, ii. p. 107. But we do not quite believe in the much-dwelt-on grafting, since the legislation itself shows such direct protest against practices native to the Hebrews themselves ; and there really can be no kind of reasonable question about this.

Jephthah's daughter, which will show that the practice was early as well as late. The Hebrew is plain ; it is, וְהַעֲלִיתִיהוּ עוֹלָה = and I will offer it a burnt offering.

And if Mr. Andrew Lang will kindly turn to Sir R. Burton's "The Jew, the Gypsy, and El Islam," he will find at p. 11 that this fine Orientalist and daring traveller has no hesitation about the kind of offering which Jephthah made of his daughter in fulfilment of his vow. "Jephthah," he says, "'did with his daughter according to his vow'; that is, *he burnt her to death before* the Lord "—he passed her over to Jahwé through the fire. And surely Mr. Lang will admit that Sir R. Burton knew something about these things, though he asks what nation but the Jews could exult in a Jephthah for doing by his daughter according to his vow.

Two of the most extraordinary mistranslations on any book are to be found in the Authorised Version at Isaiah lxv. 11, where the word מְנִי is rendered number. Did this arise from a confusion of the Hebrew word with מִנְיָן, number, as found at Ezra vi. 17, or what? It is the more surprising that the right word for number comes at the beginning of next verse. מְנִי is not number, but either Meni, the Venus of Babylonia, or one of the Arabian triad of goddesses. Again, (2), because לְגַד looks a little like גַד with the ל, they rendered it "that troop," and though "troop" is the meaning given of Gad in the Bible etymologically, that is not quite correct, any more than is the Bible etymology of Levi : it is rather "good fortune, luck," as in the common phrase בָּא גָד. But it was really הַגַד, the (god of) good fortune, fate—that is, Baal.[1] So that not only do modern divines exercise their ingenuity to refine away the real significance of many phrases in the Hebrew, but the translators do. And many maledictions do they get from me when, in virtue of an old old habit, I read my chapter in the Hebrew Bible of a Sunday afternoon, with the English at my elbow. To an ordinary reader it would not seem that a reference to the Baal rite, with its accompanying and inevitable human sacrifice, lurks in that sentence, but it does, as every Hebraist will admit, and, *pace* Mr. Andrew Lang, my point again is proved even there.

[1] The process of evolution of this word or name, בד, has a curious analogy with that of the Vedic भग (B'aga), and Zend بغ (Baga). The fundamental idea of both is *to bestow, to give;* and from them come the words expressing fortune, prosperity ; precisely as here. B'aga, the son of Aditi, is fortune, happiness, wealth, prosperity ; and hence the derivation *b'agavat*, adorable, and *bagobak'ta*, god-given, *bagodata*, god-made, of which, indeed, *Bagdad* is but a slightly shortened form.

It is surely very remarkable, in connection with this, that शिव, the god Siva, and शिवा, the wife of Siva, in the Sanskrit, are also "prosperous, fortunate."

Quite as remarkable it is that in Arabic وهاب, Vahhab, in precisely the same sense, means Bestower, Prosperer, and is precisely the Semitic equivalent of the Aryan भग, B'aga, and has passed through precisely the same process.

" בַּעַל גָּד, so called from the worship of Gad, that is, Fortune " (see Gesenius, *ad loc.*). גַּדָּה is the ordinary Hebrew word for fortune, and הַצֵּר גַּדָּה is court of fortune.

Why, even in the American edition of Smith's Dictionary of the Bible we read under Baal-Gad, בַּעַל גָּד : " It was in all probability a Phœnician or Canaanite sanctuary of Baal under the aspect of Gad or Fortune " (i. 209).

Syriac, ܓܕܐ, gado, fortune ; Arabic, جد, jad, fortune.

" But ye are they that forsake the Lord, that forget my holy mountain, that prepare a table for the Baal, and that furnish the drink offering unto Meni."

Baal's table—that was the offering-table, the altar ; so that the prophet's words have a very direct reference here. For nothing less than this would such curse have followed :

" Therefore will I number you to the sword, and ye shall all bow down to the slaughter, because when I called ye did not answer ; when I spake ye did not hear, but did evil before mine eye, and did choose that in which I had no delight." For they were " a people that provoked me to anger continually to my face ; that *sacrificed in gardens*, and burned incense upon altars of brick."

גַד, in the sense of good fortune, appears in many proper names, some of them compounded with El, as in גַדִי, גַּדִי, גַּדִיאֵל, &c., &c.

The word for gardens in the above is גִּנּוֹת, which is used mostly in later Hebrew, and as the more correct rendering of the word was grove, some confusion with Ashera may be presumed in the use of this word. Ashera also was used in the sense of grove, and is so translated, and very wrongly, in the Authorised Version.

The Revisers, in their attempts to put right, here as elsewhere compromise a bit, and only make confusion worse confounded. Indeed they do. They render the latter part of the verse and the first part of the next verse thus : " That prepare a table for Fortune, and fill up mingled wine unto Destiny : I will destine you to the sword, and ye shall bow down to the slaughter." And they put a reference at גַד

(Fortune) to Gen. xxx. 11, where we have, "And Leah said: Fortunate! and she called his name Gad."

More utterly helpless, flabby, and misleading emendations were surely never penned. I do not lay any weight on the bad English—that is to be expected; but the Revisers apparently fancied that מְנִי and מָנִיתִי were connected as noun and verb formed from it, the one being *Destiny* and the other *to destine*, while they are really nothing of the sort: the suggestion of a helplessly poor play on words being given, where surely it is much out of place. The truth is, the word מָנִיתִי is connected with the root מָנָה, to number, to divide out, and is thus associated with the מִנְחָה, whereas מְנִי traces either to the Babylonian, or, it may be, to the Arabic مناة, their goddess of fate or death.[1] Anyhow, the idea of Fortune and Destiny thus personified is utterly alien from the Jewish conception, and it is hardly conceivable that such a curse would have been pronounced on them as we have already partly quoted, for devotion to such mere generalised abstractions. No, no; *pace* the Revised translators, Jahwé and his prophets sought grounds more relative—some deity actually taken over from some neighbouring people, and with more appeal to human weakness or perversion than merely generalised abstractions of their own invention, like Fortune or Destiny, could ever have. מִמְסָךְ, besides, implies spicing of wine as well as mixing or

---

[1] Conf. Sura liii. of Koran, where we have the words: "What think ye of .... Menah?—that other third goddess"; and in Sura iv. she is also referred to in the clause, "the infidels invoke beside him [God] only female deities."

Dulaure speaks of Menah as "la même divinité que la Méni adoré par les Juifs et dont parle le prophète Esaïe."

mingling—therefore more correctly " drink-offerings "
than " mingled wine "—which is every way a bad and
clumsy translation.

Hosea, too, in his dread declarations against
Ephraim, at one place exclaims, " Ephraim, as I
saw Tyrus, is planted in a pleasant place: but
Ephraim shall bring forth his children to the murderer. . . . All their wickedness is in Gilgal: for
there I hated them " (ix. 13 and 15).

Now, what can this mean? Who is the murderer
to whom the children are to be brought out? and
why is their wickedness in Gilgal? Our idea of it is
that their sacrifice of their children was associated
with the stone worship inseparable from *the* stone-
circles which the phrase הַגִּלְגָּל as distinctly inti-
mates as does the Gaelic clachan. And there were
great stones at many places, Gibeon for one.

Scores of other passages might be cited. The
higher consciousness that had been developed in the
Hebrew Prophets which led them to try to raise the
people to the idea of Jahwé as pure and superior to
service of sacrifices, struggled vainly against the use
that had become a second nature. And it is clear
that the Prophets had no notion of the existence of
the so-called early codes of legislation, for they speak
directly too often in face of what these codes lay
down; they do not seem to have any idea that in
the passage we have already quoted Jahwé demanded
that the firstborns should be passed over to him,
and they draw no distinctions such as we can find
available as between the service in this respect of
Baal so called and Jahwé—a fact which, as we shall
see, Mr. Montefiore, in his Hibbert Lectures, dwelt

on and admirably illustrated.   But it is abundantly
clear that if, as Mr. Andrew Lang suggests, the
passing through the fire was a " harmless rite " among
the Hebrews, much in the Levitical and Deuteronomic
legislation needs to be wiped out, and a very great
deal in the Prophets demands such a gloss as to make
it no less than a noisy "much ado about nothing ; "
while, as we shall soon see, one Psalm at least wants
to be deleted and some sentences in Numbers.

III.

If any doubt can still remain, surely this unexpected
utterance, or series of utterances, in that altogether
noteworthy cvi. Psalm, would settle it.   Listen :
" They joined themselves unto Baal-peor, and *ate
the sacrifices of the dead* " (v. 28), which last clause is
a correspondent to "given them for food."   "And
they served their idols which were a shame unto
them.   Yea, they sacrificed their sons and their
daughters unto the demons [devils].   And *they shed
innocent blood, even the blood of their sons and of their
daughters whom they sacrificed unto the idols of Canaan ;
and the land was polluted with blood*" (vv. 37, 38).[1]

---

[1] Bishop Perowne thus translates this passage, leaving no doubt
that he is no believer in harmless rites :

"And they sacrificed their sons and their daughters to (false) gods,
    And shed innocent blood.
The blood of their sons and their daughters
Which they sacrificed to the idols of Canaan,
And the land was polluted with bloodshed."

He also points out that Hupfeld objects that in Numbers xxv. 2,
the same sacrifices are called sacrifices of their gods, and that sacrifices to the dead would scarcely be accompanied by sacrificial feasts.
Dr. Perowne well says decidedly that "this last objection has no
force."   After all, the expression is not sacrifices *to* the dead, but

This is but a kind of poetical rendering of Numbers xxv. 2 and 3 :

"And they called the people unto the sacrifices of their gods, and the people did eat "—[What ? The Psalm above and the correspondent " given them for food" are absolutely clear what it was]—" and bowed down to their gods. And Israel joined himself unto Baal-peor."

Here we see there was no exception to the eating of the flesh offered : so that, besides passing through the fire, there were eatings of human sacrifices, and the Hebrews were cannibals. And every Hebrew scholar knows well the meaning of this פְּעוֹר, of which בַּעַל is lord or master, just as Siva-Arganatha is lord of the boat-shaped vessel= Yoni. Baal-peor is precisely, on the male side, what Siva-Arganatha, lord of the boat-shaped vessel, is on the female in the Hindu religion : exactly what the erect stone or phallic emblem is to the moon crescent or the lotus. Peor is really Peorapis= Priapus ; and the rites associated with the worship all round were beastly. The inclination of the Jews for this is enough to prove either that all the claims they make for special revelation to them are lies, or that they were so foul and so little prepared to receive it as to wallow worse and worse in their filth after light had

of the dead—a different matter : so even Dr. Perowne translates it, and I adhere to my reading of the text still : it means, they ate of the bodies sacrificed, as is distinctly stated in Jeremiah xxiii. 37, to devour them=given them for food ; and Numbers xxv. 2 and 3, and "the people did eat."   The Irish version of the Douay Bible has, " They also were initiated to Beelphegor, and ate the sacrifices of the dead "—with this note to *initiate* : " That is, they dedicated or consecrated themselves to the idol of the Moabites and Midianites called Beelphegor or Baal-peor.

been fully revealed to **them—either** they lie, or they were so low and filthy as to take **no** benefit whatever from such wonderful **revelation. And the** words of the Psalm are a very faithful **rendering of** the Hebrew, as this—the original—will attest.

וַיִּצָּמְדוּ לְבַעַל פְּעוֹר וַיֹּאכְלוּ זִבְחֵי מֵתִים.
וַיִּזְבְּחוּ אֶת־בְּנֵיהֶם וְאֶת־בְּנוֹתֵיהֶם לַשֵּׁדִים וַיִּשְׁפְּכוּ דָם
נָקִי דַּם־בְּנֵיהֶם וּבְנוֹתֵיהֶם אֲשֶׁר זִבְּחוּ לַעֲצַבֵּי כְנָעַן וַתֶּחֱנַף
הָאָרֶץ בַּדָּמִים.

There can be no question that to sacrifice here means to slaughter, and to leave **no doubt** the word slaughter itself is used, and also the actual and common word for eating is used—a word about which no Hebrew **scholar can be in doubt for a moment.** It is the same word (הָעֲבְרִים) which is used in the expression **to pass over children to Moloch as is** used in the passage **already quoted from** Leviticus **to pass** over **to Jahwé; so that if the** children of **Israel passed** their children through the **fire to** Moloch, it was the destination that was wrong, not the process; **for** they were directed in the Levitical Law by the selfsame word to pass them over in the same way **to** Jahwé. **Dr.** Robertson Smith held, and gave good ground for his holding, that the Moloch to whom human sacrifices were offered **by the** Jews before the Captivity was Jahwé himself.

וַיַּעֲבִירוּ is the **first** word used in **17th verse of 2 Kings** xvii. **It is the same word that is used** in the close of verse **10 of 2** Kings **xxiii.,** in the clause " to **pass** through the **fire** to Molech."

And **the** sacrifice **of Saul's sons** (grandsons) by David, through the Gibeonites, be it noted, took

place, of all possible times, at the beginning of barley
harvest, which was, of course, the time of the
Passover feast.

The hangings up *in the sun* before **Jahwé**, as we
have seen, were only other forms of "passings through
the fire," the exposure to the sun fire of which the artificial fire was but the symbol.   Then the Gibeonites
were Amorites, worshippers of Baal—how do they
come to pass over to Jahwé as the Hebrew says?

This is a question Mr. Andrew Lang would do well
to answer, with the aid of his critical Hebrew advisers,
and the versatile and most learned Editor of the
"Contemporary Review"—who has the Review all
at his disposal—the whole Review—precisely for
the purpose of answering such questions—happy,
happy man!   And perhaps Mr. Quiller Couch, who
so adores Mr. Lang's style, may come in and help.

Kalisch is not a man to try to make Judaism
blacker than it was; yet he is very clear and very
decided about the hanging up before Jehovah by the
Amorites of the seven sons of Saul, with David's
sanction, if not a good deal more than sanction.
"Thus," he says, "human sacrifices were presented
to Jehovah by one of the most cultivated minds that
adorned the history and literature of Israel."   And
if David, the man after God's own heart, who had
actually pledged himself by solemn vow, to protect
these heirs of Saul, sworn before Jahwé to protect
them, was guilty of this, what, I ask Mr. Andrew
Lang, is so dreadful in saying that Ahaz, the wicked
one, burned *his* sons in the fire?

At Deut. xii. 31, we read: "Their sons and
daughters do they burn with fire to their gods."   And

on this clause Mr. Addis has the following note
(" Hexateuch," ii. p. 88) :

" Here we have one of many clues to the date
of Deuteronomy. The practice of offering children
in sacrifice was of Canaanite origin. But it was
apparently only in the later days of the Kingdom of
Judah that such a practice was introduced into the
worship of Jahwé. At all events from the age of
Manasseh and onwards we find this corruption of
Jahwé worship noticed and denounced. So here
' Thou shalt not do so,' &c., and Micah vi. 7, Jer. vii.
31, xix. 5, Ezek. xx. 25, seq. Jeremiah, it is true,
regarded such sacrifices as offered to Baal. But it
is plain from his own words, xix. 5, that such was
not the intention of the offerers."

So here Mr. Addis, probably without glimpse of
the results to which it inevitably leads him, gives
ground for believing that the longer the Jews lived,
despite their boasted revelation, the worse they were,
taking up human sacrifice—passings through the fire
—not harmless rites, nigh to the end of their course
as a people in Judea. That is not our idea, but we
commend Mr. Addis's reasonings to the notice of
Mr. Andrew Lang.

Even the exceedingly cautious Samuel Sharpe,
referring to Manasseh's passing his son through the
fire, speaks of it as a superstitious ceremony, *which
was often used as a cover for infanticide.*[1] Even he does
not quite go with Mr. Lang to declare it "a harmless
rite "—" it was *often* used as a cover for infanticide "
—" passing through the fire."

But look what the more critical Canon Venables

---

[1] " History of the Hebrew Nation," p. 139.

has written.   His words certainly give little support
to the idea that Hebrew " passings through the fire "
were " harmless rites " :

   " The fiendish custom of infant sacrifice to the
fire-god seems to have been kept up in Tophet, at its
south-east extremity, for a considerable period.   To
put an end to these abominations, the place was
polluted by Josiah, who rendered it ceremonially
unclean by spreading over it human bones and other
corruptions, from which time it appears to have
become the common cesspool of the city, into which
its sewage was conducted, to be carried off by the
waters of the Kedron . . . Robinson declares
' there is no evidence of any other fires than those
of Moloch having ever been kept up in this valley.'
From its ceremonial defilement, and from the detested
and abominable fire of Moloch, . . . the latter
Jews applied the name of this valley Ge-Hinnom =
Gehenna—to death, the place of eternal torment,
and some of the Rabbins here fixed ' the door of hell '
—a sense in which it is used by our Lord himself."

   The researches of Colonel Conder in Syria and
Palestine, and other regions of the East, have led
him to a very different conclusion from that of
Mr. Andrew Lang.   Over and over again in " Heth
and Moab," and " Syrian Stone Lore," he says that
" human sacrifice appears to have been universal
among Asiatics " ;[1] and adds that, in addition to what
we have in the way of proof in the Old Testament,
it is attested by explicit direction of an Akkadian
inscription ;[2] and there can be no doubt that the

---

[1] " Syrian Stone Lore," p. 77.
[2] *Ibid.*, p. 46.

prevailing form of it was **passing the victims through**
the fire to the Fire-God, **or** hanging them **up to the**
sun, which is but another form of it.

Bishop Perowne, **in his notes on Psalm cvi., has**
not much doubt **about** the passings-over **as some-**
thing else than **"harmless rites." "Of the** abominations of **the heathen, that of human** sacrifices, **as in**
the **worship of Moloch, is** especially dwelt on.   This
was **an offering to** FALSE GODS (Heb. Shêdîm), lit.
'lords,' **like** BAALIM, Adonim, **and then** applied to
gods (as the forms *Shaddai*, *Adonai*, were confined
to Jehovah); see the same word **Deut.** xxxii. 17, for
which in Jud. ii. 11, *Baalim*.   **The LXX.** render
δαιμονιοις, and Jerome *dæmonibus*, whence the English
version has 'devils.' . . . **The** land, the **very**
soil itself, **was polluted, as well as the inhabitants "**
(ver. 39).

Mr. Montefiore, **speaking of the** Manasseh **lapse**
and Ahaz's idolatries, goes on to add :

"**While both the authors of the** Book of Kings
and the Prophets regard the barbarous offering as
rendered **to the** Canaanite god Melech or 'the
King,' **the actual** sacrificers probably fused the two
deities together, and devoted [or passed over] their
children **to** Yahweh under the **name** of Melech.
Manasseh, like Ahaz, sacrificed **his** son, and many
another during his reign must have followed the
example of the court."[1]

Mr. Montefiore is quite on the other **side of Jordan**
from Mr. Andrew **Lang and his " harmless rites."**

Some, besides those **referred to by** Mr. Montefiore,

---

[1] " Hibbert Lectures," p. 169.

have fused the two deities together. Bethel and
Gilgal and other areas clearly became places where
Moloch was served by human sacrifices—the people,
as Mr. Montefiore says, very probably "fusing"
Moloch and Yahweh into one deity. For scarce
other offence, surely, could Yahwé have declared
through Amos, "I will visit the altars of Bethel,
and the horns of the altar shall be cut off and fall
to the ground" (iii. 15 and 16). And again at vv. 4 and 5
we read, "Seek ye me, and ye shall live : but seek
not Beth-el, nor enter into Gilgal, and pass not to
Beersheba ; for Gilgal shall go into captivity, and
Beth-el shall come to nought " (v. 5), which surely
would have been too severe if all that was special to
it was that the king's court and the king's chapel
were there.   No, but passings-over were there, and
not "harmless rites " either.   Bethel was surely
among the sanctuaries of Israel, מִקְדְּשֵׁי יִשְׂרָאֵל, which
there most clearly means idolatrous sanctuaries.

Sir George Cox does not have much reserve
about it :

"The '*passing through*' of children meant (at least
in most cases) burning their sons and daughters in
the fires of the high places of Tophet, as well as
on those of Baal (Jer. vii. and xix.), and this in the
days of Josiah."

Nor has Renan :

"David and Mesa were religiously and intellectually
on the same level. Yahvé was essentially a local
Baal, caring only for his own little portion of Palestine,
*and his followers firmly believed that he delighted in
human sacrifices like Chemosh*, and therefore did the
Yahvists at once fall back from their siege of Mesa's

fort when they saw **that king offer up his son to**
Chemosh."[1]

Colenso says : " We turn with **loathing from the**
fiendish brutality of Mexican worship, **but we have**
scanty grounds indeed **for thinking that Israelitish**
worship **in the days of Josiah was less cruel and**
bloodthirsty."

IV.

Let us now look at some significant Hebrew words,
and see if from them and the light they throw on
each other when, like precious stones, they are a
little cut and facetted, we can **get to** any clearer
notion of the *Hebrews* and the *passings* **over. Language**
itself **is the most conclusive of** all **testimonies, if we**
can but **get the materials.**

Goldziher is very firm on the point that the word
"*Ibhrim*," **or Hebrews, is derived from the word** *ábhar*,
and denotes not merely *transire*, " **to pass through**
a land or to cross a river," but rather "to wander
about " in general. Confirmation of Dr. Goldziher's
view, so far as he goes, might **be** found in many
circumstances. **Here is one** instance : עָבְרִי, from
עָבַר, **is a passer-over, a wanderer through ; indeed**
the word **is used** for walking through, **or** wandering
through, or *passing over*, and **is thus given even in**
Davies's Reading Exercises **in English translation of**
Gesenius's Grammar (p. 381) as the word to use in
translating the phrase " **wandering through " this**
world-vale in Bunyan's " **Pilgrim's Progress."**

But if separate **words are to be laid any** weight
on, I would fain raise **a question about the** way in

[1] " Hist. Israel," ii. p. 207.

which epithets in some cases came to be formed
from substantives, and I shall here deal with one
which has a suspicious nearness to this very עברי.
It is אָבִיר, strong, which became even a title of God
—Strong One. Now manna itself is called לֶחֶם אַבִּירִים,
food of the strong, the mighty; and I should much
like scholars like Dr. Fairbairn and Mr. Lang,
and the versatile and learned Editor of the "Contemporary," to satisfy me about this: Was manna
" food of the *mighty*" during the wilderness wander-
ings, or was it food of the god, and, on their principles,
does this אבירים merge into the other עִבְרִים or what?
If it does, what is the difficulty about merging both
in הֶעֱבִיר passing-over?

And what is really the ground for saying, in face
of these peculiar evidences of language, that the
Hebrews learned this bloody practice from the
Canaanites? Von der Alm holds that the whole
300 years of the period of the Judges was a time
during which the Hebrews and Canaanites, under
various leading influences, were blended into one
people. The Israelites at length got the upper hand
as regards external power, but the Canaanites in
religion, morals, and customs. When they came
forward as one people under David and Solomon,
their whole worship was Phœnician. Phœnicians
built the temple at Jerusalem, and the national
deity then became IAO, or IHVH.

But were the Hebrews so likely passively to
copy the religious observances of peoples whom they
despised and hated? Colenso at one place asks,
and there is a profound motive for his so asking:

" Is it possible that circumcision may have had

in its origin a religious meaning, expressing the dedication of all males to Jehovah by the sacrifice of a part for the whole ? " [1]

That surely suggests going back a long way, for the observance, of which circumcision is but the ceremonial symbol, goes back far beyond Abraham. The sign of admission into the covenant of Jahwé is specifically circumcision, for which even the stranger may, under certain circumstances, qualify —the stranger and all his family. Now, if Mr. Andrew Lang would call this also a "harmless rite," I persist, in opposition to him, that it, like the ceremonial " passing through the fire," inevitably pointed backward, and far backward too, to something more " harmful."

Ceremonial imperfection as summed up in the opening of Deut. xxiii., and, with some modification only, at Lev. xxii., close of verse 20, is significant alike of inconsistency on the part of a non-procreative god, and of survival from a time when certain offerings were still made and required—offerings of which circumcision remained but the ritualistic expression.

Either this ; or else this peculiar legislation points to a time when as yet the Hebrews, like many other early races, had festivals in celebration of the principle of generation or fertility, which wound up with " promiscuity," in which, of course, those who were impotent could not indulge. But I should be glad to have Mr. Andrew Lang's explanation and that of the Editor of the " Contemporary," and, failing them, of Dr. Fairbairn and Archbishop Temple.

I do not for a moment dwell on the untoward

[1] " Pentateuch," **vi.** p. 415 (*note*).

suggestion of the utterly forced and inconsistent notion of celebrating a wonderful escape in Egypt by sacrificing innocent lives in Canaan. It was the first-born of Egypt who were slain for the deliverance of the Hebrew firstborn : why, on grounds of consistent ritual or mythology, not to speak of reason, should Hebrew children for this have been offered up ? Dr. Colenso had his own notion of it, and honestly said so :

" When we take all these things into account, it seems highly probable that the Pesach meant originally the *Passing-over of the firstborns* of man and beast to the sun-god, and that the Canaanites, *i.e.*, the Phœnicians and others, did actually, at this spring festival, on the 14th day of the month, *i.e.*, the eve of the full moon, sacrifice their firstborns to that deity, from whom the Israelites adopted the practice of sacrificing their firstborns to Jehovah (Jahwé).[1] And there are only too good grounds for believing that even so late as the days of Jeremiah and Ezekiel no such redemption-money as is indicated was ever paid; but the firstborns of men, if dedicated at all, were simply sacrificed, and the people quoted the old laws as enjoining the practice." [2]

Professor Sayce, it is true, in No. 4 of " Trans. of Soc. Bib. Arch.," would fain prove that it was from the Turanian Akkads, with their high places and sacrifices in high places, that the Hebrews derived the practice of human sacrifices originally, and not from the Phœnicians; but Professor Sayce does not attempt to refine away the " passings-over " into " harmless rites." In a note by the English translator of Bleek, at ii., he says :

---

[1] Colenso, " Pentateuch," vi. p. 430.
[2] *Ibid.*, p. 431.

" It appears almost as if עבוים (1 Sam. xiii. 3, 7)
were meant to point out the Israelites east of Jordan.'
(Bleek, note by Editor, p. 77.)

Now, when we turn to the Hebrew, here we find
something very suggestive. It is clear that only the
Israelites east of the Jordan *were* meant, and this is
proved, abundantly proved, by the 7th verse, where
we have וְעִבְרִים עָבְרוּ אֶת־הַיַּרְדֵּן אֶרֶץ גָּד וְגִלְעָד.

The Authorised translators artfully put in here
"*some of*" before Hebrews; but this is mere patchwork,
and won't do. Clearly, the idea of any derivation of
Hebrews from the patronymic Eber is thus ruled out,
as Eber would thus only be name-giver to the section
of Israelites east of Jordan. And our theory is that
the later editors of Samuel were anxious—too anxious
—to bring out some pet point of theirs. They wished
to give a geographical basis to the עִבְרִים, and forced
in the crossing of Jordan as the name-giving fact
—a point again which the Authorised translators
did not like to face, and made a mixed mess of it
with the most unjustified " some of." When looked
at from our point of view, here we have indirect and
circumstantial evidence that there is something to
hide; and this was that עִבְרִים came not from anything geographical at all, but from a custom, a rite
—the passing-over, first to the sun-god, and afterwards to Yahweh, or, as Mr. Montefiore has it, to a
god fused of Moloch and Yahweh. To translate
בְּעֵבֶר הַיַּרְדֵּן as " on this side Jordan " is, as Bleek
rightly says, " against the usages of the language,"
and that utterly. It certainly cannot be correct to
write in the one case " beyond Jordan " in the land
of Moab, and in the other, " on this side Jordan in

the land of Moab," as it is at verse 5. "Beyond Jordan" clearly must mean to the west of it in the sense of having passed over it in march from the east ; for otherwise the Hebrews to the east of Jordan would be Hebrews but not passers-over in that sense, and yet passers-over.

Then again, if it is, as Bleek says, that the form given above was an established equivalent for the country lying eastwards of Jordan, how comes it that at v. 25 of 3rd chapter, we have from Moses: "I pray thee, let me go over and see the good land that is beyond Jordan, that goodly mountain (or rather mountainous land) and Lebanon "—that clearly is spoken by one still in the east of Jordan speaking of the land to the west of it, who had not yet in the permanent sense passed over, as he clearly longed and aspired to do.

Gesenius (*see* especially Hebrew Grammar, p. 9) finds good reason to doubt about the whole business of עברי and the Jordan, and would fain carry it back to very early days on the Euphrates and apply it to those who were on the other side of that river ; but this, to our mind, reduces the geographical idea *ad absurdum*, and the effort is in our favour, and for the holding of it as coming from a custom, a rite, and not from any such fact at all.

"The history of the Exodus is connected with the account of the institution of the Passover, and analogy may lead us to surmise that the national imagination had been busy in explaining the origin of an immemorial rite."[1]   What this rite was, I have

---

[1] Goldwin Smith's "Guesses," p. 66.

tried to reach. It could not have been what the Hebrew writers themselves say it was, for reasons into which I need not go further here; but it is clear that it was something that had origin and had celebration in times very remote—remote even beyond the date assigned to the selling of Joseph by his brethren, and the oppression in Egypt—though tendencies toward it lingered long after the accepted era and legislation of Moses.

The direction to "pass over" to Yahweh indeed suggests that this sacrifice was common long before Yahweh was adopted or revealed.

One very bold critic indeed has gone a step further than Colenso, and suggested that the result of all the discussion about the origin of the term *Hebrews* is to be found in the הֶעֱבִיר, *passing-over.* He grounds his claim mainly on this, that this phrase is found at a very early period, that even as met with then it points clearly to long-continued practices. His conclusion is that the name Hebrews is more probably derived from the passings-over than from anything else.

And as the term Hebrews is thus by some derived from the "passings-over" to the god of the Ashera, so, by others, the very term Ishrael is derived from the Ashera which was always associated with the passings-over as representative and symbol of the presence of Baal or Moloch,[1] as though, indeed, the Hebrew race were first and most persistent in this practice from which others borrowed. Gesenius goes back to find the origin of Hebrews in the days when they were on the Euphrates.

[1] *See* Forlong, "Short Studies," pp. 364-5.

Another instance of the use of the original for Hebrews is found at Job xxi. 29, where we have:

הֲלֹא שְׁאֶלְתֶּם עוֹבְרֵי דָרֶךְ וְאֹתֹתָם לֹא תְנַכֵּרוּ

This in the Authorised Version is: "Have ye not asked them that go by the way? and do ye not know their tokens?" where the word דָרֶךְ gives a fine reduplication of idea if we translate, as some have even done, "them that travel by travelling." But the true translation is undoubtedly "the travelling Hebrews" or "passers-over," since, as has been well pointed out, it was most likely that the Hebrews on their way from Egypt, passing through part of Arabia, should be inquired of on such a subject as death and the after-state of man and the justice of God, rather than any merely chance traveller who might pass along the road, the more especially that the chance traveller was not likely to have *miraculous signs* or *wonders*—which should be substituted for the almost unmeaning *tokens* in our version—and of these certainly the Hebrews, on their own showing, had many, among them the stories of plagues, death of Egyptian firstborn, destruction of Pharaoh's host— all which bore directly on the passing-over, according to them. But here is the difficulty that, in this sense, the idea of travelling or "passing-over" lay in the very word Hebrews.

At Exodus xii. 11, for the Lord's Passover we have פֶּסַח לַיָחוֶה; but the very first words of the next sentence recall us to our position. Jahwé says: "And I will pass over [or through] the land of Egypt," and the Hebrew there is וְעָבַרְתִּי בְאֶרֶץ מִצְרַיִם. Their Jahwé himself, then, was the first passer-over to make victims of firstborns. Here, as else-where, they but followed where he himself showed the way, and they were passers-over in this sense too.[1]

As for Mr. Lang's South Pacific cases, much will be explained with regard to them when it is remembered that Dr. Wyatt Gill and his co-missionaries found so many correspondences to the Hebrew or Semitic in the language, the customs and ritual of the South Pacific islands, that they came to the conclusion these islands had been originally peopled from Asia !

As for so-called miracles, Mr. Lang might have found further abundant evidences of magical or medicine-men passing through the fire had he sought for them—doubtless due to precisely such knowledge and resources as our "Fire-Queens," &c., possess. Thus, not to speak of "Bureaus of Ethnology," &c., &c., at p. 431 of Sir George Robertson's "Káfirs" we read that "among miracles usually related, there are those of men, under super-natural protection, standing for some minutes in the centre of a large fire without being in any way injured." And in the case of at least one people we are told of the preparation that was used to enable them to do so.

With the Druids, again, we find the passing through the fire remaining, as one might say, half-and-half between the old sacrifices and the mere "harmless rite," as a kind of ordeal in which lay omens. We read that the chief Druid, wrapped in the skin of the animal sacrificed, waited while a nobleman, with the entrails of the sacrificed animal in his hands, walked

---

[1] וַיַּעֲבֹר] is the word used at Genesis xii. 6, for *passing through* the land.

barefoot over the expiring fire thrice to bring them to the Druid. If the nobleman escaped harmless, it was reckoned a good omen; if not, not—of course, a form of survival of passing through the fire, only here the rite might be harmful as well as harmless; hence the whole significance of the ceremony.

If Mr. Lang had possessed all the knowledge that he affects, or if he had been as philosophical and scientific as he would fain appear, he would have at least referred to the vast array of survivals in the form of passing children through the sun-stone with lights all around, symbolising fire, of which a very fine type is found in the holy holed stone near the ruined church of Kolossi, between Kurun and Limasol in Cyprus, as described by Dr. Max Richter and others.

V.

Now for some proofs of Baal worship and *passings-over* in our own country. We might give many; here are a couple of very suggestive and striking ones:

The late Rev. Donald McQueen, of Kilmuir in the Isle of Skye, wrote:

"The Irish have ever been worshippers of fire and of Baal, and are so to this day. The chief festival in honour of the sun and fire is upon the 21st of June, when the sun arrives at the summer solstice, or rather begins its retrograde motion."

And he goes on:

"I was so fortunate in the summer of 1782 as to have my curiosity gratified. At the house where I was entertained, it was told me that we should see at midnight the most singular sight in Ireland, which was the *lighting of fires* in honour of the sun.

Accordingly, at midnight the *fires* began to appear, and on going up to the leads of the house, which had a widely extended view, I saw, on a radius of thirty miles all around, the fires burning on every eminence which the country afforded. I had a further satisfaction in learning from undoubted authority that the people danced round the fires, and at the close *went through these fires, and made their sons and daughters, together with their cattle, pass through the fire*, and the whole was concluded with religious solemnity."

The Irish before St. Patrick offered the firstborns of everything to an erect stone called Crom-Cruach, capped with gold.

The Beltane fires on the 1st of May are still kept up in the Isle of Man, or were quite recently (*see* Train's " Isle of Man," i. p. 328), as well as in some parts of Scotland—not all remote ; and these suffice to tell that even in those northern regions human sacrifices — passings-over—and similar observances took place at the same season of the year. In the " Statistical Account of Scotland," the clergyman of the parish of Callander tells that it was customary for the people to assemble on the moor round a fire, where, he says, " they baked a cake, which they divided into as many portions, as similar as possible to one another in size and shape, as there were persons in the company. They daubed one of these portions all over with charcoal until it was perfectly black. They put all the bits of the cake into a bonnet. Every one, blindfolded, drew out a portion. He who held the bonnet was entitled to the last bit. Whoever drew the black bit was the devoted person who was to be sacrificed to Baal (or Bel), whose favour they meant to implore in rendering the year productive of the sustenance of man and beast. There is little doubt of these inhuman human sacrifices having been once offered *in this country*, as well as in the East, although they now pass from the act of sacrificing, and only compel the devoted person to leap three times through the flames, with which the ceremonies of the festival are closed."[1]

This inference I humbly think is more philosophical and well based than that of Mr. Andrew Lang. Let it be noted, too, as a point of interest and significance, that the cake baked at the open fire on the moor, and divided into so many parts as there are persons present, is clearly similar to the unleavened bread of the Passover of the Jews, while the charcoal daub is nothing but a substitute for blood. Here we have most clearly a survival of an observance (just as Mr. Lang's Bulgarian cases are) which was common to Phœnicia, to Israel, to Syria, to Mexico and Central America, and many other places at certain times and periods. Very wonderful and suggestive, truly, to find illustrations and survivals of old Eastern Baal[2] rites at our own doors. Here there is no priest ; that office is performed by those present. In Israel each head of a family or household could kill the Passover lamb, and the qualification of the whole nation as holy (Exod. xix. 6) most probably alludes to this ancient universality of the priestly privilege.

The record does not end here. Many learned men find hint of these old and strange observances in place-

---

[1] Vol. ii. p. 62.

[2] The ancient Mexicans worshipped the god of fire, and passed their children through the fire in honour of him on the fourth day after birth.

names throughout Scotland. Here is one suggestive instance of it : Culsalmond = Kil-Saman (according to Lord Southesk), "temple of Baal-Saman," a Phœnician, otherwise Oriental god. Samhan answers to Mithras. The ancient Irish viewed him as the merciful judge of souls. The evening of the first day of November, still called "Oidche Samhna," or "the night of Samhan," was kept as his festival. (Higgins, p. 174, quoted by Lord Southesk, p. 7.)

With regard to Bel fires in Scotland, proved by Ardentinnys in Argyle, Renfrew, &c. = Ard-an-teine, "the height of the fire," Craigentinny, " the rock of the fire," in the county of Edinburgh, and Auchendinny, " the field of fire;" Lasintulloch, from Las-an-Tuloch, "the knoll of the flash of fire;" Tulliebeltane = Tulach Beil-teine, "the knoll of the fire of Bel," see "Gaelic Topography of Scotland," by Colonel James A. Robertson, pp. 111–113, who adds, "These examples prove that the object of these places of fire was for the worship of the heathen god Bel."

Dundee is really Dun-dé, and means "the fort of the god," that is, the fort dedicated to the god " Bel," which was, no doubt, situated at the top of the hill now called "the Law." (Robertson, p. 307.)

There is also a place-name in Argyle, Dumbarton, Ayr, and Perth; in the latter twice, namely, in Rannoch and Blair-Atholl, namely, Achantiobart, which is a corruption of Achadh-an-t-iobart, "the field of sacrifice."

VI.

Mr. Andrew Lang's argument, carried to its ultimate, is that these never were real "passings

through the fire" at all, at any time or anywhere.
opening the question about how the phrase could
have originated. If after such deliberate statements
respecting Israel from historians, prophets, and
poets it can be said that probably all " passings-
over " there were "harmless rites," then it is not much
to get rid of the Phœnician " passings-over," since
in their case we have but tradition or indirect and
outside testimony compared with what we have in
the Hebrew Scriptures. The Phœnicians, if they
produced any such systematic scriptures, did not
leave any to enlighten us on these points, as the
Hebrews did. Yet we read in serious history:

"In former times the Phœnicians had sacrificed
their own children to Baal, but had fallen into the
custom of buying victims; and when they were
defeated and besieged by Agathocles they ascribed
their disasters to the wrath of Baal on this account.
So to appease Baal 200 children of the noblest
families were picked out, and 300 more volunteered
to die for their country by 'passing through the Fire.'"

Does Mr. Lang say, as logically he ought to do, that
probably Phœnician and even Akkadian " passings
through the fire" were harmless rites too? And
we must go yet further. If the Jewish " passing
through the fire" was a mere rite—a harmless rite
in all cases — then, to be consistent, all human
sacrifice must be given up. And what does this
imply? The real significance of all sacrifice whatever,
and the real need for it. All, becomes one mere hocus-
pocus of empty, airy formulas without bases. Why?
Because nothing is clearer than that animal sacrifice has its force and significance only because it is

substitutionary. How else should temples all over the earth have been turned into reeking shambles, save through the belief that a crowd of cattle and sheep could only make up for a few human lives? and again, that innocent cakes of flour and oil, or of rice and ghee, should suffice to be put up to God instead of animal life ?

The proposition of Mr. Andrew Lang truly leads us a long way—to read history backward, to put the cause before the effect, to see in ceremonial institutions no real root in human necessity, and to deny the existence of any real basis and the true meaning of all " survivals."

So far as language can testify, it is clear. In the Sanskrit we have *asvamedha*, horse sacrifice, *purusha-medha*, human sacrifice, and *sarvamedha*, sacrifice for universal rule; and nothing could possibly be clearer than many passages in the " Satapatha Brâhmana " to the effect that whatever may be in fact offered, in principle *the sacrifice is a man*, and the altar, whatever may be offered on it, is, in size, that *for a man*. All else are substitutes, and this could be proved in the same way as true over a wide, wide area.

VII.

Mr. Andrew Lang, notwithstanding his confessed dependence on others for aid in Hebrew, ventures on the assertion: " I am inclined to think that Chronicles exaggerates the action reported in Kings, and that Ahaz did not make a burnt-offering of his family." Now every one knows that Chronicles is a Deuteronomic or priestly attempt, made probably by a Levite of Jerusalem at a late date, to improve in

every possible respect on Kings, and not the reverse :
and it will, perhaps, surprise Mr. Lang to learn that
he is the victim of a variety of translation rather
than anything else—which just shows how risky it
is to meddle with such subjects without knowledge
of Oriental languages.[1] The phrase in 2 Kings
xvi. 3 is הֶעֱבִיר בָּאֵשׁ (which even the conservative
Dr. B. Davies is inclined to explain is " probably
derived from the turning over of the children in
sacrifice "), and the phrase in Chronicles is this
וַיַּבְעֵר אֶת־בָּנָיו בָּאֵשׁ כְּתֹעֲבוֹת הַגּוֹיִם = " he devoted, consecrated, passed his children through the fire, after the
manner of the heathen." [2]   Here arises an indirect
argument in our favour (despite the Rabbins and their
dodges, as we shall at once see), that the translators
of the Authorised Version by so translating did not
agree with Mr. Andrew Lang ; and, further, that if
the Jewish " passings-over " were " harmless rites,"
so also were all those " after the manner of the
heathen "—result, awkward, very awkward, for Mr.
A. Lang, that there never were aught but " harmless

---

[1] " The writer of Chronicles is *deliberately reconstructing the history
of his people, as known to himself in the older records, and doing this in the
interest of the Levitical and priestly body*, to which, in all probability,
he himself belonged, as any one may see who will compare the
Chronicles account of David's last words (1 Chron. xxix.), or the
story of Jehoida's proceedings (2 Chron. xxiii.) with the corresponding
portions of the Books of Kings." (" Pentateuch," vi. p. xxvi., &c.)

[2] If Mr. Lang had even taken the trouble—the slight, very slight,
trouble—to glance at a Polyglot Bible, it would have dawned on him
that other translators had not quite followed ours.   The Douay
Version—which in many points is superior to ours, if in some behind
it—has, " he *consecrated* his sons in the fire."   The Vulgate has, " et
lustravit filios suos in igne ; " and the Spanish, " E hizo pasár sus
hijos por el fuego, segun el rito de las naciones " = " and he passed his
sons through the fire according to the rites of the heathens."

rites" or "passings-over" anywhere, or any time prior to or contemporary with the date of Chronicles, that is, 300 to 250 B.C.

Professor Buchanan Gray, in his "Hebrew Names," indirectly attests the modern dates of Chronicles by the very apt and clever manner in which he applies tests to the lists therein given, to show which are, and which are not, derived from ancient sources.

The whole method of these fellows is summed up in this passage from Mr. Walhouse—ignorant special pleading of the worst kind:—" The Rabbinical commentators have strongly repudiated the common interpretation [yes, they didn't want Judaism to look quite so bad as it was, and the Massorites even changed words by cleverest dodges to help the Rabbinical wish], and insisted that in all the Scripture passages on the subject, there is no word used to *burn* or *destroy* [*but there is*—שָׂרַף for one—over and over again, as we have quoted], but 'to pass' and 'to offer,' and they ask whether, when so wise and beneficent (?) a king as Solomon is spoken of as permitting his strange wives' 'worship of Molech,' it can be believed he would have sanctioned the murder of little children "—which is simply a gigantic *petito principii*.

This, indeed, is really very admirable dust-throwing in our eyes on the part of a man like Mr. Walhouse, aided and abetted by Mr. Andrew Lang. Solomon! well. I quote from a writer who knows: " The *first* act of the new king was to free himself from all danger of rivalry by putting Adonijah and Joab to a cruel death, and deposing Abiathar from the office of priest. He also cruelly put to death old Shimei, and some others of less note." I know very well the theologians will say, "the spirit of the period," &c., but the man who thus inaugurated his accession to the throne by blood, was not likely, in my idea, to be very particular about offering up, at a time when infanticide was common all over the earth, a few children more or less to please a wife with whom he was pleased, even were she of Moab with כמש, or of Ammon with בעל and מלך. But if Mr. Andrew Lang had read even with ordinary care his own authorities, he would have found a reason for not making the remark he does about the exaggeration of Chronicles. It is to be hoped he is more reliable in his Greek, &c., than in his Hebrew.

But there is one thing that Mr. Walhouse is careful to tell us about passing through the fire in India, which it did not quite suit Mr. Andrew Lang to reproduce, any more than to note Mr. Walhouse's remarks about no words used for burn or destroy. In vol. vii. p. 126, of the "Indian Antiquary," we read that " the fire-treaders there [in India] pierce their eyelids, tongues, the fleshy parts of their arms, &c., with long slender nails, having a lighted wick attached to each end." Now, is this, I ask Mr. Andrew Lang, a "harmless rite" attached and bound up with a "harmless rite"; and how does he account for it accompanying the performance? I wait, I wait for his reply.

Mr. Walhouse and Mr. Andrew Lang would not lay much weight on the assertions of the Persians and Kurds, that when they come out at certain hours and stand gazing at the sun, they literally mean nothing by it; those two gentlemen would at once say that this is a relic and survival of old sun or fire-worship preserved in an empty custom or fossil of rite, to use Mr. Andrew Lang's excellent phrase. But why, oh, why should he apply absolutely a different test and principle here from what he does to later merely ceremonial " passings through the fire "?

With regard to Mr. Andrew Lang's notion and absolute assertion of the exaggeration of Chronicles, there is more to be said ; and at least one point to which to direct his attention. This point will most assuredly be enough to send him on a long voyage of inquiry, and happily also of discovery, which, if he but follows it up faithfully, will occupy much of his spare time for the next year or two. It is this : That the Books of Kings and Chronicles are exactly alike on one matter, which has a very powerful indirect, if not direct, bearing on what has just been said. And to introduce this matter more effectively, I shall crave the aid of a great Biblical scholar— Bleek. He writes on this point :

" In the Books of Kings and Chronicles, it is always pointed out as blamable, that even these pious kings (Asa, Jehoshaphat, Joash, Amaziah, Uzziah and Jotham) should have allowed the worship in the high places to remain. But this is merely the verdict of the authors of these books, which in no case would .have been composed before the Babylonian exile." [Certainly, we believe Chronicles was not composed till the third century B.C.] " As the kings above-named are depicted in everything else as such zealous servants of Jehovah, we can scarcely think that they would not have aimed at putting a stop to the wor-ship at high places, where sacrifices were offered to

Jehovah at other altars besides the Temple, if the Deuteronomic law, so expressly showing this service to be contrary to the will of Jehovah, had been known or acknowledged by them as Mosaic." [1]

I should much like Mr. Lang—who is so eager to deliver himself about Chronicles—to tell me what position he takes in this all-important matter, bearing so closely as it does on " passings through the fire " among the Hebrews.   Does he hold that these pious kings persisted in their " blamable practices " in spite of a clear legislation against all such practices, or does he hold that they were wholly and entirely ignorant of that legislation, which professes to have been in existence long before their day? Here, again, I wait, I wait for his reply, and when he has definitively given it, then I assure him I shall, either way, have something more to say on that matter with strict reference to his own definite statements.   I would also venture to press the question on Professor Sayce, as bearing very directly from a special and important point on his statement about the literary character of the Mosaic age, and the complete production and publication of the Mosaic records and legislation.

The great problem for Mr. Andrew Lang and his Hebrew-scholar friends who so kindly advised him in the matter, is to find proof that this worship of the high places, which even the most highly-praised kings in the Books of Kings and Chronicles alike still practised as if the Deuteronomic law was unknown to them, or was regarded as non-Mosaic or of non-effect, was something very different from

[1] Bleek, i. p. 328.

what worship of the high places was elsewhere. If it was, and was **purely** Jehovistic worship, why then should the writers of the Books of Kings and Chronicles so thoroughly agree in condemning it as they did? If it was **not, and was what we** understand **by the** worship **of the** high **places—** worship **of Ashtaroth** and Baal **(which** were **always** associated)—then, why should **Mr.** Andrew Lang have **tried to** make a charge against Chronicles of **exaggeration as to** Ahaz, and the practice **of** sacrifices inevitably associated with the worship of the high places, as compared with Kings, when both Books plainly declare that even Asa,[1] Jehoshaphat, Joash, Amaziah, **Uzziah, and** Jotham—the **men** after the purest pattern **in Hebrew** history—were themselves guilty **of** offering **on the high** places; **or, at all events, of** tacitly approving, of sanctioning, **or of allowing it.** Azariah, **too, the son of** Amaziah, "**did right . . . save that the** high **places were not removed:** the people **still sacrificed** [how and **what, Mr.** Lang?] **and burnt** incense **in the** high places" (**2** Kings xv. iii.).

Mr. **Andrew** Lang may try to find a crevice of escape by taking quarter with Mr. Montefiore, in affirming that the gods Jehovah **and** Baal became

---

[1] "Howbeit the high places were not taken away [in the time of Asa]: *for as yet the people had not prepared their hearts unto the God of their fathers*" (2 Chron. **xx. 33**). But Chronicles *may* exaggerate. **See** also about Jehoram (**2 Chron. xxi.** 12-15); but why was Jehoram **dealt with** in so dreadful **a manner?** Perhaps Chronicles does exaggerate there! **Asa** destroyed **the idol which** his mother Maachah had made, **and burnt it by the brook Kedron** [the idol on which she had put "**a figure of shame**"], "**but the** high places were not removed: **nevertheless Asa's heart was** perfect with the Lord all his days." (**1** Kings xv. **14.**)

in the people's minds wofully "mixed," as Artemus
Ward, the witty, would have said; but, if so, is
our position not good still as against Mr. Andrew
Lang for accusing the writer of Chronicles of
exaggeration about Ahaz, who certainly is not set
before us as having any of the good points of those
kings named above, who indulged nevertheless in
high places, or, at the least, left alone and condoned
the worship and sacrifices there.

If *they* went so far in a *blamable* way, as good
Bleek says, is it possible that Chronicles could
exaggerate about what Ahaz was likely to have
done in the same *blamable* way? Come, come, Mr.
Andrew Lang, if you do not show a good reason
for the faith that is in you about passing through
the fire, then please do, at all events, show that you
have read something of Hebrew history, or are, at
least, willing to learn, and to be put on the right
path, even now, to learn it; though it is, it is indeed,
a little late for a man who spoke with such posi-
tiveness of his full conviction that it was *probable*
the "passings-over" of the Hebrews were merely
"harmless rites," and who, as we shall soon see,
slipped cunningly down to the remote and more
doubting "*possible*" the very first chance that he
found to correct and alter and tone down his first
and very strong impressions, as published in the
"Contemporary Review" under the patronage of
Mr. Percy Bunting.

VIII.

Looked at from Mr. Andrew Lang's old, bold
anthropological standpoint, this sentence with which

he closes his "Contemporary Review" article on
" Passing through the Fire," suggests an endless array
—a long perspective of contradictions, crowded and
ominous, which I rather fear that he, with all his
unbounded ingenuity and cleverness, will find it
hard to clear out.

Look at a few cases: When dealing in a passing
way with god-eating, he thus sets it down:

" The custom of god-eating is common among
totemistic peoples, who, except on this solemn occasion, abstain from [eating][1] their totem. Müller
mentions (Ur-Am-Rel.) a dog-tribe in Arkansas
which sacramentally eat dog's flesh. *This rite may
be regarded as a commutation of cannibalism.*"[2]

He writes with such fine gusto thus:

" It has been shown that the light of the anthropological method had dawned on Eusebius in his
polemic with the heathen apologists. Spencer, the
head of Corpus, Cambridge (1630—93), had really

---

[1] By the way, this awkward kind of elision in Mr. Andrew Lang's
style appears too often — only too often — in many cases giving
openings even for doubt as to meaning, but Mr. Quiller Couch, a
most versatile, immaculate man, says it is complete and perfect—
the best to-day to be had. Style and method are the man,—
L'homme même. While I am on style, might I be allowed to ask
Mr. Quiller Couch whether he regards the following at p. 34 of
" Modern Mythology" as perfect: "Everybody *has* observed that
the stars rise up from off the earth, *like* the bees *sprung* from the
blood of Ouranos"? Also, I should be obliged if any one would tell
me who the John *Fergus* MacLennan was to whom Mr. Lang dedi-
cates his " Modern Mythology"? John Ferguson MacLennan I
knew well, and through my hands indeed passed, with no ill results
to it, the very first little essay he published on a subject relating to
" Primitive Marriage," but of John *Fergus* MacLennan, I have never
heard. The *Ferguson* in the name of the author of " Primitive
Marriage" was one of which he was rightly proud.

[2] " Myth, Ritual, and Religion," i. p. 74.

no other scheme in his mind in his erudite work on Hebrew ritual. Spencer was a student of man's religion generally, and he came to the conclusion that Hebrew ritual was but an expurgated, and so to speak, divinely 'licensed' adaptation of heathen customs at large,"—excluding human sacrifice— "passing through the fire," did he say?

Mr. Lang here most dextrously closes one gate by which he might have made a feint of returning to his old standpoint. But here are specimens of his true anthropological reasoning, to which Jewish "Passing through the Fire" should have furnished no exception.

He sets it down that the custom of leading the dead soldier's horse behind his master to the grave is a relic of days when the horse would have been sacrificed.[1] I do not remember if he also sets it down that our dislike of horseflesh as edible is to this day a result of the tabu on horseflesh through its being sacred to Odin, precisely as was camel's-flesh to some tribes of Arabs, and only to be eaten sacrificially. How eloquently he writes:

" That Greeks should dance about in their mysteries with harmless serpents in their hands looks quite unintelligible. When a wild tribe of Red Indians does the same thing, as a trial of courage with real rattlesnakes, we understand the red man's motives, and may conjecture that similar motives once existed among the ancestors of the Greeks."[2]

So we might paraphrase:

" That Bulgarians, Fijians, and Scotch folk in

[1] "Custom and Myth," p. 4.
[2] *Ibid.*, p. 21.

Stirling and Perthshires should after various ceremonies go leaping through an expiring fire, and in
some cases driving their cattle through, looks quite
unintelligible. When we find wild tribes of Semites
actually making devoted ones to 'pass through the
fire,' *i.e.*, be burned, and Phœnicians, &c., passing
the first-born of everything to conciliate the god and
to secure something much wished for, then we can
understand their motives, and may conjecture that
similar motives once existed among Bulgarians and
Fijians and our own forefathers as among Jews and
Phœnicians."

Yet this is the result of his researches in " Passing
through the Fire ": "At present I think it highly
probable that the Jewish ' Passing through the Fire '
was a *harmless rite*." Yet it remains a fact that even
in the most orthodox Hebrew Lexicons, Mr. Lang
might have read under מֹלֶךְ : "pr. n. of an Ammo-
nitish idol to which the idolatrous Israelites offered
human sacrifices, 1 Kings xi. 7 ; Jer. xxxii. 35, &c."
כמש literally means firer or burner. Here is a
passage from one of the latest and most valuable
works on the Hebrew Bible :

"The expression מִלֶךְ, as it is pointed in the
Massoretic text, occurs eight times, and with one
exception has always the article, which undoubtedly
shows that it is an appellative, and denotes the *King*,
the King-idol. The appellative signification of the
word is confirmed by the Septuagint which translates it ἄρχων, *prince*, *king*, in five out of the eight
instances. As this, however, was the title of Jehovah,
who alone was the true King of Israel, and, moreover, as the Jews had frequently fallen a prey to the

worship of this odious king-idol, *with all its appalling rites of child-sacrifice*, the authoritative redactors of the Hebrew text endeavoured to give a different pronunciation to these consonants when they denote this hideous image. Hence the Massorites, who invented the graphic signs, pointed it מֹלֶךְ, *molech*, to assimilate it to the word בֹּשֶׁת, *shameful thing*, the name with which Baal was branded."[1]

By this single sentence Mr. Andrew Lang, if he has not eaten his own head off anthropologically and metaphysically, has barred the way for his further consistent advances along the line he has traversed in "Custom and Myth," and in "Myth, Ritual and Religion." By this single sentence he has really discounted all that he has done, turned the corner and gone backward, and has at last rendered one - half of his results of non-effect. Instead of the ardent scientific anthropological speculator, he has come down to the level of the too perplexed orthodox theologian, eager only to get Israel excepted from the scope of ordinary anthropology ; and if he gain anything by this reversion in the way of *bunting* (that is, κυδος, fame, advertisement) or of money, he must pay for it hereafter in the difficult business of preserving his consistency in scientific thinking. He has shown the weak point in his armour to the mythologists who, if they do not wound him, will certainly exult in the weak point, and lose no chance of aiming at it. Gubernatis,

---

[1] Dr. Ginsburg's Introduction, p. 460. The italics are mine, to emphasise the fact that Dr. Ginsburg does not think the Hebrew Passings Over to Moloch were "harmless rites," as Mr. Andrew Lang does.

in his explanations of the inexhaustible as a cow, an inoffensive cow, that must not be offended, is hardly in it with him; for he advanced so splendidly, and held his own so well, and went up so high and brilliantly, and has come down on the fatal Jewish Christian-theological stick of his own rocket in " Passing through the Fire."

Mr. Andrew Lang, as is all too clear, alas! is much more familiar with his Homer, not to speak of Mr. Rider Haggard's "She" or "Solomon's Mines," than he is with his Bible and Solomon's sacrifices. His, however, is no uncommon case. When we find even " a great scholar and thinker " like the late Dr. Thirlwall, with the ceremony of the Red Heifer before him in his sacred Book, not to speak of the Feast of Tabernacles, and that notable pouring out of water before the Lord by Samuel, and the direction, too, in certain circumstances to pour out blood *like water*, seriously writing that "water was worshipped for its *value in use*," and Bishop (then Dean) Perowne making no note or comment on it, as is the case in Thirlwall's Remains, then we need not be much surprised at anything in this kind. To discover the main facts about Hebrew " Passings through the Fire " does not need a knowledge of Hebrew, though that may aid to conclusiveness in some ways; but only an honest reading of the Authorised Version. For one passage, let it be Lev. xx. 2 to 5:

" Whosoever he be of the children of Israel, or of *the strangers* that sojourn in Israel, that giveth any of his seed unto Molech: he shall surely be put to death: the people of the land shall stone him with stones." (For the performance of a harmless rite, be it noticed, according to Mr. A. Lang.)

" And I will set my face against that man and will cut him off from among his people ; because he hath given of his seed unto Molech, to defile my sanctuary, and to profane my holy name.

" And if the people of the land do any ways hide their eyes from the man when he giveth of his seed unto Molech, and kill him not :

" Then I will set my face against that man and against his family, and will cut him off, and all that go a-whoring after him, to commit whoredom with Molech, from among their people." And all for a "harmless rite," according to Mr. A. Lang. Heavens, we need help somehow !

Whether we regard this part of Leviticus as early or late, the point against Mr. Lang's position is clear. If early, then it shows how absolute was the conviction of the existence of Molech sacrifices then among the Jews ; if late, it shows how firm was the belief on the minds of Jewish scribes that passing through the fire of Molech-Jahwè — was common even in Mosaic times. And really the Editor of " The Contemporary Review" should not have allowed even Mr. Andrew Lang to wind up his article by writing such ill-informed nonsense in his usually sober, accurate and learned pages, which in old days, as I can remember, bore the very antidote, as if by finest prophetic forecast, for the very bold and novel and destructive heresy suggested in it now.

When I pointed out the close of Mr. Lang's article to a very old and learned minister, he said " Humph, I thought Isaiah and Jeremiah and

Ezekiel knew more about that than Andrew Lang!"
and changed the subject, as though the thing
deserved no more notice, although published in the
"Contemporary." Well, if Isaiah and Ezekiel and
Jeremiah did not, Mr. Lang is the prince of destructive critics—he "takes the cake" from Kuenen and
Kinkel, and Kittel and Stade, not to speak of his old
friend and benefactor, Preller, and Wellhausen and
Colenso. For the historical and prophetical books,
and even long passages in the poetical books, are
thus proved by him to be not only contradictory and
patched up, but a long series of lies, fabrications,
humbug and the work of humbugs, Mr. Andrew
Lang having by *ipse dixit* proved them nowhere.
But in the language of my friend, the old and
learned minister, "Isaiah and Jeremiah and Ezekiel
knew more about that than Mr. Andrew Lang!"
Yes, we will hold to that same, and believe that Mr.
Andrew Lang was for once forgetful (oh, by-the-bye,
though, he did run into great, great blunders over
Queen Mary), wrote hurriedly, and wrote ignorant
nonsense for once, if he never did it before in the
course of all his hundred and fifty odd volumes.

It is almost funny to find Mr. Andrew Lang, who
actually devoted some passing paragraphs to " God-
eating " in his Mexican chapter in " Myth, Ritual,
and Religion," not only make thus an end of " Passings through the Fire " among the Hebrews as
aught but " harmless rites," but also sets aside the
clear and invariable record of the eating of these
sacrifices, unmistakably set down alike in historical,
prophetical, and poetical books. For a man who
had written of " God-eating " this is passing strange,

and can hardly signify that Mr. Lang's "passage
through the fire" of biblical investigation has been
severe—"a harmless rite" in very truth, since,
according to these scriptures, if the "harmless
rites" were not followed by "god-eatings," then
were the Hebrews cannibals on their own showing;
only Mr. Lang would here grandly save them from
themselves. "God-eating," indeed! Yes, we will
say that.

P.S.—I have now read Mr. Lang's "Modern
Mythology." All Mr. Lang's efforts here are to me
vitiated by his desire not to see what he certainly
ought to see in the Hebrew—survivals, there as
elsewhere, of savagery, of which the "passings
through the fire" as "innocent rites" are certainly
instances. Why does he turn his blind eye on that?
Why does he, a disinterested inquirer, so clear on
facts elsewhere, so blink at this and humbug, or try
to humbug, us over it? But much should I like to
cross-examine Mr. Andrew Lang, in presence of a
jury of competent men, on the way in which he can
reconcile the root-idea here with what he wrote
on Jewish "passings through the fire" as always
"harmless rites":

"Our system," says Mr. Lang, "is but one aspect
of the theory of evolution, or is but the application
of that theory to the topic of mythology. The
archæologist studies human life in its material
remains; he tracks progress (and occasional degeneration) from the rudely chipped flints in the ancient
gravel beds to the polished stone weapon, and
thence to the ages of bronze and iron. He is guided
by material 'survivals'—ancient arms, implements,

and ornaments. . . . The anthropological method
in mythology is the same. In civilized religion and
myth we find rudimentary survivals, *fossils of rite* and
creed, ideas absolutely incongruous with the environ-
ing morality, philosophy and science of Greece and
India [and Judea ?]. Parallels to these things, so
out of keeping with civilization, we recognise in the
creeds and rites of the lower races, even of cannibals,
but *there* the creeds and rites are *not* incongruous
with their environment of knowledge and culture.
There they are as natural and inevitable as the
flint-headed spear or marriage by capture. We
argue, therefore, that religious and mythical faiths
and rituals, which, among Greeks and Indians [and
Hebrews] are inexplicably incongruous, have lived
on from an age in which they were natural and
inevitable, an age of savagery."

Fossils of rite ! Pray, Mr. Andrew Lang, where
could you find a more definite instance of it than in
the later phases of ceremonial " Passings through
the Fire."

Indeed, it is something more than amusing to
think of Andrew Lang, so eager to prove the presence of survivals of coarse savagery everywhere
that he can—in Greece, in Rome, &c., &c.—so very
anxious to get rid of them *here*—to show that the
Hebrews were clear of the faintest suggestion of the
vices which are shadowed forth in Chronos, of which
he makes so much. What, what can be the motive ?
Is Mr. Andrew Lang blind or half-blind, or has he
some interest to serve in the accomplishment of
so grand a work ? However that may be, I hold,
in opposition to him, that it is highly probable

"passings through the fire" as "harmless rites" were utterly unknown to the Hebrews, and that all "passings through the fire" as "harmless rites" are survivals of something very different and very harmful, which the early Jews did practise—a position which is exactly in keeping with Mr. Lang's own position when he is dealing with any analogous observances of any other people.

I am not aware that any attempt has hitherto been made to deal exhaustively and critically with Mr. Andrew Lang's pseudo-scientific *nonsense*, which just shows how much truth there was in the main statements of Mr. Myers's *Catholic Thoughts*, and what a vile and far-extended conspiracy exists to throw dust in people's eyes by trying to make out this Judaism to have been quite other and better than it really was.   The most learned and versatile editor of the " Contemporary " returned to me my article saying, " I do not *think* I can publish this article," as though it had nothing in it, and as though Mr. A. Lang's had had everything in it, which perhaps it had—false, ignorant, and superficial, as well as true ; but——

Mr. A. Lang, however, shows movement, as we have just hinted, though it may be like that of the crab (even from his own point of view, backward). The " *probable* " in that characteristic closing sentence of C. R. article very significantly dwindles down to the " *possible* " in the more deliberate " Modern Mythology."   If Mr. A. Lang goes on cautiously, consistently on this line, he will by-and-by *be with us*, for, going backward in his approved style, he will have described almost a circle, adroitly described a

circle, turned over, "passed over," and got nearly
back to what should have been his true starting-
point. He is not, like some of our great modern
scientific men, "cocksure"; but if he does not afore-
thought leave it, he adroitly makes a little opening
in the fence behind him by which he may return.
The sudden drop from " probable " to " possible " is
a long stretch, longer far than you would think at
first glance. After that for an exact and critical
man of science, even an anthropological mythologist,
anything is " possible," if not " probable." But did
Mr. Percy Bunting, without my consent, show Mr.
Lang this article in MS. (which, by-the-bye, was kept
by him more than three weeks), and is that change,
and at least another, and yet another, in any way due
to that glimpse he had of another man's work and the
results of his research ? It is almost unaccountable
otherwise. Mr. Lang and his editor (who, by the
way, did not edit) are the Castor and Pollux of the new
era. Yes, they hang together high, high up, and no
doubt will hang as a wonderful sky-sign (not totem
beast). But I will say that I wish them no worse
luck than that the one should be at once made
a Q.C. and the other a D.D. (which the reader may
interpret as he pleases—any way between the
" probable " and the " possible ").

May I venture, however, to give what seems to
me the " probable," or it may be only " possible,"
process of thought in Mr. A. Lang's mind on this
matter ? " If," said he to himself, " I delete wholly
both the assertions of this belief of mine, that might
be too definite a proof of how I have been influenced,
and might be pounced upon. But see now what a

deft literary magic-man I am ; by changing 'prob-able' into 'possible' I can gain something in qualification and caution, don't you see, and yet nobody may notice it—not even the man who has mediated the change." The coming D.D. is worthy of his title, the more that he is a layman—for the two words are a little alike, and have exactly the same number of letters. But in a severe scientific treatise how different they are, or "possibly may be," to use his own cautious, modified phrase. I recommend to him for his next effort a treatise on theories of probability and possibility reconciled.

In the very last conversation I had with Prof. Robertson Smith, not very long before he died, he did smile—smile in his own quiet meaning way—at the idea of any such thesis as that Mr. Andrew Lang has boldly undertaken being maintained, and went over a series of points directed against it, which I wish I could recall and set down exactly as he presented them. Some day I may try, for they are well worth preserving, and would give Mr. Andrew Lang a good deal more to think of than will even arise upon him in reading this article.

And for a last word, I think I have sufficiently proved that Mr. Lang should not have made any such statement as he did make about the *probability* of passings through the fire with the Jews being "harmless rites" till he had taken the time and the trouble to have mastered as much Hebrew, at least as to enable him to verify the accuracy of transla-tions of texts, as, indeed, by his own acts he now admits. No; Mr. Andrew Lang should have waited a few years and given toilsome hours, and days, and

nights to Hebrew as others have done; and then I
am certain he would never have needed to go dodging
and jukeing—a word he knows right well—"juke
and let the jaw gae by," ye ken—between the
"probable" and the "possible." "But he is a
master of style and *method*," cries Mr. Quiller Couch
—gets great κυδος, goes on coining money and pub-
lishing nonsense. But even by his dodging and
conjuring a table top cannot stand without legs or
pillar to support it, nor a tree wave its branches
in air without a root in earth, nor a statue stand
without a pedestal—nor can there be innocent survivals and "harmless rites," indeed, without something less innocent and harmless having gone before
them—a thing Mr. Andrew Lang is so amazingly
quick to show everywhere save in Hebrew, in which
he is not an expert and has to take his cue from
others, bold man!

II.—TATTOO-MARKS, CUTS, AND SEXUAL SELECTION.

I CANNOT help thinking that Darwin's doctrine of sexual selection has been much overdone. When, through Westermarck and others, it is attempted to explain away all tattooings, marks, cuttings, and mutilations as mere decorations, " to aid in successfully courting and being courted," then I am almost inclined to say it has been done to death. There can be no doubt about the universality of the custom of tattooing and painting and mutilating, whatever may have been its cause or its source. Darwin says that " no one great country can be named, from the Polar regions in the North to New Zealand in the South, in which the aborigines do not tattoo themselves." At a certain period of human development it is, it seems, inevitable. And, though it may vary with tribes very closely related to each other, there is but little variation within the tribes themselves. What, indeed, has most astonished many travellers is the remarkable sameness. Among a hundred you will not see two that at first seem in the least to differ, and yet, when you examine more minutely, you are surprised to find that no two are identically alike. This implies, in many cases, a high perfection of art in its own way, which attests that those peoples had long emerged from what we are often pleased to consider mere savagery.   It means a long period of practice and great proficiency in a difficult art: it suggests also very complex conditions of tribal existence and relations with other tribes ; and one of my reasons for so decisively questioning Westermarck's chief positions in his Chapter IX. of "Human Marriage," titled " Means of Attraction," arises simply from this fact, though, as the reader will soon learn, there are others.   The subject is of importance, because, if Westermarck's theory is correct, then the analogy between the lower animals and man is not only confirmed, but, by inference from his arguments, increases the more that tribal life is developed and rendered complex.   I think Westermarck is wrong—wrong in his main position as he certainly is on several separate points—and under four sections I shall proceed to give my grounds for saying so.

I.

It cannot be denied that Westermarck is most interesting in his wide range of facts, and in the way he uses them ; but his reasonings are often open to criticism.   Let us look at some of these, for a few moments.   He thus summarises Frazer's results :

" In order to put himself more fully under the protection of the totem, the clansman, according to Mr. Frazer, is in the habit of assimilating himself to it, by the arrangement of his hair and the mutilation of his body ; and of representing the totem on his body by cicatrices, tattooing or paint.   Thus the Buffalo clans of the Iowa and Omahas wear two

locks of hair in imitation of horns, whilst the Small
Bird clan of the Omahas "leave a little hair in front
over the forehead for a bill, and some at the back of
the head for the bird's tail, with much over each ear
for the wings;" and the turtle sub-clan cut off all
the hair from a boy's head, except six locks which
are arranged so as to imitate the legs, head, and tail
of a turtle.   The practice of knocking out the upper
front teeth at puberty, Mr. Frazer continues, is, or
was once, probably an imitation of the totem; and
also the bone, reed, or stick which some Australian
tribes thrust through the nose.   The Haidahs of
Queen Charlotte Islands have always, and the
Iroquois commonly, their totems tattooed on their
persons, and certain other tribes have on their bodies
tattooed figures of animals, which Mr. Frazer thinks
likely to be totem-marks.   According to one authority
the raised cicatrices of the Australians are sometimes
arranged in patterns representing the totem; and
among a few peoples, the totem is painted on the
person of the clansman.

Mr. Frazer's theory, he goes on to say, is supported
by exceedingly few facts, whereas there is an enormous
mass of cases "in which we have no right whatever
to infer a connection with totemism: it is, indeed,
impossible to see how most of the practices considered
in this chapter could have originated in this way."
And then he proceeds to lay down the law that all
such decoration was for sexual stimulation; "to aid
in successfully courting and being courted."

One difficulty, however, at once suggests itself.
Westermarck is very decided on the point that habit
speedily overcomes any sense either of pleasure or

surprise, or, indeed, strong feeling of any kind.   He is almost eloquent on the utter mistake in associating nudeness with excitement of sexual passion, or any feeling so strong as complete or partial concealment would evoke.   Yet the principle, it would seem, handily works by opposites.   He sets down at a later page : " Through long-continued use covering loses its original character and becomes a sign of modesty, whilst perfect nakedness becomes a stimulus."   He insists that ornament, painting of the body, tattooing, &c., could not have originated in any religious idea such as its association with totemism implies ; but, at the same time, he holds that these marks, cuttings, disfigurements, had no other primary incitement than that of attracting the regards of the other sex ; to excite admiration, and desire, in fact, by means of novelty.   But the more permanent the effect aimed at, the introduction of novelties, after the first start, was ruled out ; and he himself has shown how soon any impression such as he upholds, goes off on habitual beholding of the ornament or effect.   What else is the final result of his own writing at p. 200 ? " These practices evidently began at a time when man evidently went in a perfect state of nudity.   The mutilations, *as the eyes became accustomed to them, gradually ceased to be interesting, and continued to be inflicted merely through the force of habit or from a religious motive.*   A new stimulus was then invented ; parts of the body, which formerly had been exposed, being hidden by a scanty covering."   He quotes Prof. Moseley to this effect : " A savage begins by painting or tattooing himself for ornament.   Then he adopts a moveable appendage which he hangs

H.   F on his body, and on which he puts the ornamentation which he formerly marked more or less indelibly on his skin.   In this way he is able *to gratify his taste for change.*" [1]

It will be noted that, while the tendency of marks and mutilations "gradually to cease to be interesting" is laid down as a general law applicable to all cases, his exception here of the innovation of a scanty covering "to secure novelty," is quite an exception—simply an accidental case referrible only to certain tribes of which he there speaks; and that Professor Moseley lays down this tendency to gratify his taste for change as a universal law.   But it is not so.   Many tribes have, as Westermarck himself emphatically tells, never risen to the idea of any covering whatever either in men or women, in others the women are slightly covered and the men stark naked; and this was so in many cases after the white men and missionaries had been long in contact with them; and for ages on ages the system of marking or tattooing had been absolutely unchanged, fixed and uniform.

Darwin himself admits that, "the taste for certain colours or other ornaments would not remain constant with the human being whatever it may have done with the animals." [2]

Even Starcke, whose inquiries have led him to doubt the universality of totemism, and to seek to qualify a good deal in Maclennan's views, writes thus, showing the unchanging character of these marks, and the serious issues for the

[1] " Human Marriage," p. 412.
[2] " Descent of Man," p. 571.

tribe that might hang on the very slightest change
in them :—

" The tattoo marks make it possible to discover
the remote connection between clans, and this token
has such a powerful influence on the mind that there
is no feud between tribes which are tattooed in the
same way. The tattooing, which usually consists
in the imitation of some animal forms, may lead to
the worship of such animals as religious objects.
However this may be, tattooing is a plastic art
which may be modified and altered; and if similar
tattoo marks unite peoples together any alteration
of these marks may make the breach which has
taken place between them irreparable. Tattooing
may also lead to the formation of a group within
the tribe. At all events, among the Kainumas the
different families or hordes are distinguished by the
tattoo marks of the face. Among the Guaycurûs a
caste of nobles seems to have been formed this way." [1]

Vanity of mere adornment, or markings and
mutilations to attract the other sex, if we may judge
the caprices of individual human nature in the
savage no less than in the civilized, would by itself
lead to variety; to novelty, to manifold experiment
and improvement, in fact, to divergent competitionary
efforts.[2] But it is not so. The fixedness of custom
is the remarkable thing within the clan or tribe.

[1] " The Family," p. 43.

[2] So we find it among the Criminal populations— the savages of
civilization. See Mr. Havelock Ellis's " Criminal." But so we find
it, too, among the recherché people, who undergo elaborate tattooing
at the hands of Mr. Macdonald, of Jermyn Street, who is certainly
an artist. Extremes meet. Here the individual vagary has full play,
each sitter indulges his own caprice, and the adornment has no

They tattoo themselves according to the custom of
their ancestors, that being often the only reason they
can give for the practice.   They say "to please the
women," urges Westermarck. But the more perfect
they are in their tattooing, which is indelible and is
the most laborious of all kinds of decoration, as we
have said, there is henceforth the less room for
novelty; and it is the novelty and not the striking-
ness—the beauty or the ugliness—in itself that
pleases and excites.

Westermarck himself, if we remember right, refers
particularly to the case of one chief who had tattooes
on his breast, a certain number of dark lines running
partly parallel to each other, one for each enemy he
has killed; which suggests indeed a whole series of
such body memoranda directly traversing his main
position.   In this case we have, without doubt, a
direct association with the old idea which led the
savage to fancy that the power or agility of the
defeated passed into him; and these marks were
something in the nature of a symbol of this fact;
any way, these stripes point very far away from

reference to anything in the way of rule or principle.   One person
has painted on the back the "Last Supper," another one "Orpheus
and Eurydice," another a flight of birds, and a fourth an eagle;
now, if the name of the latter was Osprey, and an Osprey was
painted, there we should have some meaning, more meaning than
is conveyed even by the case of the very flowery individual, who is
not content with any symbolism—of name, crest, or aught else, but
plainly has prominently tattooed on his belly his name in staring
capitals, as if all his individuality was in that reclaimed from the
rich and wild and tortuous waste of his other decorations.   The only
persons who in the least approach to the motive and idea of the
early men are officers of regiments who have the crest or arms of
their regiments tattooed on their arms—by these marks they could
be identified, even if stripped, on the battlefield.

Westermarck's assumptions of "courting and being courted," unless it may be in a somewhat forced and secondary way.

Again, not without surprise, we read :—

"Among savages it is, as a rule, the man only that runs the risk of being obliged to lead a single life." Yet it does not appear that, though this law is practically universal in savagery, the women in the least act as though it were—in a great many cases they put themselves to no end of trouble and suffering to secure that of which they are assured— to attract the men ; when they run no risk like the men, of being obliged " to lead a single life." Never- theless, the women, in many cases, surpass the men in the marks they put upon themselves. "Among the Nagas of Upper Assam, for instance, it was the custom *to allow matrimony* to those only who made themselves as hideous as possible by having their faces cut and elaborately tattooed."[1]

"*To allow matrimony!*" Then, here is a case which Westermarck does not, so far as we can see, properly explicate. There were here, and there may have been, nay, probably were, in many other of the cases he cites, elements of tribal law coming in to modify wholly such free courting as he favours, in which, as he holds, ornament was used merely that they might "court successfully and be courted." What were these laws? Westermarck does not tell us, nor does he to our satisfaction make even a guess. In this regard his work, laboured and complete as it is, needs, and indeed loudly calls for, a supplementary chapter, maybe more than one.

---

[1] Dalton "Ethnology," p. 39.

On the opposite side a question arises. Why, if this is a universal law, why, in so many cases, do the women, as Westermarck himself tells us, content themselves, as he says, " with their natural charms " ? On his principle, this thing ought not so to be. Westermarck, in some measure unconscious of the bearing of these markedly exceptional and in degree contradictory cases, gives a selection thus :—

" It has been suggested by Darwin that the plainer appearance of the women depends upon their oppressed and despised condition, as well as upon the selfishness of the men. But it is doubtful whether this is the true explanation. Savage ornaments, generally speaking, are not costly things, and even where the state of women is most degraded, a woman may, if she pleases, paint her body with red ochre, or put a piece of wood through her lip, or a feather through the cartilage of her nose. In Eastern Central Africa, for instance, the women are more decorated than the men, although they hold an inferior position, being viewed as beasts of burden, and doing all the harder work. ' A woman,' says Macdonald, ' always kneels when she has occasion to talk to a man ' (*Africana*, vol. i., p. 35). Almost the same is said of the female Indians of Guiana, whereas in the Yule Island, on the coast of New Guinea, and in New Hanover, the women are less given to personal adornment than the men, although they are held in respect, have influence in their families, and exercise, in some villages, much authority, or even supremacy. Of all the various kinds of ornamentation tattooing is the most laborious. Yet in Melanesia it is chiefly women that are tattooed, though they are treated as slaves; whilst in Polynesia, where the *status* of women is comparatively good, this practice is mainly confined to the men. In Fiji, where women were fearfully oppressed, genuine tattooing was found on them only."

So that the poor Fijian fellows had no Westermarckian aid whatever to their courting!

Westermarck's theory wholly fails to meet or to cover certain of the dreadful mutilations both in men and women—to several of which he has himself referred, and with good taste and reserve used Latin in writing of them.

Another point: Westermarck elsewhere is keen to prove jealousy as universally prevalent. If so, was it to have all expression after marriage on "proprietary principles"? and was it to have none before it when the courting was being done? The jealous married man, if his jealousy was well founded, had his remedy; not so certainly the jealous courter, and jealousy grows with what it feeds on! Did the jealous courter never resort to means of showing his jealousy which superseded or overstept the limits tribal law allowed in his adornments, or did it not? Was the tribe ever prevailing in such matters, or did the individual in this way also assert himself and break away, or did he not? I should like from Dr. Westermarck an answer to this question, because if individual fancy had free play in the matter of free courting, as we understand it, and if jealousy is universally prevalent, then I should look for some phenomena with not a single instance of which has Dr. Westermarck presented us.

That story of the origin of tattooing in Tahiti does

not look so decisively in Westermarck's direction, as, at first sight, it might seem ; and Westermarck makes this bold statement : "This legend is especially instructive, because it shows how a custom which had originally nothing to do with religion may in time take a more or less religious character." But hosts of legends bear in the same direction, as in the South Pacific, New Zealand, &c., &c. Let us, however, look for a moment more particularly at his instance. The daughter of the god and goddess Taaora and Apouvaru was kept very strictly enclosed with the idea of protecting her chastity. Her brothers, as a last resource, tattooed themselves, and showed themselves to her. She broke from her enclosures, was like them tattooed, and by them seduced. The two sons of Taaora and Apouvaru became gods of tattooing. The suggestion is that tattooing originated in the time when intercourse between those of the same family was still permissible or just at the point where it was beginning to be disallowed. Prayers, we are told, were addressed to the images of the sons of Taaora and Apouvaru in the temples where the art of tattooing was practised. We are not informed what these images were, nor whether they were accompanied by birds or beasts or symbols sacred to them ; but a good deal in savage development would lead us to believe that they were, and that these birds, or beasts, or symbols were the things more or less effectively tattooed on the bodies of the worshippers.

In the cases of hair cut off on marriage to which Westermarck refers, this suggestion may be allowed. He speaks of hair as having been by many savage peoples looked on as promoting sexual desire. The cutting off of the hair was an offering to the god— the hair that in many cases had been arranged so as to suggest totem-forms, as he himself has indicated in speaking of certain tribes.

Some of the Abyssinian women, for example, remove their eyebrows, and in their place put crescents, tattooed in blue ink. They also stain their gums a deep indigo-blue.[1]

If Maclennan's theory of tattooings, paintings, marks, cuttings, cicatrices as totem-marks, will not satisfactorily explain everything, so certainly Wester- marck's very bold attempt to reduce all those to mere ornamentation to attract and to excite sexual desire, will not explain everything either ; and, after all, we return provisionally, and not without some satisfac- tion, on Mr. Herbert Spencer's deliverance that tattooing and other forms of mutilation were practised originally as a mere means of expressing subordination to a dead ancestor, or ruler, or god.[2]

II.

In this second section I shall present under four headings groups of typical classes selected from a wide range, which certainly do not, at all events primarily, come under Westermarck's principle of attraction between the sexes,—" to aid in successfully courting and being courted." Our first section shall deal with tattooing on infants and young children.

1. *Tattooings and Marks on Infants and Young Children.*

Among the Otomi tribe of Mexico, as Bancroft tells, if the little one was a boy, one of the old men

---

[1] Donaldson Smith, p. 77.   [2] "Sociology," ii. p. 72.

took it in his arms and painted on its breast an axe, and on its shoulders a bow and arrow. If a girl, the women took it, and the figure of a flower or plant was traced, tattooed, over the region of the heart, while on the back of the right hand, a rude spinning wheel was pictured, and on the left a piece of wool." [1] Again, of another tribe in Mexico, we read that, after some ceremonies, " the priest carried the child to the altar, where he drew from it a few drops of blood by a cut meant to form a small cicatrice of certain form, and then he threw water over it, or plunged it into a cistern or bath. With the Guaycurûs of Paraguay, the boys are painted black till the age of fourteen, and afterwards red till sixteen, and, at the age of twenty, on the degree of veteran, as they call it, being attained, they are, in the most sensitive and private parts, pricked and painted, the blood from the wounds being used to rub the head, and one of the crowns or tails of hair being pulled out by the roots.[2] One part of this observance has, in our idea, to do with the circle of phenomena with which circumcision is allied—circumcision which, as we shall see, Westermarck is fain to show, is a mere decoration " to aid in successful courting and being courted "—despite the Jews.

Sir R. Burton tells that, despite Mohammed's legislation, three lines are cut with a sharp instrument on the cheeks of Arab children of certain tribes to-day.[3]

In Abyssinia the child, as soon as born, is washed

---

[1] " Hist. of Mexico," i. p. 634.
[2] Charleroix, " Paraguay," i. pp. 87-89.
[3] " Pilgrimage," ii. p. 75.

with cold water and perfumed, and then a woman
moulds its head, and the different features by pressing
them with her fingers, while a man from the outside
of the house pokes a lance into its mouth if it is a
boy to make it courageous.[1] With the Tupinambas
of Brazil the first operation on the child is to flatten
its nose with the thumb and finger, and the lip is
then bored. If it is a boy, the father paints or tattoos
him black or red, and lays beside him in the hammock
a club and a little bow and arrows, with an image of
the god.[2] A certain tribe in Australia, whose totem
is the sand-lizard, light a fire over a quantity of
prepared sand. The newborn babe is then deposited
therein, perfectly nude, and buried up to the very
chin, and is kept there for two hours and afterwards
painted.[3] In Madagascar, the names of animals are
often given to children of even the best families, as
" mamba," the crocodile, "voalavo," the rat, and
so on.[4] At Maiva, South Pacific, quite young girls
are tattooed all over, except the face, which is tattooed
after marriage.[5] In the Port Moresby district, New
Guinea, it is the custom to tattoo from head to foot
every female. Commencing from infancy, they are
marked with strange designs and figures, until, when
they are grown-up, there is no space for more.[6]
Solinus tells that they (the ancient Britons) had
shapes of beasts artfully cut in mere youth in their
bodies, so that the prints in their flesh might grow

[1] Parkyns, ii. p. 35.
[2] Southey, i. p. 248.
[3] G. T. Lloyd, p. 465.
[4] Little, p. 66.
[5] Chalmers and Gill, p. 261.
[6] Captain Webster's " Through New Guinea," p. 248.

and increase as their bodies did.[1] The Guaycurûs
pull the hair out of the heads of the children, making
the girls completely bare, and on the boys' heads
leaving only a tuft on the crown.[2] Some quite young
girls on the Solomon Islands wear a little mother-of-
pearl bird, which is fastened in a hole at the extreme
tip of the nose.[3] Here is a very peculiar custom :
The Zapotees of Mexico give to each of their
children what, is called a "tona" or second self.
This was a certain animal, and, when the child
grew old enough he procured an animal of that kind,
took care of it and ornamented it, as it was believed
that his health, strength, and even existence depended
upon it—were bound up with that of the animal—in
fact, that the death of both would be simultaneous.[4]

The Dieri of Australia, as Fison and Howitt tell
us, remove the two front teeth at eight years, and
other tribes do the same by their children.[5] The
Andamanese, begin to tattoo their children about
their eighth year. Among the Australian tribes,
at the famous Kuraweli-wonkana, the ceremony of
circumcision is performed, when a boy is about nine
or ten ; and another ceremony afterwards is notable. Each of the old men draws blood from his
body and sprinkles it over the body of the boy,
till he is perfectly covered with it, in order that he
may learn to have no fear at the sight of blood.[6]

With many tribes knocking out or filing of the

---

[1] Camden, i. pp. 1-3.
[2] Charleroix, "Paraguay," i. p. 87.
[3] Coote, p. 120.
[4] Bancroft, i. p. 655.
[5] Anthro. Jour., xx. p. 80.
[6] Kamilaroi & Kurnai, p. 174.

teeth is a very strict observance. Many difficulties have been raised at one time or another about this. But precisely as the cutting and arranging of locks of hair to imitate the turtle among the turtle tribe of Red Indians, or the leaving of small tufts to imitate tail and head of Small Bird clan of Omahas; so the filing down of the teeth, like the running of horns through the nose, was to imitate the totem animal.

It is most distinctly suggested by Ali Effendi Gifoon, a Shilook Negro-arab, in the *Cornhill Magazine* for June, 1896, that the Fertits and Resirra or hyena tribes of the Soudan, as they, at certain times, so imitated the totem in their movement and cries, also had their teeth kept sharp by filing in imitation of the teeth of the hyena. [1]

Sir George Robertson says that, among the Kafirs of the Hindu-Cush, he has seen boys under twelve smeared with blood, and the horns put in the hair, at the Sanowkun celebration or feast—boys who certainly had not yet reached the age of puberty.

The Dume pigmies of Central Africa make discs of zinc, which they hang on the forehead, and from the ears and the bored septum of the nose, which makes it difficult really to see their features; the mouth being in most cases completely covered, and this is begun when quite young.[2]

The Kere twist their hair round a stick that points directly upward, or they dress it with clay, others similarly raise it up, and they wear zinc discs suspended from their ears like the Dume.[3]

---

[1] P. 600.
[2] Donaldson Smith's " Through Unknown African Countries," p. 273.
[3] *Ibid.*, p. 307.

The Bangala of Africa dress their hair fantastically, allowing one or more pigtails to grow a foot long, and stiffening the plaits with wax to give them the appearance of horns. They also cut and re-cut the skin from the root of the nose upwards to the hair, the cicatrix thus formed being often an inch high, and resembling a cock's-comb.[1]

Miss Kingsley finds the tattooing of West Africa is not any way decorative, but is in origin connected with initiation into secret societies which are at basis totemistic. Much is suggested by this. Initiation ceremonies go much further and deeper than Dr. Westermarck has yet seen; but this subject would want express and lengthened treatment, and must wait. This is what Miss Kingsley most significantly says :

"Tattooing on the West Coast is comparatively rare, and I think I may say *never used with decorative intent only*. The skin decorations are either paint or cicatrices; in the former case the pattern is not always kept the same by the individual. A peculiar form of it you find in the Rivers, where a pattern is painted on the skin, and then when the paint is dry, a wash is applied, which makes the unpainted skin rise up in between the painted pattern. The cicatrices are sometimes tribal marks. They are made by cutting the skin, and then placing in the wound the fluff of the silk cotton tree. The great point of agreement between all these West African secret societies lies in the method of initiation. The boy, if he belongs to a tribe that goes in for tattooing,

[1] Hinde, p. 110.

is tattooed and handed over to instructors in the society's secrets and formulæ." [1]

Dr. Freeman paid close attention to marks and cuts and mutilations among the tribes of West Africa, and is certain that, if some desire for ornamentation may now and again play a part in the body marks, the face-marks have invariably some special significance, tribal mostly. He gives at p. 425 a drawing of the tribal marks of Moslie (five long curving lines running alongside each other right down the side of the cheek from top to bottom).

The Mabode have excisions in patterns caused by cuts and removal of little bits of skin, and in all cases these are begun on certain parts at an early age.

Messrs. Spencer and Gillen distinctly tell us, with regard to certain mutilations among the Central Australian tribes, that "These cicatrices are often the result of self-inflicted wounds, made on the occasion of the mourning ceremonies which are attendant upon the deaths of individuals who stand in certain definite relations to him " [the mourner] . [2]

The Aïnos of Japan—the hairy people—by some set down as the " missing link," have some very peculiar customs. Among them tattooing is practised only on the women, or more properly, females— the face being sometimes tattooed with the figure of a flower ; the little girls only have a small patch or fragment, the *elaborate* tattooing being all done after marriage, and in most cases the tattooing is begun before the child is weaned—before the third year at latest.[1]

2. *Tattooings after Marriage.*

In the Marquessas Islands, Melville observed many women who had the right hand and left foot most elaborately tattooed, while the rest of the body was free. He learned that this was done after marriage, and was the distinguishing badge of wedlock.[2]   In New Guinea a girl, on being engaged, is tattooed on the chest with a figure of triangular shape ; after marriage the spaces within are filled up with figures, and lines of tattooing are carried down to the knees.[3]   Here the most elaborate tattooing was done after the need for it, according to Wester-marck, had utterly ceased, and cases of this sort are many.   At Banate, in the Caroline Islands, Lutke tells that women have sometimes tattooed upon them marks standing for the names of their hus-band's ancestors—done, of course, after marriage, which, according to Westermarck, should aid court-ship.   In Japan, the married women alone enjoy the privilege of staining their teeth a deep black.[4] Among the Aïnos of Japan, when a woman marries they tattoo her upper lip, and sometimes the under one also.   A favourite pattern has the ends curled just in the way exquisites frequently curl up the

[1] See " The Aïnos," by D. MacRitchie, in " International Archiv für Ethnol," 1889.

[2] " South Pacific," p. 211.

[3] " Anthropological Journal," vii. p. 481.

[4] " Trans. Ethnological Soc.," vii. p. 18.

ends of their moustaches.[1] In Formosa there is a
Malay-looking race called the Kweiyings, which live
in the mountains, and we are told that, among them,
"The unmarried men and women tattoo a square
mark on the forehead, the married men also on the
chin, and the married women right across the face
from ear to ear."[2]

Now that cannot possibly be regarded as an
improvement; and one of the motives to it is
most likely and most naturally the very opposite
of what Westermarck says is *the* object of all
tattooing.

In North-West California, as Schoolcraft tells,
the woman after marriage is entitled to have a
tattooing on her face extending above the corners
of the mouth.[3] The married women of the Guay-
curús of Paraguay are tattooed a dark blue under
the eyes.[4] Lindt says that in New Guinea all the
women are tattooed, and that a peculiar necklace-
like mark, ending in a peak between the breasts,
indicates those who are married or engaged[5]—
according to Westermarck, to aid courtship and to
attract the men! Just as though, with us, a wed-
ding-ring were a signal of invitation or of solicitation
—which in exceptional cases it may be, but, thank
God, that is not its original purpose or general
effect.

In the Hawaiian (Sandwich) Islands a widow had
the name of her dead husband pricked into the tongue

[1] Trans. Ethnological Soc. vii. p. 27.
[2] Swinhoe, p. 7.
[3] "Indian Tribes," iii. p. 175.
[4] Knight, "Cruise of the Falcon," p. 225.
[5] P. 67.

—a very strange and a very permanent kind of widow's weeds truly. The *rationale* of the custom seems to have had origin in much the same idea as the Hindu suttee—the consecration, by outward mark in this case as by burning in the other, to the *manes* of the dead husband. Many forms does one idea take—so many and varied that it is hard at first to see any affinity; but surely Westermarck would not say that this was decorative!

3. *Tattooings where the Motives are Mixed.*

Among the Esquimaux we find one kind of decoration or tattooing which certainly admits of a mixture of motives besides the exclusive one favoured by Westermarck. The harpooner after a successful day's work is a great personage, and is invariably decorated with the Esquimaux order of the Blue Ribbon—*i.e.*, he has a line of blue drawn across his face over the bridge of the nose, and to *this is attached* the privilege of being allowed to take another wife.[1] The only parties among the Dasuns of Borneo who tattoo themselves are those who have killed an enemy. The tattoo is invariably a broad band from the navel to each shoulder. A smaller band is carried down each arm, and a stripe drawn transversely across it for each enemy slain. One young fellow had no fewer than thirty-seven stripes across his arms.[2] So also in Hood Bay, New Guinea, and in other parts of New Guinea. In these cases the primary motive was certainly not what Westermarck says, and, according to him, what of the rest of the

[1] McClure, p. 93.
[2] Ro. Geo. Soc. Pro. 1858, p. 348.

Dasuns not tattooed, in their courtship? Poor fellows! In this they could not succeed save by killing, as indeed is the case with some civilised castes. Captain Webster gives a picture of a chief in the interior of New Guinea, with his upper lip slit and each half sewn up into his nostrils, as he says, for ornamentation;[1] but surely " for ornamentation," in any true sense, it could not be. The Catties are a sort of half-Hindoos. Doararca is a small island containing a temple resorted to by pilgrims, who, among other ceremonies, receive a stamp on the body with a hot iron, on which are engraved a shell, ring, and a lotus-leaf, the insignia of the gods. *A pilgrim is sometimes stamped for an absent friend.*[2] Surely there is full enough suggestion of religious motive here—vicarious stamping in some cases, where the courting would need, like that of Miles Standish, to be done by deputy!—though it may be in some cases the women, too, are attracted to the wrong man!

4. *Exceptional Tattoo and other Marks.*

But the strangest sort of totem and totem-marks are, perhaps, to be found among the priests of the Moxas of Brazil. They were initiated by abstaining wholly for a year from fish and flesh; and it was necessary that the aspirant should have been attacked and wounded by a jaguar, and show the marks of it. The jaguar is the object of their worship, and they consider him, therefore, as setting his mark upon those whom he chooses to be his priests. After long

---

[1] " Through New Guinea," p. 65.

[2] Malte Brun, iii. p. 67.

practice as a snaker (by which term they were called from the mode in which they attempted to administer relief), they were raised to a higher grade in the priesthood. To attain this degree it was necessary to undergo another year of severe abstinence, at the end of which the juice of certain pungent herbs was infused into their eyes to purge their mortal sight, and also to change slightly their colour.[1]

A Blackfeet Indian boy at the age of fourteen will wander away from his father's lodge, and absent himself sometimes for four or five days, lying on the ground in some remote or secluded spot, crying to the Great Spirit, and fasting the whole time. When he falls asleep, the first animal, bird, or reptile of which he dreams he believes the Great Spirit has designated for his protector in life. Coming home, he does not long remain, but sets out again with weapons and trap to procure the animal thus indicated; and, having found it, he preserves the skin entire, and ornaments it according to his fancy. He carries it with him through life as his strength in battle, and in death as his guardian spirit. It is buried with him, as it is believed to conduct him safe to the beautiful hunting grounds.[2] Among the Abipones boys of seven years old pierce their little arms in imitation of their parents, and display plenty of wounds.[3]

It is almost impossible that the raised cuts, ridges as thick as the wrist, caused by earth or ashes or some other substance having been introduced under

[1] Southey, iii. p. 202.
[2] Catlin, " North Amer. Indians," i. 36, 37.
[3] Herbert Spencer, " Cere. Institutions," p. 178.

the flesh immediately after the cutting, could at first
have been regarded as ornamental. At Eboe, on
the Niger River, some of the women are quite
mutilated with marks on their arms and breasts,
having the flesh raised nearly an inch, presenting
stripes and figures of animals.[1] This practice could
not indeed have begun with the earlier progenitors
of the race : it had a beginning in a much later
period. We know perfectly well that for all such
"ornamentations" certain instruments and pigments
are needful—and assuredly so for tattooing and
the finer paintings. To what indeed are properly
primeval men, or indeed utterly savage men, they
are out of the question. Then at what point did
they begin ? Ornament is not likely to have been
much in demand with human beings whose whole
business was as yet merely to find subsistence,
shelter, and escape from wild beasts.

We talk of savages and savagery, and are but too
inclined to group all under one class : with the
result that beautiful thoughts arising now and then,
special faculties cultivated almost to perfection in
certain directions, are either overlooked or do not
receive the attention they deserve. We want to
distinguish more, and indeed to classify. As all
civilised peoples are not equally advanced, so as to
have escaped in like measure from the dominance of
"survivals," so all heathen peoples are not equally
savages by any means. "Survivals" in their case
are just as significant for the student as in ours ;
and it is as needful with them as with ourselves to
distinguish between what is a "survival" and what

[1] Laird and Oldfield, ii. p. 32.

a vital element in present faith. To absorb all
" survivals " into a certain atmosphere which would
explain them on grounds or influences which are
existent or operative to-day as other influences that
are past were operative hundreds of years ago, is not
a very advanced philosophy, nor is it likely to carry
us very far. There is surely a great distinction
between the washing with red ochre and rubbing
with grease and soot, and such highly artistic
performances as Cook has told us of in the way of
tattooing. If both were meant to aid courtship,
they certainly exhibited very different conditions
and artistic tastes. Cook tells that, of tattooed
persons in New Zealand, of a hundred which at
first sight appeared to be exactly the same, no two
were, on close examination, found to be exactly
alike. Southey writes: "Some of the tribes of
Brazil, notably the Xarayes, were artists. Both
sexes stained themselves from the neck to the knees
with a blue dye, which they laid on in such exquisite
patterns that a German who saw them doubted
whether the best artists in Germany could have
surpassed the nicety and intricacy of the designs."[1]
Thomas thus describes South Pacific Islanders on a
labour ship : Some had their skins blistered up into
the similitude of flowers and ferns, cameos in living
flesh, really pretty. Others, again, were ornamented
with fish and lizards. The skin is cut, and earth
and hot ashes placed inside, when the flesh grows
into the forms into which the artist dresses the
sores.[2] In Burma the principal tattooing is confined
to the portion of the body from the navel to the

[1] I. p. 140.   [2] P. 337.

knee. The figures consist of animals, such as lions,
tigers, and hogs, with crows, some fabulous birds,
rats, and demons. The figures are first painted on
the skin, and afterwards punched in by needles
steeped in pigment.[1] Many of the ladies of Fez
are tattooed with the name of God, among flowers,
circles, &c. In the Society Islands the cocoa-nut
palm is a favourite subject, and exquisitely rendered.

Speaking of Abbeokuta, Mr. Burton admits himself puzzled by the rules strictly observed amidst
the greatest diversity. " There was a vast variety of
tattoos and ornamentation, rendering them a serious
difficulty to strangers. The skin patterns were of
every variety, from the diminutive prick to the
great gash and the large boil-like lumps. They
affected various figures—tortoises, alligators, and the
favourite lizard, stars, concentric circles, lozenges,
right lines, welts, gouts of gore, marble or button-
like knobs of flesh, and elevated scars, resembling
scaulds, which are opened for the introduction of
fetish medicines and to expel evil influences. In
this country every tribe, sub-tribe, and even family
has its blazon, whose infinite diversifications may
be compared to the lines and ordinaries of European
heraldry."[2] This indeed is the principle that unites
or explains all the variety : each clan or sub-clan of
a tribe has its clan-marks, subordinated to the true
tribal ones.

Here are some testimonies as to the natives of New
Guinea from Dr. Wyatt Gill :

" As the ordinary tattooing would not show on the

[1] Crawford, " Ava," p. 96.
[2] " Abbeokuta," i. p. 104.

dark skins of the natives of New Guinea, a sym-
metrical scar is made on the shoulder of all males in
Mauat and in the Straits."[1]   "Our first impression
of the Redscar Bay women was that they wore
tasteful, close-fitting, lace-like garments. But it
proved to be merely the exquisitely-beautiful tattooing
with which they are covered. They wear a neat
girdle of leaves reaching nearly to the knee. The
men are but slightly tattooed in their faces and necks,
exactly reversing what we had seen in Polynesia.
The girdle of the men is made of the paper-mulberry,
but is a mere pretence as a covering."[2]   "While at
Mauat," Dr. Wyatt Gill goes on, " I remonstrated
with some of the chiefs for not wearing a little
covering. They straightened themselves up and
replied, with offended dignity, 'Would you have us
to be like women? Clothing is only for women.'"
The Papuans of South-western New Guinea have
exactly the same idea, and, oddly enough, the women
in the Andaman Islands think the same about the
men. Here we have cases in which, if adornment
is, as Westermarck says, merely for sexual attraction,
the men did not conform to the same law as the
women, though there are good reasons why, ethno-
logically, the positions in the former case should
have been exactly reversed ; and, be it noted, they
had nothing of Professor Moseley's external painted
appendage.

We may say, therefore, that Professor Moseley's
dogmatic generalisation, which Dr. Westermarck
quotes with such approval, and on which he so much

[1] " Life in the Southern Isles," p. 241.
[2] *Ibid.*, p. 248.

relies, to the effect that a savage begins by painting
and tattooing himself for ornament, and then adopts
a moveable appendage, "which he hangs on his body
and paints as he had before painted the body," is a
handy assumption, but far too wide and wide of the
mark, because we have given cases—and there are
many others—both where there was no moveable
appendage, and where the moveable appendage is
painted without any painting whatever on the body
having gone before—an end without a beginning, so
to say, an effect without a cause, according to Drs.
Moseley and Westermarck! The latter agrees that,
in many cases, tattoo marks make it possible for
savages to distinguish their clansmen, though "I
cannot think with Chenier,"[1] he goes on, "this was
their original object"—that many of them are trophy-
badges or ornamental substitutes for them, and others
are carried as signs of opulence. "Nevertheless, it
seems beyond doubt that men and women began to
ornament, mutilate, paint, and tattoo themselves in
order to make themselves attractive to the opposite
sex, that they might court successfully and be
courted."

Among the Australian tribes we find the practice
of cutting scars or cicatrices in certain forms on
children, so that with growth the scar should grow
into certain figures, and yet we have this fact clearly
set down by Sir George Grey in his "Journals in
Australia":

"Female children were always betrothed within a
few days after their birth; and from that moment the
parents cease to have any control over the future

---

[1] Quoted by Heriot, p. 293 (note).

settlement of their child. Should the first husband die before the girl has attained the years of puberty, she then belongs to his heir. A girl lives with her husband at any age she pleases; no control whatever is in this way placed upon her inclinations. When a native dies his brother inherits his wives and children; but his brother must be of the same family name as himself. The widow goes to her second husband's hut three days after the death of the first."

Not much room for free courting here, any more than in hundreds of savage cases beside.

Darwin has, in his own frank and characteristic way, noted this fact, and does not miss the real possibilities on the other side:

"With many savages it is the custom to betroth the females while mere infants; *and this would effectually prevent preference being exerted on either side according to personal appearance.* But it would not prevent the more attractive women being afterwards stolen or taken by force from their husbands by the more powerful men [of other tribes? Certainly tribal laws would not allow fights for women]; and this often happens in Australia, America, and elsewhere."[1]

Now this, from the pen of the great master himself, is finely conclusive of the utter failure of Dr. Westermarck's theory to cover all the facts of the case—to cover large sections of them; but the value of tattooing to render recognition of a stolen wife easy surely gives a wholly efficient and clear motive to clan-marks on the women, especially in those cases where we find the women are tattooed and not the

[1] "Descent of Man," p. 593.

men. Where the men are not tattooed, while the women are, we have facts which suggest one objection to Mr. Herbert Spencer's theory that all marks, mutilations, and tattooings have their origin in the attempt on the part of the boys and young men to imitate the scars borne by the warriors and veterans of the clan or tribe. In such cases the old men bore tokens of battle just as in others, but the boys and young men did not, from whatever reason, in those cases imitate them. Again, from the risk, as Darwin says above, of the more attractive women being carried off by enemies, may there not be something in the reason urged by several tribes that tattooing of women, as we shall see, is done to make them repellent and ugly? Not much in favour of Westermarck's theory, surely ! [1]

According to Westermarck, circumcision owes its origin to the same cause ;[2] and this leads us to a little excursus Australia-ward.

Dr. Stirling, in his section of the Horn Expedition Report on the Anthropology of Central Australia, says :

" Both sexes, when uninfluenced by civilisation, are practically nude, though in the groups that assemble about the stations, the women, and particularly the younger ones, cover their nakedness with miscellaneous odds and ends of garments acquired from whites. Almost all the men habitually wear a conventional covering in the form of a small

[1] Aiolos, according to Kahn, variegated = tattooed, warriors, —Rawlinson. Aryan, — extreme simplicity, variegated, highly coloured, &c.
[2] " Human Marriage," p. 201.

fan-shaped tassel made of fur string, and not much larger than a postage stamp. This is attached to the pubic hairs, and is much less efficient as a covering than the vine-leaf of the sculptor. Its grotesque inadequacy, in fact, rather serves to attract the attention to the parts which it pretends to conceal."[1] Here certainly you have evidence of the savage care for mere ornament.

Dr. Stirling, of a truth, leans strongly enough to the side of Westermarck ; but certain of the phenomena there make him pull up and declare that they cannot at all be covered by Westermarck's theory—certainly one of the most powerful though unintended blows it has yet received—and that from the hands of a friend. He is fain to find that scars, knocking out of teeth, and boring of the nasal septum are due merely to love of decoration ; but he has to admit that the piercing of the septum and the knocking out of teeth are very frequently done at a much earlier age than puberty, and scarcely gives such full force to this as he should have done.[2] Moreover, he cannot find any ground for saying that circumcision, as practised by many tribes, can be decorative, much less the horrible practice of subincision, where the incision itself is certainly not visible. He has to fall back on the idea that this was practised with the view of reducing population, and putting bars in the way of adding to it. "The limits," he writes, "being primarily those required and defined by the food supply, and secondarily by the special trouble and difficulty in rearing children under the circumstances of their nomadic lives—and attempts have been made

---

[1] " Horn Exp. Report," p. 18.   [2] *Ibid.*, p. 31.

to show that those tribes which do carry out this singular practice are those most liable to the conditions which bring about these difficulties. The same view is not unfrequently either directly stated or implied by the natives themselves, and Mr. Kempe, manager of the Peake Station on the west side of Lake Tyre, informs me that certain individuals are there deliberately left without operation, so that they may be free from the disabilities of their mutilated fellows."[1] And after considering some difficulties arising from the fact that this practice prevails where the land is fruitful, and does not prevail where it is not so, he goes on to say : " I am satisfied that though subincision may be reasonably supposed to operate in the direction required by the Malthusian view, it is by no means an effectual hindrance to procreation " ; and, significantly enough, Dr. Stirling is not alone in this conclusion or inference.

Sir Richard Burton, in dealing with exactly the same custom among certain tribes of Arabs, tells that they assert it is for the purpose of limiting the number of children, which he ridicules, giving instances of large families begotten by men so subincised,[2] precisely as Dr. Stirling does, and as, yet more emphatically, Messrs. Spencer and Gillen do in "Australian Aborigines," though Sir Richard certainly tells his story with a great deal more *abandon* and subacid (=*subincisive*) humour than Dr. Stirling does.

Messrs. Spencer and Gillen emphatically write on this point : " The Arunta natives have no idea of sub-

[1] *Ibid.*, pp. 33, 34.
[2] " Arabian Nights," viii. p. 109.

incision having been practised or instituted with the idea of preventing or even checking procreation. It does not do this. Nor has the food supply question anything to do with it. It is infanticide that keeps down the number of a family."[1]

But here we are in a region that demands yet fuller investigation, and the application of comparative methods in a much more systematic way than has yet been done. Only this much is to be said, that surely Dr. Stirling is right in declining, in view of these, to go the whole hog with Professor Westermarck, whom, in our idea, he celebrates just a little too loudly.

Of Professor Westermarck's theory of circumcision (not to speak of subincision), in face of phallic worship so widely spread, and mutilations for the god so common, it is bold; but on this other statement we must make a remark or two: "This conclusion" [Mr. Herbert Spencer's, that circumcision originated in trophy-giving to the god or chief] "Mr. Spencer draws from *the single fact* that among the Abyssinians the trophy taken by circumcision from an enemy's dead body is presented by each warrior to his chief." Westermarck is wrong here as to the fact. Indeed, he is doubly wrong—wrong (1) as to the facts generally; wrong (2) as to Mr. Herbert Spencer's statements in reference to the facts. Let us look at these two points.

I. Certainly it is very far from a "single instance." Anthropological record presents a very wide array of facts—so wide an array that any loose statement like

<hr />

[1] "Australian Aborigines," p. 264.

this should make **us slow to accept** a writer's other statements without our having first carefully examined not only his authorities, but the whole range, **to see** how he uses, and selects, and manipulates. **There** is first and foremost the case of the Hebrew David finding **100 (or was** it 200 ?) Philistine foreskins for Saul (**1 Sam. xix.** 25, 27, **and 2** Sam. iii. **14), which were given "in** full tale **to** the king," **as** we are **told ; and,** from **the** whole circumstances, one is assuredly quite **as** much justified as Westermarck is **in** many of his inferences, in inferring that this **is a** survival, and that foreskins were **in** old days presented as trophies to the Hebrew kings or to the heads of Hebrew tribes, **as was** decidedly the case with some Arab tribes **as** well **as Abyssinians and** Berbers. And am **I not** justified **in claiming that** victory of **the sons of Jacob over** the **Shechemites as, in one aspect at least** symbolically, an offering **first of foreskins, even if it were** but through fraud, though more **than the** foreskins followed through fraud **too?** Why, it is surely not too much to say that **we have** this very trophy-rendering in the act **of** Zipporah, when she conciliates Jahwé and saves Moses her husband from Jahwé by casting her son's foreskin at Jahwé's feet.

Then there **is** the very significant case of the Izedis, of whom **some** authors have written as devil-worshippers *pur et simple.* But **it is** clear that **this term** poorly **describes them or their** belief, since they believe **in God, but deem Him as** being in the meantime **of** little **practical importance** compared with the **more** active **evil** personality—Shaitan—a belief not professed, perhaps, but really held by many people who pretend to more enlightenment than the Izedis. Kelly, Rawlinson, and Dr. Grant have traced them to Jewish origin, and surely it is, at all events, significant to find that in their murders of the Turks, whom they intensely hate, it is easy to distinguish those slain by them from the victims of ordinary robbers, because of the " horrible mutilations " they invariably inflict to secure a certain trophy—that is, the trophy identified with early circumcision.[1]

Then turn the eye to the Antipodes. Among the Australian tribes, and especially among the Dieri, who have been very closely studied by Messrs. Fison and Howitt and Mr. Gason, this observances survives. No doubt the trophy was in early days taken from enemies, and even now the trophy is yielded to the head or chief or god by members of the tribe at a certain age at what are called Kurawile. And a very remarkable association is here set up with rain. We read words which force us to conclude that here it was especially the offering or trophy of the rain-god, as in Mexico and Peru :

" The foreskin which is carefully kept from the Kurawile is supposed to have great power in producing rain. The foreskins are carefully kept, wrapt up in feathers and rubbed with fat of the wild-dog and carpet-snake. If no rain follows, the explanation is that some neighbouring tribe has influenced Muramura not to grant it them."[2]

The intimate connection of all the phallic emblems with rain and water has not, so far as I know, been

---

[1] Kelly, " Syria and the Holy Land," pp. 47–51 and 127.
[2] Anthro. Jl. xviii. p. 561.

yet properly investigated and systematically set forth. It appears more or less decisively in all—from the divining rod to the smooth stone—from the earliest forms of the cross to the mast of the " boat-shaped vessel."

" During times of partial drought the Dieri do not feel anxiety if they possess one of these foreskins, believing that with its aid they can cause rain to come before long.   No matter how Mr. Gason scoffed at this belief, they were quite immovable in it, believing that the foreskin has an affinity to the clouds and rain." [1]

Further, if Heliogabalus brought to Rome from Syria the custom of throwing human foreskins or human phalli at the round black stone—symbol of the sun-god Elagabal—as had been done in Emesa,[2] I would venture to ask Dr. Westermarck where and how they were procured ?   Did they make multitudes of eunuchs of their own tribe or nation, or did they take the foreskins or phalli of dead enemies or of living prisoners ? [2]

Further still, up till and perhaps after the year 1876, at the Nangas in certain hill portions of Fiji, an important part of the observances had to do with the rite of circumcision, as most probably in early times something very closely corresponding was observed at the maraes all throughout the South Pacific.   This rite was either a part of the *Solevu ni Vilavou*, or New Year festival, or of special celebrations which were consequent on the sickness of a chief or of a warrior or man of note.   In the first,

---

[1] Anthro. Jl. xviii. p. 591.
[2] Döllinger, " The Gentile and the Jew," p. 431.

the young men, or *vilavou*, were brought up for circumcision; or, in the second case, a son of the sick man or a nephew was presented to the *vale lamba*, or god's house, as a *soro*, or offering of atonement, that his father or uncle might recover (clearly a survival of human sacrifice), and usually, for reasons of convenience or other reasons, other young lads went up with him to be circumcised. *The foreskins, we are told, were stuck in the cleft of a split reed, and were presented to the chief priest, who, holding the reed in his hand, offered them to the ancestral god*, praying for the sick man's recovery. After this followed a feast of revelry and open promiscuity. One of the old men, who told about the Nanga worship and ceremonies, himself confessed that, "while it lasted, we were just like pigs." Dr. E. B. Tylor, in view of the whole circumstances, regards it as "a proof and instance of consanguine marriage kept up as a mere ceremonial institution."[1]

So here, in spite of Dr. Westermarck and his "one instance," was offering foreskins to a god practised, perhaps, in hidden corners in Fiji, almost up to the date of his writing, and, what is yet more, in fine irony on the experts who deny early promiscuity, promiscuity practised in witness of the other promiscuity, up to quite the other day in Fiji too! Wherever offerings of this kind were made to kings or gods, a still more prevailing offering was held to be that part in conquered enemies.

Among the savage mountaineers of Formosa, as Dr. Mackay tells us, there is a regular practice of hunting for Chinese heads—heads of their traditional

---

[1] "International Archiv für Ethnographie," 1888.

enemies who have never subdued them—and that these heads are highly prized as trophies. When a party has been successful in this enterprise, a sound, never used at any other time, is made at a certain distance from the village. All the people turn out to meet the hunters; a ring is formed exactly at the point where the hunters and the village people meet; and there are celebrations and dancings round the heads set on spears stuck in the ground.[1] Another authority suggests that sometimes another trophy is taken as well as the head, if indeed Dr. Mackay does not hint it between the lines.

Mr. H. O. Forbes in his account of Timorlaut tells us that the bodies of those who die in war or by a violent death are buried, and if the head has been captured [by the enemy] a cocoa-nut is placed in the grave to represent the head of the missing man, and to deceive and satisfy the spirit.

So that here it is certainly not too much to adopt and adapt Dr. Westermarck's own words in reference to Mr. Frazer's thesis and say that his theory is supported by very few facts, and that many facts there are against it and in favour of that of Mr. Herbert Spencer, notwithstanding Dr. W's. conceited and ignorant deliverances and his *ipse dixits*.

Dr. Remondino's arguments directed against Israelitish circumcision having originated from phallic worship or any trophy-giving, because of the strict law against mutilation of anything sacrificed, or the admission of any one mutilated as a member of the congregation, is simply absurd. The two things have no connection whatever with each other,

[1] "Far Formosa," p. 268.

as could be proved by the survivals which attest that the taking of trophies—heads, phalluses, etc., etc.— was common with the early Jews as with other races. Besides all which, Dr. Remondino's arguments are refuted by language—by the very fact, for one thing, that the עָרְלַת was used with regard to David's trophies taken from the Philistines; this word being in strictness phallus as well as foreskin, the word being elsewhere translated foreskin, as though the foreskin strictly still existed in the circumcised. So it is used at Habakkuk ii. 16; the translators, both Authorised and Revised, being far more anxious than as disinterested men and scholars they ought to have been in rendering very plain words by euphemisms, and as the good Mr. Myers of Keswick said in "Catholic Thoughts," "Christianising Judaism as far as they could."

In spite of the efforts of the lexicons, I would connect this word עָרְלַת with עוּר, nakedness, which, of course, would cover circumcision (making naked or unsheathing), and, indeed, so we have it in the ending phrase of Hab. ii. 15, עַל־מְעוֹרֵיהֶם, or their nakedness. The two phrases must there, at all events, be taken the one in the light of the other, and to translate עָרֵל in the next verse as foreskin is a mere euphemism, and ridiculous, giving the part for the whole, and a part, too, that has vanished, been cut off, and, as Artemus Ward would say, "has no existents, is a myth."[1]

Here is another point well worth notice and further

---

[1] Both מְעֹר (for מֶעְרֶה), nakedness, privy part, and עֶרְוָה, nakedness or privy part, are from the same root, עָרָה, to be bare or naked.

investigation and comparison with others in which
may linger disguised survivals: " Among the Basutos,
at the time fixed for circumcision, all the candidates
go through a sham rebellion and escape to the woods.
The warriors arm and give chase, and, after a sham
battle, capture the insurgents, whom they bring back
as prisoners, amidst dancing and great rejoicings,
which is the prelude to the feast." [1]

Do we have here any suggestion of the origin
of circumcision (in that part, at all events), in the
survival of its being carried through in imitation of
securing a trophy from enemies ?   The point is not
without importance, in view of other things.   Certain
benefit or profit secured in prisoners or slaves, from
whom a trophy of this sort only was taken, instead
of their being killed to secure the head itself.

With regard to this form of offering, we trace it
as having originally been given voluntarily to the
god of fertility or increase, in not a few cases
identified with a deceased chief or king.   Thus the
Marquis de Nadaillac, in his account of the sacrifices
of the Mayas, a Yucatan tribe, and the orgiastic
celebrations which follow them, says :

" The sacrifices were always succeeded by several
holidays, dancings round engraved stones, banquets,
and brutal drunkenness ; husbands had to refrain
from all intercourse with their wives . . . and the
devout pierced the tongue, ears, and *other parts* of
their bodies and smeared the lips and beards of the
idols with the blood from their wounds.   At other
times the blood was drawn from the male organ,
some grains of maize were sprinkled with it, for the

---

[1] Remondino, p. 42.

possession of which the assistants disputed eagerly, believing it to be an aphrodisiac." [1]

Here is something to match from Nicaragua:

"At these processions the Nicaraguan priests blessed Indian corn, which had been sprinkled with the blood of their genitals, and threw it at the stone representation of their god."

East and West here shake hands:

"Among the Canaanites of Syria it was the highest and most acceptable service of priests and laymen to make themselves eunuchs in honour of the virgin goddess. During the festival of Astarte it was the custom for young men to spring forward, seize the ancient sword which lay on the altar of the goddess, and therewith mutilate themselves." [2] The same was customary at the festival of Rhea-Cybele or Agdistus in Phrygia.

II. Now with regard to Mr. Spencer's statements in the "Ceremonial Institutions." Will it be believed that Mr. Spencer specifically cited, besides "the single instance," several cases, and suggested a great many others? He referred to Phœnicia, to Egypt, to Israel, etc., etc. Here are his words about Egypt, with reference to a fresco:

"Along with the heap of hands thus laid before the king there is represented a phallic heap, and an accompanying inscription, narrating the victory of Menephtheh I. over the Libyans, besides mentioning the 'cut hands of their auxiliaries' [3] as being carried on donkeys following the returning army, mentions

[1] P. 268.
[2] Duncker, i. p. 366.
[3] "Ceremonial Institutions," p. 45.

those other trophies as taken from men of the Libyan nation."

And then about Phœnicia and San Salvador:

" Among the Phœnicians, as Movers tells, circumcision was a sign of consecration to Saturn, and when proof is given that of old the people of San Salvador circumcised in the Jewish manner, offering the blood to an idol, we are shown just the result to be anticipated as eventually arising."

And then he gives full illustration of it among the Jews, mentioning expressly the case of King David cited above.

Dr. Westermarck indeed proves only too little here, but it must be said that he proves too much elsewhere, and more especially when he says that the girls in Ponafé consider the boys handsomer for having undergone a process of semi-castration. That is not quite so good as it would be to say that the Hottentot women think their lords the handsomer for having when boys of six or seven been deprived of one testicle. No; handsome is as handsome does, and as the one testicle is taken to prevent, as they fancy, the begetting of twins and too many children coming, perhaps some of them would fain the man were intact. But that testicle, there is the best ground for believing, was given as offering when the child was a certain age to the rain-god.

" The facts stated seem to show that the object of tattooing, as well as of other kinds of self-decoration and mutilation, was to stimulate the sexual desire of the opposite sex." In opposition to this I say—and I think I am justified in saying, from the facts I have given, and to which I could add almost indefinitely—that tattooing and decoration and disfigurement originated in nothing of the sort, since they were applied in numerous cases to children, to new-born infants even, and, what is more, to children betrothed in infancy, for whom there was absolutely no courtship whatever in our sense of it; and that, if it came to be an element in stimulating sexual desire, this was a secondary element among other secondary elements, whatever the primary one may have been. To stimulate sexual desire by processes tending to produce incompetence, and indeed aiming at it, seems to be about as illogical as it would be to say that men may fly the better from being tied to earth! And certainly some suggestion of a primary religious meaning is derived from this fact, that we know in many tribes the priests were the tattooers, probably in all in the earlier days; and that, as the South Pacific legends of the origin of tattooing show, the process was accompanied with religious rites.

Mr. J. G. Scott, in his "Burman," very carefully tells us about the *Baw-dee-that-do* connected with the remarkable process of tattooing against snake-bite in Burma. When undergoing this process the man must eat chunks of human flesh, while the tattooer indulges in incantations many. He has much to say about the peculiar results on the *Baw-dee-that-do*, producing in some cases exceptional powers and tendencies, which may be the results of inoculation or may not be. But this remarkable custom most distinctly suggests a survival of sacramental or ceremonial eating of human flesh—undoubtedly only another form of god-eating, and as decisively telling of an original religious basis for *this* tattooing, at all events. Was it originally an initiation into a serpent or poisonous snake-clan or tribe?

Or, look again at the peculiar customs in this respect of the Talaings of Burma.

The Talaing men tattoo breeches on themselves, from the waist to below the knee, with sessamun-seed soot. The figures traced are ogres, tigers, monkeys, spirits, and each is surrounded by a border of mysterious cabalistic letters, while magic squares and lucky marks are also commonly introduced. Vermilion figures are also tattooed on the chest and arms and back, with special superstitious purposes. *The women are not tattooed.* The origin of the custom, of which the people are very proud, is exceedingly obscure.[1]

Now, how does Dr. Westermarck account for this peculiar custom? Does he deny the superstitious purposes, or does he say that they are all subordinate to the sexual attraction, or what? And how does he explain that the women in such case go untat-tooed? Do they want no aid in their amours? We should have thought that they, in this case, should have "worn the breeches," and had marks "for special superstitious purposes" on their breasts and backs. But no. Once again the aids to sexual selection are all on one side, and not the side that most wants them either, according to all natural and rational cal-culations. Every mark in tattooing has a significance, though we may not fully understand them any more than the savages themselves often did, and an illus-tration of this, very clear and decided, from Captain J. G. Bourke, will be quoted under another section.

[1] " Burma as it was and is," p. 9.

Further yet :

The mortuary masks of the Indians as given in the Report of the Bureau of Ethnology (Washington), vol. iii., 1881–2, are painted feathers, and in some cases with tribal cuts imitated, and teeth knocked out or filed down or filed sharp. In Peru also such masks are found, and one is given in fig. 188, vol. iii. p. 509, Report, Bureau of Ethnology (Washington).

At p. 76 of vol. iv. of Report of Bureau of Ethnology (Washington) a drawing is given of an Australian grave and carved trees round it, and, in explanation, a passage is quoted from Mr. I. C. Russell in " American Naturalist," vol. xiii. p. 72, where he remarks that these hieroglyphiss are connected with the tattoo-marks ; and he goes on to say that the desire of the Maori for ornament was so great that they covered their features with tattooing, transferred indelibly to their faces complicated patterns of carved and spiral lines, *similar to the designs which they put upon their canoes and their houses, and even their grave monuments.* [1]

But the very fact announced here proves that mere personal ornament was not the great exciting cause, because in New Zealand images carved on house-posts and on grave effigies were marked in imitation of the tattoo-marks, as was the case also with several of the Indian tribes of Central America. Here is another very unexpected testimony from a first-class authority on all such matters :

" Painting the body is the simplest mode of ornament. Tattooing, or any other permanent interference with the surface of the skin by way of ornament, is practised only to a very limited extent by the Indians

[1] P. 76.

of Guiana ; is used, in fact, only to produce the small distinctive tribal mark which many of them bear at the corners of their mouths or on their arms." [1] Now, what inference can be drawn from this distinction between tattooing and painting here ?

Mr. James G. Swan also sets down a confirmatory passage about the Haidas of Queen Charlotte Islands :

" The tattoo-marks of the Haidas of Queen Charlotte Islands are heraldic designs or the family totem, or crests of the wearers, and are similar to the carvings depicted on the pillars and monuments around the homes of the chiefs which casual observers have thought were idols." [2]

These Haida totem-posts and carved columns in front of the chiefs' residence are in many ways striking and grotesque ; but they certainly serve to sustain us in our position that the tattoo-marks mainly reproduced there have a significance far beyond what Dr. Westermarck and others choose to discern in them—so great that I should esteem it a special favour if Dr. Westermarck would kindly tell me how he reconciles these outstanding facts with his theory of mere ornament " with a view to aid in successfully courting and being courted "?

Again, Professor Brauns of Halle reports ("Science," iii., No. 50, p. 69) that among the Ainos of Yaso the women tattoo their chins to imitate the beards of the men.

Schultze tells us that among the Kaffirs the warriors are rendered invulnerable by means of a black

---

[1] Everard F. im Thurn on " Indians of Guiana," p. 137.

[2] Report of Bureau of Ethnology (Washington), vol. iv. p. 67.

cross on their foreheads, and black stripes on the cheeks, painted by the Inyanga or fetish-priest.[1]

The Sioux Indians believe that if a person is not tattooed in the middle of the forehead or on the wrists, the spirit will not go direct to the " Many Lodges," but may be thrown from a cloud or a cliff, and fall back to this world, to join the souls of those that wander on the earth, and can never travel the spirit road again.[2]

In New Zealand Mr. I. C. Russell says that the Maori formerly tattooed the bones of enemies —quoted in Report of Bureau of Ethnology (Washington), iv. p. 73.

Rawlinson, as seen already, says that, according to Kahn, *Aiolos* means variegated = tattooed warriors.

Now, in these cases, does Dr. Westermarck find any trace of support for his theory ? These are cases—and they might be multiplied indefinitely— which show that, if sexual selection had any part in the matter, it was a most secondary and indirect one, and was wholly crushed out by other interests, unless, indeed, Dr. Westermarck will find a peculiar inverted backward-going one in the case of the Ainos of Yaso, where the tattoo on the chins of the women imitates the beards of the men. " Bearded " women are not usually deemed by men to be thus additionally attractive sexually ; but, of course, there may be exceptions in race-tastes as in individual tastes, and Dr. Westermarck may be an exceptional case himself and find " bearded " women attractive. Perhaps Dr. Westermarck would retort on me here with

---

[1] " Fetishism," N. Y., 1885, p. 32.

[2] Report of Bureau of Ethnology (Washington), xi. p. 486.

the remarkable instance of the male concubines among the Kadiahs, who have their chins tattooed exactly like those of the women. This, however, is an exceptional and very curious manifestation, and my explanation of it, which meanwhile I reserve, does not go to support his theory, after all !

The taking of human heads is the inveterate custom of the Nagas, Garos, Kukis, Lushais, and other tribes of South-eastern Bengal, and has clearly existed for ages. It may not always mean that there is hostility, though sometimes there is. To obtain this " certificate of manhood," they must present their Rajah with a human head, and generally belonging to a tribe not related. On presenting this head to the Rajah, the young man is tattooed with the *ak* or mark of *that* tribe, and henceforth is a man. Raids for heads often lead to warfare.[1]

Here the case is definite : in addition to any of the proper tribal marks, the young man now has added the *ak* of the tribe to which the head has belonged, and thus, in tribes practising this custom, a variety of devices over and above the fixed tribal devices of their own, which, with the individual totems as explained by Mr. Frazer, would go far to account for such variety as Sir R. Burton and others have noted. If all this was *primarily* to attract or please the women, our way of reasoning on such matters is very different from that of Dr. Westermarck.

The Northern Was of Central Africa are said to be cannibals. You pass through their villages by a grisly avenue of posts, each post bearing a human skull—that of an enemy slain in battle—the flesh of

[1] Jour. Anthro. Inst. iii. **p. 477.**

the body in most parts having been eaten, and the bones burned or buried—but not a certain other part !

The Macas Indians of the Equador actually sew up the mouth of the heads of their dead enemies secured, that they may not make any answer, and this though the heads have been boiled, dried, and prepared. The Mundurucus of the Upper Amazon do the same, adding strings of various kinds.[1]

And, then, what about tattooing of enemies' bones ?

Another noticeable case :

At Oakley Springs, Arizona, totemic marks have been found, evidently made by the same individual at successive visits, showing that on the number of occasions indicated he had passed those springs, probably camping there, and such record was the habit of the neighbouring Indians at that time. The same repetition of totemic marks has been found in great numbers in the pipestone quarries of Dakota, and also at some of the old fords in West Virginia. In this respect there seems to have been in the intentions of the Indians very much the same spirit as leads the civilised man to record his initials upon objects in the neighbourhood of places of general resort. But these totemic marks are so designed and executed as to have intrinsic significance and value, wholly different in this respect from vulgar names in alphabetical form.[2] One very marked peculiarity of the drawings is that within each particular system, such as may be called a tribal

---

[1] Jour. Anthro. Inst. iii. p. 30.
[2] Report of Bureau of Ethnology (Washington), vol. iv. p. 17.

system of pictography, every Indian draws in precisely the same manner—no play of individual taste allowed.

III.

Then there is the argument from the Hebrew Scriptures. Professor Robertson Smith has glanced at this matter, without exhausting it, however, in his "Kinship in Arabia" and elsewhere. He finds totemism and mutilation clearly traceable. Even so late as the days of Ezekiel totem worship is to be found, not only indicated, but practised—unmistakably practised, as any one can see by turning to the book of that prophet (viii. 10 and 11). As for cuttings and mutilations and marks, the legislation shows how long they persisted. We read in Leviticus xix. 28:

"Ye shall not make any cuttings in your flesh for the dead, nor print any marks upon you: I am the Lord."

Again, we have this direction to the Levites in chap. xxi. 5: "They shall not make baldness upon their head, neither shall they shave off the corners of their beard, nor make any cuttings in their flesh." Yet again, it might well be asked what was the mark set upon the foreheads of the men of whom Ezekiel speaks in chap. ix. 4, "that sigh and cry for the abominations that be done in the midst thereof" (Jerusalem)? At v. 6 we read: "Slay utterly old and young, both maids and little children and women, but come not near any man upon whom is the mark, and begin at my sanctuary."

Many advanced theological critics now agree that

these cuttings and marks were totem-signs. The cuttings for the dead are totemistic, allied, as totemism essentially is everywhere and at all times, with the worship of ancestors—the totem being presumed to be consecrated to the dead ancestor, and indeed may be his abiding-place or body; so that he who killed or ate the object pictured or thus symbolised might be guilty of eating a dead ancestor. Clearly, Westermarck's theory would gain little support from the Hebrew testimony as to cuttings, marks, or tattooings, since there is no suggestion whatever that sexual suggestion or stimulation had any influence in their use.

Professor Robertson Smith points out the significance of the fact, in this connection, that animal names abound in the Hebrew genealogies far beyond what had been supposed; and that animal names in the Hebrew as in the Arabic point to totemism. The tribal arrangement, as he holds, was not perfected till after the conquest of Canaan, and he thinks that the earlier division was simply that of descendants of Rachel and Leah—the one meaning an ewe, and the other an antelope. Levi means a serpent, and, in a secondary sense only, something that twines like a serpent, or is wound round something—say, a garland. Hence the serpent became the totem of the priests—בני־לוי, sons of the serpent—the most sacred order of all—and this totem was no doubt imprinted on the persons of the Levites. At all events, they took care to preserve its emblem in the Temple even up to the time of Hezekiah; for we read that there stood "the brazen serpent which Moses made," and to which incense was burned;

for we further read, " He [Hezekiah] removed the
high places, and cut down the groves, and brake in
pieces *the brazen serpent that Moses had made ; for unto
these days the children of Israel did burn incense to it.*"

Professor Robertson Smith found, too, that the
totem of the *Jabsh* tribe of Arabs was a young ass.
It is evident that this also was the totem of an early
Hebrew tribe ; and in the legislation the fact is
recognised in the special and exceptional form of
redemption required for the firstborn of the ass.

The *wasm* or sign set upon the camel both by
Arabs and Hebrews was not confined to camels, but
was a form of the totem borne by the master. " I
venture to conjecture," says Robertson Smith, "that
the *wasm* was not placed on camels alone. *Wasm*
cannot be separated etymologically from the Hebrew
שֵׁם (*shem*), a name ; and there are sufficient traces
in Hebrew usage that שֵׁם is a stock, a tribe name
primarily. And this *wasm* must be connected, if
more remotely, with *washm*, tattooing. The *washm*
meant also the tattooing of arms, hands, and even
gums imprinted by women on others of their own
sex by way of adornment. But tattooing could not
originally have been mere adornment, and with the
northern Semites was practised in connection with
religion." Even with the Hebrews there was, alas !
no free courtship, in our sense of it. The wives
were bought, and were, as with many other races,
property, passing to a next heir.

Burton speaks of the *wasm* or tribal sign, and says :
" The subject of *wasm* is extensive and highly
interesting, for many of these brands date doubtless
from prehistoric ages. For instance, some of the

great Anazah nation (not tribe) use a circlet, the initial of their name (an Ayn-letter), which thus shows the eye, from which it was formed. I have given some specimens of *wasm* in 'The Land of Midian' (i. 320), where, as among the 'Sinaitic' Bedawin, various kinds of crosses are preserved long after the death and burial of Christianity."[1]

This is what he says in "The Land of Midian":

" The *wasm* in most cases showed some form of a cross, which is held to be a potent charm by the Sinaitic Bedawin; and on two detached water-rolled pebbles were distinctly inscribed IH and VI, which looked exceedingly like Europe. Apparently the custom is dying out: the modern Midianites have forgotten the art and mystery of tribal signs (*Wusúm*)."

Among the signs, however, of which Sir Richard gives drawings there are discs and crescents at all the places named, while at Hudd we meet with bird and snake—the snake in the bird's mouth; with the camel-stick and the camel at Sharm Yáhárr, where also we have what seems a lizard; and some of the signs look as like charms as tribe-marks.

It is very remarkable to find also that, as Calvert points out, over large spaces of West Australia the physical features resemble those of the Holy Land, while many observances of the natives are similar to those of the Hebrews. This is especially the case as regards what is suggested by those prohibitions of cuttings or marks on the person for the dead which we find in Leviticus and Deuteronomy. " It is very singular to remark," says Calvert, "that

[1] "Arabian Nights," vi. p. 163.

when the women among the Aborigines do cut
and disfigure their faces for the dead, it is always
between the eyes, just as was explicitly forbidden
by Moses."

Elsewhere the prophet Isaiah reprehends the
custom of remaining among the graves, which is to
this day a prevalent custom among the natives of
Western Australia :

"A people which provoke me to anger," etc.,
which "remain among the graves and lodge in the
monuments."

IV.

We know from many sources, not even excepting
the Hebrew, how in ancient warfare it was a custom
to carry off the heads of those slain as special
memorials and prizes, or, as in the Bible, to heap
them up at the gates of cities. Now, Colonel Robley
tells us that it is said tattooing on the bodies was for
the purpose of identification in case the head was cut
off by an enemy in battle. Sir George S. Robertson,
in his " Káfirs of the Hindu-Cush," assures us that
it was a point of honour with these tribes to bring
back the heads of those of their tribe slain in battle
or raid, and that they were carried in processions,
and dances—special dances—gone through to celebrate their presence. " At the close of war," writes
Colonel Robley (p. 136), "an exchange of heads was
an indispensable article of a treaty of peace among
the Maories. . . . It was a point of honour with the
Maories to try to save the heads of those slain of
their tribe from the grasp of the enemy."

If moko was used merely to promote sexual

attraction, this is a queer result of it. Dr. Turner also tells us that when the Samoans returned from war they brought back with them to the ancestral graves the skulls of their dead.[1]

Rutherford, quoted by Colonel Robley (p. 25), states that " in the part of the country where he was detained in captivity and tattooed in 1816, the men were usually tattooed on the face, hips, and body, sometimes as low down as the knee, but that none were allowed to be decorated on the forehead, upper lip, and chin, except the great ones of the tribes. Priests were either exempt or were forbidden the latter." An untattooed person on the field of battle was treated with utter brutality—the head battered till unrecognisable.

Now, from all this, it is clear that if sexual attraction, as has been so dogmatically urged by Westermarck and others, was the primary motive, and indeed almost the sole motive, in tattooing, then the crowd of men just as much needed the full aid as did the chiefs ; but the reason of the distinction here is at once apparent when we think of the marks and badges by which officers are distinguished in our own army according to their rank. And why should priests have been exempt or forbidden ? Not because they did not, we can well believe, wish to lack attractions for the other sex, but because they were not belligerents strictly, their duty being to pray to their gods for success at some distance, and their in so far untattooed persons, with other marks of their sacred office, meant to other tribes what our white or red cross does on the field of battle. No ;

[1] " Nineteen Years in Samoa," p. 230.

the tattooing is a kind of soldiers' regimentals, as well as standard or heraldic device.

Another point: The tattooed mark on the chin of the Maori women indicated that they were married, and were post-nuptial (p. 46). Besides, the women at funerals, married and unmarried, cut and gashed their faces, necks, arms, and bodies with sharp shells until they streamed with blood; and yet we are further told that soon afterwards the *narahu* or moko dye was often applied to their wounds, and the stains commemorated the scenes at which the women had mourned—the gashes, even without this, making a sort of moko to perpetuate the sign of their grief.[1] And though the Colonel remarks that these cuttings at mournings were often done with considerable method and regularity, so as to make the scars ornamental (!) rather than otherwise, there is no suggestion that the thing was done with any idea of sexual attraction. Besides, with the Maories idols at pas and wooden effigies of deceased persons were carefully mokoed and hung up in appropriate places, and even Westermarck surely will not hold sexual attraction applied here. If an effigy or god were carried off by enemies, it bore the insignia of the tribe, and there was the same call to use every effort to bring the effigy or god back as there was to bring back the heads of the slain—a thing to which we have a parallel in the case of the Hebrew Ark and its sacred stones, rods, etc., etc.

And is not this hanging up of mokoed effigies and the carving of the crest-signs on sepulchral monuments or on trees near the grave very like the hanging

[1] Robley, Moko. p. 45.

up of a knight's insignia in the chapels of certain churches or cathedrals, or the inscribing on the back of his stall or memorial plate his name and merits, with his crest or arms ?

Here is a further testimony from the New World :

" If killed by an enemy, the heads of the untattooed were treated with indignity and kicked on one side, while those which were conspicuous for their beautiful moko were carefully cut off, stuck on *turuturu*, a pole with a cross on it, and then preserved; all which was highly gratifying to the survivors and the spirits of their late possessors." [1]

What is the significance of the cross here on the pole which bears the tattooed head ?

The truth is, the marks and tattooings were symbols of tribal descent, or asserted descent, either by the figures themselves or by signs standing for them. As Captain John G. Bourke explains:

" If, say, the clan or gens be that of the eagle, the totem will be the eagle, and the dancer will be decorated on breast or back with some conventional symbol, recognised by the whole nation as the gentile emblem of the ' Eagles.' " [2]

V.

Now for some general remarks. Primitive or early man has, no doubt, some resemblances to animals and their ways. He, like them, for a long time finds it enough merely to procure food and shelter, to protect himself against enemies, wild beasts, etc. He is not, and cannot be, as some scientific specu-

[1] Report of Bureau of Ethnology (Washington), iv. p. 49.
[2] "Snake Dance," p. 117.

lators have inclined to represent him, a poet, of imagination all compact, concerned to interpret the universe from a lofty ideal standpoint, or a creature who can indulge in playful exercises and invent abstract terms. Not at all. He is by necessity of circumstances a utilitarian *pur et simple*, or, as one writer has said, his attitude at highest is that of the *naïf*. His first contact with Nature is one of stern resistance and effort ; and, when he has conquered his first aids, rude tools and weapons of defence, and has by this purchased a very little leisure, he is still overborne by ideas of resistance and self-preservation. Language itself is an unvarying witness to this. When we pass to primitive language, it is in all cases a record of the kind indicated. Trees are named by the tools or weapons of defence they furnish. Even in the Hebrew it is so, and Hebrew is not a savage tongue. בְּרוֹשׁ, a fir or cypress tree, for example, is also a spear, because the wood of this class of trees was used for spears ; and there are many other instances, among them צִנָּה, which stands at once for a thorn and a fish-hook.[1]

Next, when the family has been formed, or, in other words, rather when progeny has been begotten, the utilitarian cares are and can only be increased ; and when we come to the clan, or later to the tribe, still we have the same sense of absolute and continual resistance and effort after the mere necessities of the day. And the aim of the tribe in its first form, at all events, is to provide against a common danger rather than to ensure any higher common interest.

---

[1] The Saxon word *aesc* also means at once an ash and a spear, from the same circumstance.

All testifies to this : language, custom, even adornments, which now begin to appear under the first
stirrings of the æsthetic feelings. But present everywhere are tokens of the burdensome sense of possible
failure to secure the prime necessaries of life. Out
of this comes infanticide, which has very widely prevailed—the hundred and one regulations of the tribe
all directed to limit population, as assuredly some
forms of mutilation witness—mutilations which cannot be wholly dissociated from the motive that first
produced tattooing, as seen, for example, in the
Hottentots : the whole purpose of early tribal rule
being to limit the indulgence of individual whim or
desire ; so that courting in the sense we mean when
we use the word does not at all exist. That form
of marriage (of which there are survivals in India
and other places to-day) in which the man goes and
lives in the house of the father of the wife arises out
of the desire of the head to control certain tendencies.

Professor Huxley laid full hold on this when he wrote
in the " Nineteenth Century" for February, 1889 :
" The first man who substituted the state of mutual
peace for that of mutual war, whatever the motive
that impelled men to take that step, created society.
But in establishing peace, they evidently put a limit
upon the struggle for existence. Between the members of that society, at any rate, it was not to be
pursued *à outrance*. And of all the successive shapes
that society has taken, that most nearly approaches
perfection in which war of individual against individual
is most strictly limited."

The very highest animals in the scale remain
individualists pure and simple ; but man from his

very beginning as man has been something else than this. He has dropped the principle of each one for himself, and realised, however imperfectly, a certain community of interest, which, working inwards and outwards, so transforms the family, and finally the clan, that no analogy exists any longer between the animal constitutions and the human. The family is absolutely based on this ; and that no true analogy can be drawn between animals and men arises just here, as we have seen, that no animals do form families in the sense that the very earliest men do. Less highly-developed animals, as bees and ants, essay social communities, but not the family.

This has been very admirably worked out by Sir Arthur Mitchell in his Rhind Lecture, "What is Civilisation?" He holds that the true unit of civilisation is the family, while Professor Karl Pearson traces the real origin of the family to the mother-age—the mother originating that as well as agriculture, etc., etc.!

Dr. Russel Wallace has some very decided words on this matter, which he could hardly, we think, have had in his mind when he read certain sections of Dr. Westermarck's book before he so highly and unqualifiedly commended it. Here is one bit :

" But man, as we now behold him, is different from the animals. He is social and sympathetic. In the rudest tribes the sick are assisted, at least with food ; less robust health and vigour than the average does not entail death. Neither does the want of perfect limbs or other organs produce the same effects as among animals."

And the dominating reason? Man, through the

[1] Pp. 181-189.

family, at once develops powers and emotions which
are not developed among the animals—a standing
distinction and separation which, *pace* Dr. Russel
Wallace, Dr. Westermarck would fain efface—so
that patron and patronised here are at loggerheads
at once in intention and in result.

Thirdly, no greater fallacy can be indulged in than
to go upon any analogies between men's feelings and
customs now, and those of the early men—a fallacy
by which, as I humbly think, all Dr. Westermarck's
arguments and illustrations in this direction are
vitiated and turned into a kind of special pleading,
as also are many of Mr. Grant Allen's eloquent
paragraphs. Not that I would adopt here that
passage in Mr. Coventry Patmore's "Angel in the
House," in which he pictures the early man as
dragging his bride, bleeding, by the hair to his hut,
as though it were a faithful and unvarying picture.
But it represents what certainly, to a large extent,
was true ; and, assuredly, the laws of the tribe were
such as to limit so thoroughly all individual fancy and
desire that sexual selection could not have found the
play that Dr. Westermarck assumes and fancies to
have been freely operative among savage men generally.
It is here very markedly the case that men at this
point must differ from animals, and defy any analogy
as between the two. Man has no sooner been touched
by the æsthetic than he looks both before and after,
and, whether or not, in the words of Shelley, "he
pines for what is not," he fears the future. On that
fear, on the sense of common dangers that may front
him, the tribe is built. He resorts to means to attain
his ends of which the animals would never dream ;

and, since increase of population beyond a certain
point must, as he perhaps rightly conceives, affect
the food supplies, he lays down rules that have both
ends in view. In Samoa, as Dr. Turner tells, laws
were passed allowing no more than two children to
a family to survive, because of the food supplies.
Man does what, looked at from the point of simple
instinct, is unnatural, and resorts to all manner of
devices to preserve unity in the tribe. From being
a purely natural man and utilitarian, at one step,
with the advent of family, he becomes a rude thinker;
a thinker for the family first, and then for the clan
or for the tribe. All natural instincts are now affected,
modified, and limited by this.

It is, indeed, very curious that in this matter of
sexual selection not one of the ingenious illustrators
of Darwin's principle has, so far as I am aware,
dealt satisfactorily with the modifying elements that
must step in by the very fact that human beings
must form families at a very early stage—families,
and clans, and tribes following in a sense that no
animals ever form. One of the most pathetic things
about animals, indeed, is that, with but few exceptions, the moment the time of nurture is over, the
brood is practically cast adrift—not recognised as
theirs by the parents any more; so that over large
areas, as regards animals, the courting is seasonal
and unvarying—a thing which touched White of
Selborne as few things touched him. It is not so
with man; and one of the most remarkable things
is that where, for tribal reasons, individual fatherhood strictly is, as it would seem, reduced to zero,
the responsibility is only shifted to the tribe or to

the head of the tribe—a fact which affects in every direction the operation " of successfully courting and being courted."

The master himself, while he was much less dogmatic, had a far more open eye for qualifying elements than have many of his disciples. Here is the way in which he suggests the modifications certain to arise from the point on which we have now dwelt— a passage which is worthy to be put in the forefront of many of their treatises—to counsel caution and reserve of statement and less of easy, clever theorising:

" If we look back to an extremely remote epoch, before man had arrived at the dignity of manhood, he would have been guided more by instinct and less by reason than are the lowest savages at the present time. Our early semi-human progenitors would not have practised infanticide or polyandry; for the instincts of the lower animals are never so perverted as to lead them regularly to destroy their own offspring, or to be quite devoid of jealousy.[1]

Westermarck's whole arguments are vitiated, as some of Sir John Lubbock's were, by this notion of an individual freedom in tribal life, such as we civilised moderns in some respects enjoy. It is the " pathetic fallacy " in another form, transfiguring strangely the field of savage or tribal life. The Australian tribes have recently been closely studied and observed, and what have Messrs. Fison and Howitt to say on this point ?

" The individual," they write, " has no rights as distinct from the group to which he belongs; and, moreover, it is directly contradicted by evidence

[1] " Descent of Man," p. 47.

which can be **tested at the** present day.[1] . . . They maintain the tribal right against the individual with regard even to war captives as strictly as they maintain it with respect to any other women.[2] And now, with regard to war captives, **it is well known that they** must be admitted into **a clan before they can be married to** any man."

Nor is this without counterpart in the Jewish law. **A** captive woman could not be appropriated to one **man** without strict preparatory observances and rites of alliance—rites which implied sacrifice and offering. Read :

" When thou goest forth to war against thine enemies, and Jahwé hath delivered them into thine hands, and thou hast taken them captive,

"And seest among the captives **a beautiful woman,** and hast a desire unto **her, that thou wouldst have her unto thy wife ;**

" **Then thou shalt bring her home to thine house, and** she shall shave her head,[3] and also pare [or **dress]** her nails.

"And she shall put the raiment of her captivity from **off** her, and shall remain in thine house and bewail her father and mother a full month : and *after that* thou shalt go in to her and be her husband, and she shall be thy wife." (Deut. xxi. **10—13.**)

Clearly, therefore, in the Jewish law, certain **very** strict rules **and** ceremonials had **to** be complied **with**

---

[1] " Kamilaroi and Kurnai," p. 151.

[2] " Kamilaroi Marriage," p. 66.

[3] The word here for shave is גֵּב רָחָה, from בָּלַח. to make smooth or round—that is, to make bare or bald, shear or cut off, which is quite different from the word used at Job i. 20, גָּז. which implies more of tearing-off.

before a war captive could be taken as wife—that is, the captor was not free to do as he chose, but must observe certain tribal and ceremonial demands. And I should say this law was a survival of the purely tribal law expounded by Messrs. Fison and Howitt and others.

To secure the unity and inclusiveness of the tribe spoken of above, the early men adopt such simple outward marks as they can ; so that in rude warfare, no less than in hunting or adventure, there may be no danger of killing one of their own tribe : they set up laws and customs which forbid certain connec-tions, certain indulgences, which would add to the burdens and responsibilities of the tribe. A rude altruism now arises, with some most perverse and unexpected expressions, which yet, when we know the secret of them so far, are perfectly intelligible and even reasonable from the rude man's point of view. Now, the preservation of the tribe takes the place of the self-preservation of the man at the earlier stage. All forms of decoration, we insist, have their beginning and rise at this point—they are signs of the rude altruism on which the tribe is based—signs of its realised solidarity and self-interest. Religious ideas superpose themselves on this. All the elabo-ration that comes after through alliances, etc., is secondary, and wholly secondary the elements which can in any way be construed as bearing on sexual selection in a condition where free courtship, as we understand it, is wholly out of the question. In one respect, indeed, the tattoo-marks and mutila-tions on savage tribes stand for regimentals—the only regimentals these poor men know (each of them being practically a fighter); and though, indeed, we admit that a red coat even now attracts the women, he would be sadly out of reckoning who would say, far less argue, that the first purpose of a red coat is to aid sexual selection, or, as Dr. Westermarck would put it, "to aid in successfully courting and being courted."

To this it might be objected that as, in a great many cases, the women are tattooed, or painted, or mutilated as well as the men, and sometimes are tattooed when the men are not, the case does not hold. To this I reply that if the women do not actually fight (some of them have done so now and then), they are involved in the results of war as civilised women cannot be; and that here, too, the clan or tribal markings are of use in preventing the possibility of certain mistakes which, in their idea, would be fatal.

Fight? Yes; there are definite enough records of savage women fighting. And it is on this ground as well as on others, suggesting some of them modifications of the idea of female infanticide in many cases, that Mr. Fison writes of the Australian tribes:

" So far from being an incumbrance on the warrior they [the women] will fight, if need be, as bravely as the men, and with even greater ferocity. Of this I could give some shocking examples which have come within my own knowledge." [1]

William Buckley (the " wild white man "), who lived thirty-two years among the Port Philip tribes, says, when mentioning that those he lived with were

---

[1] Fison, p. 136.

attacked and in danger of being worsted by a numerous hostile party: "They raised a war-cry, on hearing which the women threw off their rugs, and, each armed with a short club, flew to the assistance of their husbands and brothers. . . . Even with this augmentation our tribe fought to great disadvantage, the enemy being all men, and much more numerous. . . . Men and women were fighting furiously and indiscriminately, . . . and two of the latter were killed in the affair."[1]

Among the Fiji tribes, we read, that the women fight with the men. Sometimes they inflict ugly wounds, and the men can retaliate only by flinging clay balls from the top of a stick.

Mr. Frazer writes in a note (pp. 29, 30):

"Among most of the Californian tribes, the Ainos of Japan, the Chacklhi in Siberia, it is the women alone who are tattooed. Old pioneers in California are of opinion that the reason why the women alone tattoo is that in case they are taken captive they may be recognised by their own people when opportunity serves. This idea, Mr. Powers[2] says, is borne out by the fact that the 'Californian Indians are rent into such infinitesimal divisions, any one of which may be arrayed in deadly feud against another at any moment, that the slight differences in their dialects would not suffice to distinguish the captive squaws.' There may, therefore, be a grain of truth in the explanation of tattooing given by the Khyen women in Bengal: they say that it was meant to conceal their beauty, for which they were apt to be

---

[1] "Life and Adventures of William Buckley," p. 43.
[2] "Tribes of California," p. 109.

carried off by neighbouring tribes.[1] Certainly a version of it which does not yield any support to Dr. Westermarck! any more than this:

"Among the Murlé tribe of Central Africa the women are disgusting-looking, as their lower lips are pierced, and distended by a piece of wood two inches long and three-quarters of an inch thick. You saw nothing of the lower lip except a thin piece of mucous membrane that encircled the wooden plug. Two front upper teeth are knocked out, and their tongues project from their mouths. . . ."

The only apparent reason why the Murlés thus mutilate their women is that they want to keep them from being stolen by their neighbours,[2] the very opposite of Dr. Westermarck's sexual attraction.

The Khyens of Chittagong tattoo themselves to a disfiguring extent, and say that the practice was resorted to to conceal the natural beauty for which they were so renowned, that their maidens were carried off by the dominant race in lieu of tribute. Figures of animals—totem animals—are sometimes imprinted on their flesh. The operation is so painful that the young girls are tied down when subjected to it.[3]

Thus, though I would not go wholly with Mr. Herbert Spencer in saying that probably the origin of tattooing lies in the young savage making marks on himself similar to the scars borne by the warriors of his tribe, since in some cases women only are tattooed or mutilated, and it could not have so begun

[1] Dalton, p. 114.
[2] Dr. Donaldson Smith, pp. 300, 301.
[3] Dalton, "Ethnology of India," p. 114.

with them; yet this, in my idea, comes far nearer to it than Dr. Westermarck's theory that all tattooing marks, cicatrices, and scars are "aids to courting successfully and being courted." Even old Herodotus got a step—or even two steps—beyond this when, speaking of the Thracians, he says, "To have punctures on the skin is with the Thracians a mark of nobility." It was the same with the Picts. It was their peculiar characteristic, the painting the body by puncturing, the chiefs, etc., having special marks.[1]

Well, then, this suggests once more that, in addition to the idea of regimentals, the indelible marks of tattooing and skin cutting or puncturing are, and were, and have ever been, in a very remarkable way, heraldic—the only thing the savage men had or have corresponding to our coat-of-arms.

---

[1] Skene, Pref. to "Chronicle of the Picts," p. xcvii.

III.—SIR HENRY MAINE AND HIS ADMIRERS.

I.

I OWE it to a friend's kindness that I was present at the meeting of the Indian Section of the Society of Arts, March, 1898, when Mr. Tupper, C.S.I., read a paper on "India and Sir Henry Maine." He was very clear and judicious, up to a certain point—more clear and judicious than some of those who followed him in the discussion afterwards. From what was said by nearly all the speakers, one would have fancied that not only was Sir Henry Maine an able jurist, a skilful and far-seeing administrator, an excellent legislator, and an expert in codification of Indian law, but also a great comparative anthropologist, as well as a profound and exact thinker and eloquent writer, whose books were as pure and without blemish as no doubt were his character and conduct as a man.

I pretend to no means of judging him in any capacities save those of comparative anthropologist, thinker, and writer. In his books he reveals himself as a man of very quick and acute powers of association—seeing the point of contact or likeness between what might appear distant or disparate, yet, despite this, occasionally failing to note adequately what lies

K 2

between as qualifying. Very learned along certain lines, according to the ideal of English Universities, and in manner cultivated to the highest point encouraged and most approved there. A man doubtless of the greatest charm in personal contact with him—a very fine type indeed of the highly-educated English gentleman. But his area, which, from certain points of view, was limited, he had most carefully and often traversed—so carefully that he was apt to ignore or to undervalue lines of inquiry outside it on which he had not himself embarked. At all events, he nowhere shows the least trace of that admirable sense of dissatisfaction which is often so grateful in the great and famous—the keen desire to penetrate further, which was closed in Newton's famous saying about being like a child wandering on the sea-shore picking up a few shells and pebbles, which, realised by Tennyson, gave birth to the grand lines in " Ulysses " :

> "It may be that the gulfs will wash us down,
> It may be we shall touch the happy isles,
> And see the great Achilles whom we knew.
> . . . . To follow knowledge like a sinking star
> Beyond the utmost bounds of human thought."

A gracious and benignant self-content everywhere appears. If *he* does not know aught, it cannot be very important, nor could it modify much his conclusions. His works are all so neatly cut out, finished, rounded, that it looks even ungrateful and ungracious to say that, studied in certain moods, they are unsatisfying. Was it because in reality he advanced on and looked at every great problem first as a lawyer, a jurist, or was it because of something constitutional? That remains for his friends to answer — those who can bring the commentary of looks and smiles, of gestures and expressions, to the aid of these somewhat cold, limited, error-strewn, and formal dissertations, in which the discriminating stranger can but see a superior and colossally-calm professor, who all too implicitly demands the deference of his student or reader as to a very " superior person."

But when one, having devoted long, weary years, silently and unknown, to Oriental languages and comparative studies, philological and anthropological, endeavours to bring to bear on these lectures and essays a truly discriminating judgment, it has to be confessed that, in a very supreme degree, they have the defects of their qualities; that in some points, vital and dominating, they are to appearance contradictory, and in others crassly ignorant—and that, too, as regards matters most essential to the perfecting of his *schemæ* on some sides, if that was to be in the least satisfactorily achieved. To justify so far what I have said, permit me to present you with a few notes made as once more I read his writings— read patiently, carefully, with all the eulogy and effusion of the Society of Arts' meeting in my ears.

II.

In "Ancient Law," at p. 24, we read :

" It may further be remarked that no one is likely to succeed in the investigation who does not clearly realise that the stationary condition of the human race is the rule, the progressive the exception."

How is this to be reconciled with the idea that

"when a primitive law has been embodied in a code there is an end to what may be called its spontaneous development" (p. 21).

Surely the ordinary, common-sense deduction from this would be that spontaneous progress or development had ceased in favour of some kind of artificial development or progress *ab extra;* and is this in the same sense as the other true progress at all logically? But clearness is surely not brought to the matter when we read in the fifth sentence of chap. ii., " Legal Fictions," thus :

" From the little we know of the progress of law during this period, we are justified in assuming that set purpose had the very smallest share in producing change ; " and it is immediately added that such changes as are effected "appear to have been dictated by feelings and modes of thought which under our present mental conditions we are unable to comprehend." But if we are so utterly unable to comprehend these feelings and modes of thought, how can we possibly, even in the loosest way, judge how they acted in setting up or determining set purpose or anything else ?

Further on we read :

" The study of ancient races in their primitive condition affords us some clue to the point at which the development of certain societies has stopped " (p. 23).

And yet this is in face of his own statement that " no one is likely to succeed in the investigation who does not clearly realise that the stationary condition of the human race is the rule." So that generally there is logically, with but few exceptions, neither progress nor retrogression to observe or chronicle, because "the stationary condition of the human race is the rule." That is surely philosophic, when all science, anthropology, geology, etc., day by day impresses on us that nothing can stand still or be stationary ; either it advances under laws of evolution, progress, or, by reverse, degenerates, goes back —but no, no standing still, no stationary condition, none. And even the degeneration is only travelling back, as it were, on a segment of a circle to resume a former condition with a difference—a subtle difference. That "stationary condition" beats me, as words used without due philosophic apprehension ; and I should like the gentleman who so boldly asserted at the Society of Arts' meeting that Sir Henry Maine did exactly in his own department what Darwin had done in Natural Science, to clear up this business of the human race in "a *stationary condition* as a rule."

Yet, in spite of all this, Sir Henry Maine (p. 116) finds that Montesquieu greatly underrates the " *stability* "—stability, mark you—of human nature; not stationary condition—the word " *stability* " means something different from that. " He pays little or no regard," says Sir Henry, " to the inherited qualities of the human race, those qualities which each generation receives from its predecessors, and transmits, but *slightly altered*, to the generation which follows it." Oh, ho ! and so this is a general rule that something is transmitted—something which enables human nature to be stable: the "stationary condition "! Yet, mark you, these qualities are transmitted *slightly altered*, as a general rule; and even though it be but *slightly altered*, where, pray, oh, where is the *stationary condition* of the human race as a rule? And his criticism on Montesquieu is that he underrates this something! Stationary condition against inherited qualities transmitted and slightly—even *slightly*—*altered* means, as a rule, standing still and moving or (?) making progress at the self-same moment! Or, to put it another way: If the stationary condition of the human race is the rule, what matters inherited qualities even though slightly altered, or is *stability* in the inverse ratio of *stationariness*, or what?

Once more, after remarking that "the unit of an ancient society was the family, of a modern society the individual" (p. 126), he goes on to say: " If the individual is conspicuously guilty, it is his children, his kinsfolk, his tribesmen, or his fellow-citizens who suffer with him. *It thus happens that the ideas of moral responsibility and retribution often seem to be more clearly realised at very ancient than at more advanced periods;* for as the family group is immortal, and its liability to punishment indefinite, the primitive mind is not perplexed by the questions which become troublesome as soon as the individual is conceived as altogether separate from the group" (p. 127).

This, from one point of view, might be taken in proof of Sir Henry's statement that the stationary condition of the race is the rule—only here the "stationary," if not even backward drift, which, by-the-bye, is not *stationary*, would begin precisely when, according to another dictum of his, it should have ceased. But if "stationary condition " is the general

rule, what is the good of theorising **about the** generation of new ideas and sagely remarking that **"the**
generation of new ideas does not proceed so rapidly
in all states of society **as in that to which we**
belong "? **Why, if a "stationary** condition," **as he**
has **said, is the rule, it** is all too clear **that the
generation of new** ideas does not, *as a rule*, **proceed
at all, unless like the** crab backwards, **to save, to
save** even in little, **his** consistency.

III.

In "Ancient Law" (p. 148) he actually writes:
"A female name closes the branch or twig **of the**
genealogy in which **it occurs."** But he **is not**
content with saying **that;** he **must** unfortunately
generalise all **too** boldly **upon** insufficient **data :**
"*None of the descendants of a female are included in the
primitive notion of family relationship.*" **And** again :
"It is obvious that **the organisation of primitive
societies** would **have** been confounded **if** men had
called themselves relatives of their mother's relatives " (p. 149).

We find Mr. Fenton thus writing in "Early
Hebrew Life " **(p. 7) :**
"Throughout the patriarchal legends **of the**
Hebrews, descent in the female line is an important
factor in the **purity** of blood. For instance, **the**
children of Nahor **by** Milcah are carefully **dis-**
tinguished from his children by his secondary wives.
Bethuel disappears almost entirely, **and the con-**
nection **of** the families **is traced** entirely through
the sisters Milcah and **Sarah.** Isaac and Ishmael
are familiar instances of the distinction between the

son of the bond woman and the son of the free
woman. But even Esau's progeny are reckoned
and grouped according to their various maternities."
And how much must lie, as bearing in this direction,
on the change of name from Sarai to Sarah a
princess; for a princess in those early times was
next door at the least to a goddess, and was the
subject of at least quasi-worship. This is not a
result of the most recent research, and was it too
much to expect that Sir H. Maine should have
read his Bible with even ordinary care?

In spite of all that he has so dramatically said,
however, in a later work he quotes from Sir John
Lubbock: "Although descent among the *lowest
savages* is traced in the female line, I do not know
of any instance in which female ancestors are
worshipped." And Sir Henry meets it—actually
meets it—by writing thus, notwithstanding what
he had gratuitously said in "Ancient Law" just
quoted: "Female ancestors in the direct line are
now worshipped by the civilised Chinese, but the
evidence shows that the posthumous honours paid
to women are of later origin than the worship of
men." Had Sir Henry lived to read certain passages
in Professor Rhys David's American lectures on
Buddhism, certain passages written by ourselves
on Moon and Earth Worship, and much—very much
—that Professor Karl Pearson has written, he would
not, I think, have been so certain about the later
origin ; but it was too much his habit to generalise
too quickly and to dogmatise too much. What do
I find in the chief authority to which he refers me
on Hindu law? This: that female ancestorship and

worship of female ancestors is testified in the long past by the fact that, despite a gradual linking close of marriage bonds under new conditions, it still survived—"the female ancestor," as Mr. J. B. Mayne says, " among the Aryans (Hindus) were only worshipped in conjunction with their deceased husbands."[1]

But it is a vast step to find him writing thus—always marking as though he were judicially summing up on whole and completed evidence before him, which certainly he did not have here, nor very frequently elsewhere, in spite of his pretending so:

" I attach small importance to casual expressions tending to show that their writers preserved traditions of the savage customs of tracing descent through females only. Still, as we cannot doubt the existence and prevalence *among some part of mankind* of this savage usage called mother-law "—(by the way, as hinted already, there are very clear and obtrusive traces of it in the Hebrew—women selecting for heirship second sons, their favourites; Zipporah, as priestess and head, circumcising her child, and offering to the god the trophy, to save her husband; Deborah, a judge and a mother in Israel, etc., etc.)—" it is impossible not to ask oneself the question, Did the worship of the dead bring about the recognition of paternity, or is ancestor-worship a religious interpretation of, or a religious system founded upon, an already existing institution ? "

That certainly shows an advance on "Ancient Law," only it should have been more fully and frankly acknowledged.

And there is a further remarkable proof—women-

---

[1] "Hindu Law," 4th ed. p. 63.

rule and women-descent in the Hebrew—and that is in the legislation where it is laid down that "all the males among the priests" shall do certain things, or "every male among the priests"—which, if words mean anything, mean that at a time not so far distant there were female priests, and that a female priesthood and a male priesthood had, for a certain time after, run on side by side, recognised and acknowledged, as parts of the Hebrew system. This phenomenon of women-priests does not bear in his favour.

The presence of mother-right in earlier times in the South Pacific is surely well witnessed in the New Hebrides group by a peculiar survival. In Mangaia, according to Dr. Wyatt Gill, there was often a contest between father and mother as to whether the child should belong to the clan or tribe of father or mother, and many little tricks were sometimes practised by the one against the other. The name of the child's god was declared at the cutting of the navel-string, it "having been previously settled by the parents whether the little one should belong to the father's tribe or the mother's. Usually the father had the preference, but occasionally, when the father's family had been devoted to furnish sacrifices, the mother would seek to save her child's life by getting it adopted into her own clan or tribe, the name of her own tribal divinity being pronounced over it."[1] Circumstances alter cases. Among the Hebrews we find women testifying to survival of mother-right by devoting sons to God and the Temple, when perhaps had sacrifice instead

[1] "Myths and Songs of South Pacific," p. 39.

of substitution remained they would not; mothers contriving succession for second sons, their favourites, undoing the eldest son wholly; Zipporah actually, in so far like the Mangaian women, offering a certain trophy to please the god and save her husband in place of the child.

Traces of female descent are undoubtedly found among Pelasgians, Etruscans, Greeks, and Latins. See Morgan's chapter "Change of Descent" in his "Ancient Society" (pp. 278—296). Herodotus in his time met with female descent among the Lycians, who, if Pelasgian in lineage, were Greek by affiliation. Bachofen's researches were distinctly to the same result.

Nor is this merely something ancient, and hints of it to be dimly gathered from vague survivals. It is to be found now among living tribes and races. And not only this, but the more interesting process of transformation is to be witnessed now. We have striking cases where all three forms of descent are found alongside each other—maternal, paternal, and intermediate—and the physical and geographical conditions account for much. The Kwakiutl tribes of the North Pacific coast of America have a maternal organisation, while those further South are purely paternally organised. The Central tribes show a most peculiar intermediate or transitional stage.[1]

With some of the Central Australian tribes descent is through the mother, with others through the father. Messrs. Spencer and Gillen say: " With the Urubunna descent is counted in the female line, with the Arunta in the male line," and they show in

---

[1] Report of Smithsonian Inst. for 1895, p. 375.

so far how this has come about through the very peculiar and complicated relationships.

Among certain of the Tibetans the sons take the family name of their mothers, and a son must not marry a person of the same cognomen as himself. [1]

IV.

Further, Sir Henry Maine is as far at sea, in my idea, as a man ever was, in trying to argue away promiscuity by drawing inferences as to early promiscuity producing infertility, and his illustrating of this by the modern form of promiscuity, which makes the streets of London and other of our great cities, even at midday, a disgrace to civilisation. But the friends of Sir Henry will perhaps excuse my saying that there was and could be no analogy between the two cases, because of circumstances that every one may guess at, though I cannot soil my pages by dealing with them in detail; but curious or scientific readers may find a good deal pointing toward these in a certain section of Acton's great book on prostitution. If there were any approach to a parallel to any modern conditions of promiscuity, it would be, I most regretfully say, found in the fruits of the sad rural conditions induced in my own country by the bothy and kitchen systems on farms that so long and generally prevailed, encouraging promiscuity; but because of calls of labour and life in the open air—parallel circumstances with the circumstances, of course, of early promiscuity—this bothy and kitchen promiscuity in Scotland, instead of infertility, causes, and has for centuries caused,

[1] Smithsonian Report, 1893, p. 679.

the great scandal of illegitimacy, over which ministers
of religion and social reformers have so loudly
mourned. Dr. William Alexander, in his "Life
among my ain Folk," and elsewhere, has glanced at
these conditions, and spoken very wisely regarding
them ; and some of the men who have allowed Sir
Henry Maine to influence them on this point might
do well to turn to Dr. William Alexander's pages ;
for even where he is the mere dialect story-writer
these ever move before his imagination like great
black ominous cloud-masses in the background. In
one word, early promiscuity could not have been in
any one essential like modern prostitution, for the
three very powerful reasons : (1) that it *was* early, and
due to other causes ; and (2) that it was universal,
open and acknowledged ; and (3) that most probably
it had behind it the sanction of perverted religious
ideas, that still, in all the ceremonial survivals of it,
have more or less sway. That the Rishis have such
peculiar privileges in it would be enough to prove
this, and I shall attest this by record immediately.
Mr. J. B. Mayne well remarks that British prostitution is passively tolerated and indirectly legislated
for in the fact that it is what it is ; and the nearest
approach to this existing in the East is perhaps the
prostitution, not only recognised by Indian usage,
but honoured in the class of dancing girls; the
relations between the prostitute and her paramour
being regulated by law, just as any other species of
contract.[1] The English business very characteristically does not go so far as this : it allows the contract to be freely made by the parties to it, but if in

[1] "Hindu Law," p. 51.

no other way do they offend by breach of the peace or by committing a nuisance by noise, etc., etc., it simply leaves them severely alone, and in thus far passively recognises them. I am not aware in how far infertility applies to Hindu prostitutes called dancing girls—perhaps some Indian friend of Sir Henry Maine would kindly tell me; but certain I am that there is much more analogy between Hindu dancing girls and modern British prostitutes than there could be between early promiscuity and either of them; and this simply because, if there were nothing else (which there is), the principles of physiology being better understood and made matter of every-day teaching, there are in many forms multiplied *checks* on conception, as it is evident the interest, professional interest, of both the British prostitute and the Hindu dancing girl is not to conceive, whereas we have no ground for concluding that these motives could weigh with the early women; and we certainly have some grounds for concluding that they did not, because there could not but have been then the notion of breeding for the tribe, as Plato—even Plato—recommended breeding for the nation.

Among the Scythians, for example, promiscuity, as we know, prevailed along with a form of marriage (somewhat resembling the *piraura* marriage of the Australian tribes). As with many other races, the man, under certain recognised rules, made his sign of desire to cohabit with another man's wife, and set up his sign of being with her, while yet the fatherly affection towards the children remained undiminished. [*See* Duncker and Preller.] Rather a severe blow to Sir H. Maine's notion that for the exercise of the natural paternal instinct clear evidence of or belief in physical fatherhood was essential.

Promiscuity at this moment among the **Kulus of** the Himalayas is very much of this character too. The **women are** married simply for reasons of **dower,** and neither men nor women regard **themselves as in any way bound to** each other. The behaviour at the **Nagar** Fair simply exhibits free and open intercourse **of the** sexes. "It can cause little surprise that the women, with no home ties as we know them to bind them, wander off with their lovers into the dark forest, where **in the** warm night the tall deodars spread their sheltering branches over them."[1] **So** ends the Nagar Fair, as many other fairs have ended even in our own country in past times—in orgy, the men universally, and the women sometimes, having made **themselves** drunk with **a special intoxicant then in vogue.**

We know only too well that with some peoples **their** religious festivals ended in orgy. Certain of these peoples definitively ordered that men should not go **in to** their wives for three days previously, **and** is it not strange to find that "for three days before going up to the Mount **the** Hebrew men *were not to come at their wives*" (or in the Revised Version, "not to **come near a** woman") (Exod. xix. **15**)? What possible **connection** could the coming at **their** wives, or coming **near a woman, or not, for three** days, have **had** with the going **up** to the Mount? **None.** But **it is** all reasonable and consistent enough if at one **time** the early Hebrews, like **other** races,

---

[1] F. St. J. **Gore,** "Lights and Shadows of Indian Hill Life," p. 53

wound up religious festivals with promiscuity—with orgies. No wonder the Talmudists and rabbis, as well as men to-day, feel that there is indeed a lot to hide.

Plutarch distinctly says that in his time the Jewish Feast of Tabernacles was wound up with orgiastic observances—that it was, in fact, a bacchalian festival ; and surely he knew to what feast such words could be rightly applied. So here again, as we have found and will find elsewhere, suggestions of precisely the same orgiastic observances, pointing to promiscuity, under religious sanctions, be it observed. And it is confessed in the denunciations of those who worshipped under trees and in gardens.

Here, further, is a very significant and remarkable deliverance bearing on this matter: " There shall not be among the daughters of Israel any one *consecrated* to prostitution, nor shall there be among the sons of Israel a male *consecrated* to prostitution. Thou shalt not bring the hire of a consecrated whore, nor the wages of the sodomite, into the house of Jahwé thy God for any vow, for both are an abomination to Jahwé thy God."[1] קָדֵשׁ is the the word here used for consecrated one : it is clear and plain. The A. V. neatly drops out that idea

---

[1] Deut. xxiii. 18, 19. Since this was written we read: "Everywhere we see evidence that until the growth of the moral feelings brings with it a higher ideal, the natural practice of mankind is to begin life with a grossly promiscuous intercourse, but to form in maturer years monogamous unions of fairly sympathetic type. What is the meaning of that army of over 700,000 [registered] prostitutes to be found in Europe? Does it not signify that a large part of the male population is accustomed to spend its early days in promiscuous intercourse, out of which it passes into marriage? And is not this an indication of that underlying principle of savage life which even the

altogether ; but what can the "consecrated prostitution" which existed at one time mean, save the
very promiscuity I am dealing with? It is the
fashion always to put it as though all this was
merely a protest against the habits of other peoples
to which the Hebrews had a tendency: I prefer
to believe that it was a protest against inveterate
old habits of their own ; and in this I am vastly
confirmed, I confess, by the significant and suspicious
manner in which these translators get rid wholly of
the idea certainly present there in the word קָדֵשׁ.

The Authorised Version here makes the passage
absolutely nonsensical, for why should the hire of
a whore or the price of a dog be specially in that
character brought into the house of Jahwé? But if
the prostitution of females and of males was consecrated, then the money, as was the case with other
people's, would go directly into the treasury of the
Temple. It is this that the passage legislates against,
although it would appear, from some references in
the Prophets, utterly without effect, unless, indeed,

most cultured races of our own time have left behind them after all
not more than one hundred generations, a time too short for radical
modifications of racial instincts ? There are still very many persons
who think it only natural for a young man 'to sow his wild oats,'
which in the main is only an euphemism for the grovelling delights
of promiscuity. Several medical authorities offer the estimate,
which, however, is only a guess founded on the trend of experience,
that about one-fourth of the adult male population of Europe is
at any given time living at least in the occasional practice of
promiscuity. Certainly, when one considers that in the most
cultured countries from ten to thirty-five prostitutes exist for every
10,000 of the population, or about an average of one to every 100
men, it must at least be allowed that the most cultured races still
are reminiscent of their naked ancestors." (Sutherland, "Origin
and Growth of the Moral Instinct," i. p. 187.)

Deuteronomy was not written or known when they prophesied. But, anyway, this legislation—very late legislation, we believe—proves that *consecrated* prostitution had been practised, and that there was even then a great tendency to it, so that it needed to be thus expressly forbidden.

Nor, despite the dust-throwings of self-interested professors and preachers, who put this as though it was a warning against other people's vices and not practised by the Jews, is this left to merely general impression. At 2 Kings xxiii. 7 we read: "He [Josiah] brake down the houses of the sodomites [? male and female consecrated prostitutes] *that were by the house of the Lord*, where the women wove hangings for the grove [*asherah*]. . . . And he defiled the high places where the priests had burned incense." Then, again, 1 Kings xiv. 24: "And there were also sodomites in the land."

The Revised Version does not do much to improve matters. At the word "harlot" (which it rather primly substitutes for the Authorised "whore" in the first clause) it gives in the margin *Kedeshah*, and at the word "sodomite" it gives in the margin *Kadesh*, as though the ordinary reader would be much enlightened by that. At the word "dog," כֶּלֶב, in the next sentence, it gives no note of explanation that "dog" there is clearly used for *Kadesh* or sodomite in the preceding verse, though they do well in changing the phrase "*price* of a dog" to "wages of a dog"—that is, of a sodomite. But for any real light the ordinary reader must turn to Gen. xxxviii. 21, where the Revisers give in the margin "*Kedeshah, that is, a woman dedicated to impure heathen *worship,*" which last words should have been "consecrated to temple prostitution." Dr. B. Davies actually notes the fact in his Lexicon, but he does not make the needful change in his translation of the Old Testament.

Another argument in favour of this position might be based on the legislation of Deut. xxiii. 1. That legislation is absolutely unintelligible unless in view of festivals wound up with promiscuous indulgence with actual religious sanction. If there was a strict law that men should not have at their wives [or come near a woman] for three days prior to such consecrated promiscuity, then what surprise need be felt at this view of Deut. xxiii. 1 ?

In this the Hebrews were like most other early peoples. Among the Australians men and women joined in their nakedness to perform lascivious dances, and it was in many tribes a custom during a grand corrobboree that a number of women should form a camp a little way off from the dance, to which the unmarried men could retire in the intervals to enjoy their gross embraces.[1] The Hebrews were naked in their dancings round the golden calf—that is, bull—and the close of such dancings we know; and yet Aaron speaks of this as a feast to Jahwé. David danced naked, to Michal's disgust, round the Ark.

Some of the forms of promiscuity were like the ways of the " heathen Chinee—strange and peculiar."

" In Tasmania widows, if they did not re-marry, were the common property of the males of the tribe into which they had married." [2]

[1] Brough Smyth, ii. p. 319.
[2] *Ibid.*, ii. p. 386.

Messrs. Spencer and Gillen are distinctly of opinion that with the tribes of Central Australia you have a form of individual marriage united with relations of a much wider nature, clearly pointing you back to group-marriage, and through that to promiscuity. No other explanation of certain things is to them intelligible. They point out that, "as will be seen, group-marriage, in a modified but yet most unmistakable way, occurs as an actual system in one of the tribes with which we are dealing," and proofs and survivals of it and of promiscuity under religious sanction are found everywhere.

"The woman can become, though only in a modified way, exclusively the property of one man by having passed through certain ceremonies, etc., among the Urubunna tribe ; and these ceremonials invariably suggest first group-marriage, and secondly, if more indirectly, promiscuity " (p. 94).

Again, they deliberately say, summing up certain results :

" No one has an exclusive right to any woman, only a preferential right. A group of women of a certain designation are actually the wives of a group of men of another designation, partial promiscuity thus pointing to a less restricted promiscuity in ages past " (p. 96).

Every corrobboree gives full and indubitable testimony to this :

" Every day two or three or more women are told off to attend at the corrobboree ground, and, with the exception of men who stand in the relation to them of actual father, brother, or sons, they are, for the time being, common property to all the men present on the corrobboree ground " (p. 97). " It is at certain times a clear duty of the man to send his wife to the corrobboree ground. . . .

" Every man in turn is thus obliged by public custom to relinquish, for the time being, his possession of the woman who has been allotted to him " (p. 99).

Sir John Lubbock's notion of capture giving a man the only right to monopolise a woman is thus, as we shall see, put out of court.

Westermarck's fine ideas about hospitality and the lending of wives receive short shrift from Messrs. Spencer and Gillen (p. 102), where Westermarck's error and confusion of idea on the points are well exposed, as well as his " unfounded assertions to the effect that there is not a shred of genuine evidence for the notion that promiscuity ever formed a general stage in the social history of mankind " (pp. 110, 112).

Messrs. Spencer and Gillen sum up effectively in these words :

" General intercourses during the performance of certain corrobborees are, it appears to us, only capable of any satisfactory explanation on the hypothesis that they indicate the temporary recognition of certain general rights which existed in the time prior to that of the form of group-marriage of which we have such clear traces yet lingering among the tribes. They prove the existence of wider marital relations than group-marriage " (pp. 111, 112).

And they repeat :

" We do not see how the facts detailed can receive any satisfactory explanation except on the theory of the former existence of group-marriage ; and, further, that this has of necessity given rise to the terms of relationship used by the Australian natives, and points clearly back to a period of promiscuity."

Among the Hurons, and in fact among all the Central American Indians, there were festivals when promiscuity was general (see Bancroft, i. 763) ; and it was the same with the Melanesians (Codrington, p. 23), with the Negritos, and a host of other tribes and races.

Professor Robertson Smith himself deliberately notes it, as an illustration, that "the autumn feast, usually known as the Feast of Tabernacles, has a *close parallel* in the Canaanite Vintage Feast," and we know what that was, and how it ended. And the Professor proceeds :

" That there were great similarities in the method of celebration between the feasts of the Hebrews and their heathen neighbours is clear from the Bible, especially from the undoubted fact of the admixture of elements of Ba'al worship with the service of Jehovah. The custom of holding feasts in tents or booths (Hos. xii. 9) reappears in the Babylonian *sacæa,* and elsewhere in the East (see Movers' ' Phœnizier,' i. 483, *seq.*). Again, the Hebrew technical term עצרה reappears in the worship of the Tyrian Ba'al, 2 Kings x. 20. The description of Syrian festivals given by Posidonius (Müller, ' Frag-ments,' iii. 258), the copious eating and drinking, etc., the portions carried home, the noisy music, etc., resemble forcibly what we read of the Hebrew feasts (1 Sam. i. 14 ; 2 Sam. vi. 9 ; Lam. ii. 7, etc.)."

The worship under trees and in gardens of the

Hebrews, as said already, was accompanied with immoral orgies—*i.e.*, promiscuity—even down to so late a date as the time of Isaiah and Hosea, as we find proof in Hos. iv. 13, and Isa. i. 29: " Ye shall be ashamed for the oaks that ye have desired, and ye shall be confounded for the gardens that ye have chosen." And they most certainly maintained themselves to the time of Josiah, if not far beyond it, when Plutarch can speak as he does of the Feast of Tabernacles.

Mr. Risley, writing of polygamy and other practices, says that " any check on promiscuity is better than none," suggesting tendencies to promiscuity still marked and noticeable among tribes and races of India, as well he may.[1]

On the festivals of Bilit the maidens sat in the groves with chaplets of cord upon their heads. Even the wealthy came with carriages and retinues. They sat till one of the pilgrims threw into their laps a piece of gold with the words, " In the name of Bilit " [or of Mylitta]. Then the maiden had to follow and comply with his wishes. The money thus earned was given to the temple treasury. " The good-looking and graceful maidens," Herodotus tells us, " quickly found a pilgrim, but the ugly ones could not satisfy the law, and often remained in the temple three or four years." And the goddess Nana had the very same offerings in this kind as Bilit. The analogy with the consecrated whores, male and female, in the Temple or attached to the Temple among the Hebrews, up even to a late date—the females with very significant cords, too—shows in what peculiar way the Hebrew

[1] " Tribes and Castes of Bengal," I. p. 196.

customs were akin to those of heathen Semites in Canaan and also in Mesopotamia, and, more, with those of Australian corrobborees, etc., etc. We do not go so far as to say that this is borne out or strengthened by the idea of more than one writer dealing with boomerangs, etc., etc., who suggest that Australia as well as the South Pacific Islands were all alike populated from Asia. Yet when writers like Dr. Wyatt Gill and Mr. Calvert, Mr. Macfarlane, and Mr. Chalmers are agreed, it is not too much to say that there may be something in it, and that the corrobboree, with all its accompaniments, is directly derived from Asia, from Semites.

Among Etruscans, Greeks, Arabs, early Germanic tribes, among Picts and early Celts, not to mention many other races—Malagasies, numerous tribes in India and in Africa—descent was through the mother; descent through the mother in all these cases accompanied with such phenomena that the insistent and *accepted* doubt of definite sexual fatherhood can only point one way. Robertson Smith in " Kinship " literally makes it clear that father in Hebrew and Arabic meant merely old head of a house.

There is an extraordinary instance of a survival of promiscuous intercourse working under and into the later institution of "raising up seed," to be found in Letorneau (p. 233), which I commend to the notice of Sir Henry Maine's friends—an instance which absolutely proves that the Djebel-Taggale of Kordofan literally do not know certain common facts of human nature, and act like absolute idiots, if Sir Henry Maine is right here. And, further, Grimm ells that the same thing was much in the same way provided for among the early Germanic tribes under communistic law[1]—a fact which can only point in one direction : to clan or tribal promiscuity.

And over and above all things it must not be forgotten that in the inevitable progress of the early human societies you have, *it may be*, the family, but certainly at least, in forming, the clan and the tribe, and that these two last, instead of being thrown aside as regards any institution, were not only consenting to, but operative in it—the individual even in such indulgences moving in an area defined and after all limited by these, and had no freedom outside certain well-defined lines. This is essential to the very conception of such societies, the clan and the tribe, whatever may be said of family, lying behind all along the whole line of natural development; while yet, as language unmistakably proves, the word father had no reference whatever to the facts of actual physical or sexual fatherhood. In fact, the submergence of all family relations under that of father, brothers and sisters, and absorption into these—all the males of a group being regarded not as uncles, etc., but fathers, and all cousins as brothers and sisters— must have had some origin or reason lying much farther back. What was it ?

Sir Henry Maine's explanation is certainly not very satisfactory. He thinks that the savage had not brain enough to follow complex relationships. But surely the most utter savage could have followed it at least one step farther than fathers and brothers and sisters, and the question to be answered is, why

---

[1] " Rechtsalterthumer," p. 445.

did he not, and why is there a kind of common consent on the part of savages very widely separated, not to do so? Mr. Morgan's descriptive system merely shows fitful efforts to do so.

And all this, mark you well, while Sir Henry Maine has just demonstrated to you, to his own complete satisfaction apparently, that "the unit of ancient society was the family" [not always, however, merging more into clan and tribe, but rather emerging out of these], "while the unit of modern society is the individual." The individual, thus discharged from closer dues to the family and clan and tribe in modern society, does not, to any large extent, and certainly not absolutely, appear to escape from tendencies to promiscuity ; and the let-alone principle is hardly to be assumed as favourable to the reducing of promiscuity, if certain recent returns are to be trusted. There arises the vast problem whether restrictions, as tried by recognition, inspection, etc., as in France, etc., or restrictions and inspections of a different kind more suitable to ourselves, might not be made available. But promiscuity not existent at all in early times, with this proved tendency to it in all times—in our own time ! Truly, if so, Sir Henry provided a powerful self-destroying argument to pierce his own breast with its irony, when he said that the stationary condition was the rule for the human race. There is progress—progress, truly—from the promiscuity of the early men, with some vague kind of regulation and religious sanction of clan or tribe, to the truly individualistic promiscuity of England, etc., with no control or sanction whatever. That —that is progress ! Heavens ! latent tendencies to

promiscuity prevail widely now, **even now, and find,**
under certain restrictive laws, legal and social, their
full outlet. **Sir R.** Burton on this matter has some
very plain and queer remarks now and then. **And if
in** so many cases **the tendencies to promiscuity come
out even in modern conditions, and after all education
and tradition of self-control, it is fine to hear** men
like Sir Henry Maine trying to argue it away in the
earlier days, and to deny what **is to the** credit of the
earlier time, that tribal influence, *plus* family influence,
was so strong as in degree to control it by regulation and religious sanction. With many, many men
even now the **way to** marriage lies through promiscuity as a fixed stage **of** development. If each man
is the race in little, there you have it, **"plain and flat,"**
as Biglow says.

V.

I am fully **aware that, in addition to Westermarck,
Mr. A. H. Keane (if I** remember right) **and several**
others **in** this country, like Sir Henry Maine, have,
to their own satisfaction, argued away, or tried to
argue away, promiscuity ; and, with the worthy and
trustworthy Westermarck, would fain trace human
monogamy and family life back to the loftier mammals
and higher apes, from whom primitive men received
it as a delightful legacy, which, most unfortunately,
they seem soon to have squandered, like the Prodigal,
and returned **to** their wallowings in the mire like a
dog. I always, in this connection, recall a wise **and**
shrewd **remark of Dr. A.** Russel Wallace, that men
differ **from** the lower **animals in** several respects—
especially **as** regards social sympathy and nice fellow-

feeling, etc., etc. However it may have been with primitive men or early men, men now, from all too irrefragable facts already hinted at, are only, alas! too apt to return on promiscuity; and all I would ask these able and respected ethnologists and naturalists is to tell me at what point men, and highly civilised men, so decisively, markedly, and painfully departed from the beautiful and lofty example set them, according to these worthy gentlemen, by the higher mammals, apes, and primitive savages! I think I am entitled to an answer, and a definite answer, on this point. Perhaps Mr. A. H. Keane may not disdain to lead.

In truth, all this theorising in favour of the family as the unit of most ancient societies becomes, in the light of research, more and more uncertain. The farther we go back we find—most assuredly find—that the family exists under the very vaguest and loosest ties, while clan and tribe contrive to control everything. In any form of truly monogamous marriage some idea of individual or family free action is assumed; but, in face of this, we find that the clan and the tribe literally control everything. Westermarck's apes are all very good; but men certainly develop differently. Promiscuity tells it. There is under tribal rule no such thing as individual freedom even in marriage, nor is there such a thing as family unity properly conceived. Professor Wundt has expressed this result faithfully in his "Ethics":

"The farther we trace the history of the family, the less secure do its foundations become, the less evidence do we find of an indissoluble marriage and of its prime condition, abiding conjugal affection.

Nor is it to be wondered at if, as is highly probable, the *polygamous* form of marriage preceded monogamy. Far more influential than the family in primitive times, and of far higher value in ethical regard, was the tribal union. Even at the present day its social significance is greater than that of marriage among savage races, and its original importance for the civilised peoples is proved by numerous survivals in language and custom."[1]

Why, at this moment, is it not common matter of remark that marriages in our highest classes are not usually made in heaven; that conjugally there is much to wish for as to continuance and faithfulness; and that, in a word, if there is not there marriage for the advantage of the state, there is marriage for the presumed advantage of the caste?

Proof of this—abundant proof—is found in survivals in that sphere, the Hindu, with which Sir Henry Maine ought to have been best acquainted; and if he is not to be blamed for not having in the least forecasted the results of recent researches, he is to be blamed for his high and dry theorisings and dogmatisings, conducted with all the air of a man who knows everything.

In the above passage from Wundt polygamous marriage should have been made alternative with polyandrous marriage and promiscuity. Even at this moment in civilised nations, and among the highest castes in civilised nations, as just said, the way to marriage on the part of a majority, it is greatly to be feared, is through promiscuity. Is this progress, or is it stationary condition? I earnestly ask

---

[1] "Ethics," tr. by E. B. Titchener, p. 185.

of the friends and eulogists of Sir Henry Maine, and implore one or other of them to answer me.

That thoughtful and ingenious Scotsman, George Cupples, in his endeavour to reach the starting-point of the training of domestic animals, more especially the dog, came to a very deliberate opinion, after years of research, that no effort was made or could have been made in that way before family life, with a master of a house or home, was established. He says:

"A promiscuous human horde not divided into families would thus appear to have formed the world's original and early population. . . . No wild whelp could have learnt the merest rudiments of his education so long as he had to obey more masters than one."[1]

Mr. Cupples was not at all concerned with anything but dogs and other animals in relation to man ; but he was a scholar and an antiquarian, and this was his conclusion—reached entirely from his own point of view, and with quite another order of facts before him.

VI.

And would it be believed that, when I turn to the authorities to which I am demonstratively and even ostentatiously referred by Sir Henry Maine, I find confirmation of my points of view, and not of his? Thus in J. B. Mayne's "Hindu Law," in section "Looseness of the Marriage Tie," I read:

"Other passages of the Mahabharata are referred

---

[1] "Scotch Deerhounds," p. 181. This is borne out by the most severe decisions of science. The neolithic settlers had a small kind of dog, and this little dog, towards the end of that period, becomes a larger dog; but all through the palæolithic period, and what preceded it, there is no record of domestic animals—the horse first appearing in the bronze-age settlements as an animal completely domesticated.

to which seem rather to evidence the greatest gross-ness and want of chastity, in the relations between the sexes, than anything like polyandry. It is said that ' women were formerly unconfined and roamed about at their pleasure, independent. Though in their youthful innocence they abandoned their husbands, they were guilty of no offence, *for such was the* RULE *in early times.*' This ancient custom is supported by authority, and is observed by great Rishis, and it is still practised among the northern Kurus." Dr. Muir goes on to add, " A stop was, however, put to the practice by Svetaketu, whose indignation was on one occasion aroused by a Brahmin taking his mother by the hand and inviting her to go away with him, although his father, in whose presence this occurred, informed him that there was no reason for his displeasure, as the custom was one which had prevailed from time immemorial [apparently a yet worse form of consecrated prostitution]. . . .

" The Gandhara Brahmins of the Punjaub are said to corrupt their own sisters and daughters-in-law, and to offer their wives to others, hiring out and selling them like commodities for money. Their women, being thus given up to strangers, are con-sequently shameless," as might have been expected. (Muir, A. S. T. ii. 482, 483.) In exactly the same way the Koravers of Southern India, who are not polyandrous, sell and mortgage their wives and daughters when they are in want of money (Madras Census Report, 167). Of course, delicacy or chastity must be utterly unknown in such a state of society. But these very texts seem to show that each wife was appropriated to a single husband, though he was willing to allow her the greatest freedom of action. Mr. V. N. Mandlik says of the passages cited from Dr. Muir: "To me the whole chapter shows that the northern Kurus were then what the Nairs in Malabar are now; so *that a man did not know his own father.*" (Pp. 65, 66, 4th ed., 1888.)

There are to-day a great many races who are to others as the northern Kurus are to the Nairs of Malabar now, according to Mr. Mandlik.

But, however this may be, one thing is clear, that custom and law alike had been directed to insuring "seed," without any the least respect for blood. "A man's son need not have been begotten by his father, nor need he have been produced by his father's wife."[1] Out of what conditions could this custom or law have grown, with all the implied processes of adoption, begetting by deputy, etc.? Sir Henry Maine at one place dwells much, as we have hinted, on the instincts, etc., of sexual fatherhood, which, as mere facts of nature, according to him, needed and demanded gratification. In that particular he was just guilty of reasoning from later experience to early experience, which is a most misleading and all-unauthorised process — unless indeed the stationary condition of the race is the rule —in all such respects. Here we have at once a tradition of a long past, confirmed by isolated cases even in the present, where some dominating interest, belief, or feeling wholly overrode presumed instincts of sexual fatherhood, and that in the very area with which Sir Henry Maine should have been best

[1] J. B. Mayne, "Hindu Law," p. 66.

acquainted. The indifference to it leads inevitably **to the presumption that it** derives from a **period when** to trace fatherhood was **as hard as to succeed in it** would often have been unwelcome.

Mr. J. B. Mayne writes : "A law of inheritance which assumes the tracing of male ancestors unbroken through fourteen generations, while **there** is a family **law in which** several admitted forms of marriage are only euphemisms for seduction and rape [and incest ?], and in which twelve sorts of sons are recognised, the majority of whom have no blood relationship to the father,[1] cannot but point to much in the past to which **it** stands wholly foreign, as an effort by legal and wholly artificial means to overcome and modify what was clearly of very ancient usage and bound **up with** forms **of** religious **belief and even reverence—the most inveterate of all forms of custom and usage.**"

VII.

Sir Henry Maine, in endeavouring **to take** away the **ground** on **which** MacLennan so **far** based to support **his** idea **of** scarcity of **women,** disclaims general female infanticide—doubts if it was anything **but** exceptional—and argues **that, if one** side lost **their** women **through** defeat, others must have gained **them,**[2] that it "**was a common rule** of tribal victory **to take all** the **women."** [3] **Now, we** believe that **this** leaves out wholly **a most important** factor in the **matter.** In the **Hebrew Scriptures** nothing is clearer **than the command, over and over again** repeated, as **though direct from the mouth of** Jahwé, **to kill**

---

[1] "Hindu Law," p. 79.
[2] "Early Law and **Custom,**" p. 213.
[3] *Ibid.,* p. 214.

all the women "that *had lain by man*," but to take
the virgins for themselves. Were the Hebrews in
this respect better, or were they worse, than their
neighbours? Did they stand alone in this matter,
not having even the excuse that they shared it with
tribes generally at that stage, with Eastern races
generally, or even with their own brother Semites?
The excuse, it was the custom of the time, is often
offered on such matters. What I ask is this: Did
the Hebrews in this stand alone? If they did, they
present a very remarkable phenomenon ; if they did
not, then we assume that the same custom as they
practised as regards women taken in war will do
much to account, up to a certain point, for the
disparity in numbers of men and women. Tribes
were almost in constant conflict with other tribes,
and the losses by this custom, if custom it were,
would be tremendous. *Some* of the men would fall,
but all the women that had lain by man would go.
And in Eastern countries, where puberty is early
and child marriages are common, and where single
women—old maids—were not existent, it is all too
clear that the women that had *not lain by man* were
few—that, in fact, only children or very young girls
were spared. If people like the Hebrews were guilty
of such enormities, what would make it so unlikely
among pure savages? During the continual inter-
tribal fights that went on among the South African
Bantus or Kaffirs previous to the European occupa-
tion, the women of the vanquished were invariably
carried off by the victors and became the wives of
their masters. Sir Henry Maine never glances at
these facts and at this problem, and in throwing doubt

on infanticide appears **to us** wholly to **evade the** difficulties rather than in any way to face them, and thus to make confusion worse confounded. We **could** furnish here such a list of undoubted cases of infanti-cide, **under one pretext or** another, as would **make his doubts** about it appear very capricious **and very ill-informed. He writes :**

" There is evidence that some of the islands **of the** Pacific were populated by boatfuls of men and a few women, **and it** would be no violent conjecture that the aborigines of Australia and America originally reached their present homes with the sexes in this proportion. It is needless to say what would be the character of the institutions which would establish themselves under such circumstances. **In fact, it** may be said to have been the **usages of the Australian** and **American Indians which respectively suggested the theories of MacLennan and Morgan, and it is** singular **how often, whenever a dim glimpse of** similar **institutions is** caught elsewhere, **it is** amid societies originally settled, like the Irish, by wanderers **over the sea."** [1]

And all research, comparison, and thought goes to **show that these** Australians originally derived from **Asia,** carrying **its** then customs with **them.**

The above, besides, is **a kind of reasoning so** vague, indefinite, **and** unhistorical that it emphasises the proverbial hardness **of** proving **a negative.** But **we have** some points **to** argue. The **reports of Dr. Turner at Samoa, of** Wyatt **Gill at Mangaia and other places, of** Chalmers **in New Guinea and other parts, show** that the disproportion **in the South**

1 " Early Law and Custom," p. 243.

Pacific must soon have been effaced, for from time
immemorial female infanticide has been practised.
With this result for Sir Henry Maine, unfortunately,
that any practices due to anything approaching to
promiscuous polyandry, which, physically, according
to him, cannot escape *certain* resemblances to modern
promiscuity, could not have had any tendency to infertility, as he has said, because in these areas from time
immemorial female infanticide has been common.

Sir Henry Maine's argument against infanticide
based on the demands of the paternal instinct is, like
too many other of his arguments, met by wide array
of actual facts and disposed of. The parental instinct
is intensified by infanticide—the children preserved
appearing to receive a double share of affection :
hardness of life, not hardness of heart, being the
cause.

Look at a few out of many facts bearing directly
against Sir Henry Maine's assumption.

Eyre tells that infanticide was common among all
the Australian tribes, and that some of them killed
only the females.[1] Williams says that the custom
of killing female children was very common in Fiji.[2]
In Samoa infanticide was ordered by law ; only two
children were allowed to a family, as they were
afraid of a scarcity of food.[3] In the Solomon Islands
it was the custom to kill all, or nearly all, the children
soon after birth, and they would afterwards buy
children from other tribes, and not too young.[4]

---

[1] P. 324.
[2] I. p. 181.
[3] Turner's " Samoa," p. 284.
[4] Romilly, " West Pacific," pp. 68, 69.

Brough Smyth firmly believes that infanticide, as well as the practices of circumcision and (still more remarkable) subincision, prevailed over the whole of Western Australia.[1]

If Mr. Brough Smyth is sure about Western Australia, Messrs. Spencer and Gillen have no reserve about Central Australia. " Infanticide," they say, " is practised—the child being killed immediately on birth. They believe that the spirit part goes back at once to the particular spot from whence it came, and can be born again at some subsequent time even of the same woman. Twins are regarded as something unnatural, and among the Luritcha children of a few years are often killed, the object being to feed a weakly but elder child, who is supposed thus to gain the strength of the younger one."[2]

With the Mbayas of Paraguay, as with many other tribes, the first children of a couple were always killed. Only when the mother thought she would not bear another did she rear the infant.[3]

Nor can we here, as we Britishers are so apt to do, pique ourselves on having been better than other people, for even with regard to our own Anglo-Saxon forefathers their inveterate custom of infanticide is only too clearly proved. Here is what Thrupp says, and he only repeats what all other authorities have said :

" Infanticide was commonly practised among the Anglo-Saxons. Instead of being regarded as a crime, it was meritorious and a proof of virtue. Even

---

[1] II. p. 347.
[2] " Australian Aborigines," p. 52.
[3] Washbourne, p. 42.

after infanticide positive was, under new influences, discredited, exposure of infants was still common. It was considered idle to rear a weak or sickly child, and it was worse than useless to rear a timid one, who could only be a 'nithing,' and a disgrace to a nation of brave men" [1]—facts these with which a great lawyer and Oxford professor should have been familiar.

VIII.

It is only too clear that Sir Henry Maine, if he knew a little of Sanskrit, knew nothing at all of Hebrew and Arabic; and, like Professor Jowett before the late Lord Tennyson, might have incurred rebuke, as he rather suffered by the want of this accomplishment in some at least of his lines of study. [2] For example, he ventures at page 59, "Early Law and Custom," on the assertion that "the Hebrew Scriptures contain but few allusions to this widespread practice" [worship of ancestors], [3] when, despite the all-too-interested tricks of translators, the Authorised Version might have warned him, and the Hebrew itself, could he but have read it, would certainly have taught him better. It is funny—really funny—to find him quoting Ps. cvi. 28, but leaving out of account the passage in Numbers on which it is based, and accepting meekly the dictum that what is there meant is "*sacrifices to the dead.*" It meant something different from that, as we have seen in

---

[1] Thrupp, "Anglo-Saxon Home," p. 79.

[2] *See* "Memoir of Lord Tennyson," by his son, ii. p. 167.

[3] "It has been generally allowed that the Hebrew Scriptures contain few allusions to this widespread practice." ("Early Law and Custom," p. 59.)

dealing with Mr. Andrew Lang. Then he gives, as
though there were no more, a reference to Deut.
xxvi. 14, while at various points of the Levitical
legislation there are clear warnings in different places
against eating of mourning feasts (feasts to ancestors);
against making marks or prints on the person *for the
dead ;* making cuts on the body for the dead ; marring
the corners of the beard for the dead, or rounding off
the corners of the hair for the dead—the Hebrew
word here, פֵּאָה, being one of the most expressive an
significant in the whole Hebrew Bible ; while in
the Deuteronomic code some of these are repeated
with emphasis, and "making baldness between the
eyes *for the dead*" prohibited (xiv. 1, 2). [1]

The serpent was clearly the totem of the tribe
of Levi, originally more specifically of the family of
Moses (בְּנֵי־לֵוִי = Sons of the Serpent), and נְחֻשְׁתָּן, the
symbol of ancestors of that tribe, was worshipped
in the Temple, and incense burned to it, up to the
time, at all events, of Hezekiah.[2] The teraphim,

[1] At Jeremiah xvi. 6, 7, we read : "They shall not be buried,
neither shall men lament for them, nor cut themselves, nor make
themselves bald for them : Neither shall men tear themselves for
them in mourning, to comfort them *for the dead*, neither shall they
give the cup of consolation to drink for father and for mother."
Jeremiah surely did not so write about what was only a mere
antiquity and had no existence when he wrote ; otherwise, I
seriously ask the friends and admirers of Sir Henry Maine what
the above can mean. Perhaps Sir F. Pollock will kindly tell me !
If these were merely common or ordinary mourning rites, why did
Jeremiah so denounce them ? And, if not, did he denounce what
really was no way practised when he wrote ? That is what I want
to know from Sir F. Pollock or another of Sir Henry Maine's
admirers and eulogists.

[2] And with regard to the serpent, נְחֻשְׁתָּן, was it an oracle, and
consulted as such, or was it not ? Something strange it is, anyway,
to find such proper names, specially applied to priests, or possibly

every one now agrees, were images of ancestors (even Kitto, not to speak of the rationalistic critics in Germany and at home, held this view). The teraphim that were stolen from Laban, and translated gods or images in our version, were exactly the same as we find later. Some of these teraphim were so large and lifelike that Michal, by putting one in bed and drawing the goatskin over it, managed very cleverly to expedite David's escape from her father's vengeance; so that if David himself did not worship ancestors, of which there may well be some doubt, he had good cause to be thankful to an ancestor's image! And the fact that these teraphim or images of ancestors were found in the house of David, and kept so very handy by his wife, does suggest the question that if David—"the flower of Jewish monotheism," according to the most eloquent and learned Dr. Fairbairn—consented to be so served, what must it have been with the vulgar crowd? But then again we think of David and that image from Nob (the ephod was a teraphim gilded) which he divined by—and the teraphim were used for divining by—and ask, was it, too, a teraphim? The teraphim were generally tolerated by priests and prophets and kings; scarce a word was uttered against them, if those who worshipped them but attended to the ceremonies and sacrifices of the Temple. Even the

interpreters of oracles, as פִּינְכָס, or serpent's mouth. Was that totemistic, or what—a mere accident, with no importance anyway, or was it not? Will Sir Henry Maine's friends kindly give us their theory of that, and full explanation of it? We shall be deeply obliged to them for satisfaction on these heads. Both the teraphim and ephod were consulted as oracles—does the פִּינְכָס in this point the same way? Perhaps Sir Alfred Lyall will answer that.

earlier prophets have no word to say against them.
On the contrary, they regarded them as perfectly
innocent and consistent with what they termed
Jahwé worship. Sometimes, indeed, they spoke
of them as an essential part of it. Even the later
prophet Hosea (iii. 4) says : " For the children of
Israel shall abide many days without a king, and
. without a prince, and without a sacrifice, and without
a pillar, and without an ephod, and without a *tera-*
phim." And Hosea wrote in the days of the good kings
Uzziah, Jotham, and Hezekiah. These teraphim stood
exactly to the Hebrews as the "tablets of ancestors"
stood and stand to the Chinese ; and that, too, among
a people where the Mosaic legislation was clear against
all graven images, proving how thoroughly persistent
it was.

The very word תֶּרֶף, had Sir Henry but known
it, might have warned him ; for תֶּרֶף means food,
nourishment, that on which man thrives ; and the
teraphim, if they became feeders, nourishers, were
at first the fed or nourished ones. So we see that
they were so named because offerings of food, wine,
etc., were made to them precisely as to the *manes*
among most of the peoples of the earth, wild tribes
as well as civilised peoples. Sir Henry knew Latin
well, and no doubt often mused over the *Penates*.
Well, the process with the *Penates*—from *penus=panis*,
food—implies the fed, the nourished, the word
having passed through the same stages precisely,
at last to designate images or symbols of deceased
ancestors, as the Hebrew תְּרָפִים had done.[1] Colonel

---

[1] תֶּרֶף = רֵעַ, triph, = درب, driph, = τρέφω = thrive, be
nourished, live in comfort.

Conder, indeed, in one of his quarterly articles, speaks, and quite rightly, of teraphim *or* Penates.

Again, "the chambers of imagery" which Ezekiel tells of, where the heads of the houses of Israel worshipped ancestors under intermixed figures of teraphim and totems, were temples of this worship.[1] No other conclusion can the comparative anthropologist draw from the Hebrew. Stade, the great German critic, regards El, the tree, the sacred tree itself, as a mere totem sign for an ancestor or *numen* worshipped as such.

Every stone of a circle at the Gilgal or at other circles, which were, as Joshua says, regarded as witnessing covenants, etc., was also a Beth-El—house of a deified ancestor—the upright stone being a representation of the thigh of an ancestor. So that, instead of its being as Sir Henry Maine says, it is the very opposite. The Hebrew Scriptures are full of half-veiled but still indisputable references to the worship of ancestors, and many, many, many might be cited beyond those I have now given. Worship of ancestors, direct or indirect, looms as clearly behind Mosaism or Jahwéism as it does behind Hinduism and the mixed later worships of the Chinese and Burmans—and Sir G. Birdwood is quite right about the naïfness of the Jews here.

There is, for instance, a further very remarkable expression in the Hebrew with a bearing here. It is רוּר, or, better still, דּוּר. Both mean going round or about. Now it has more specifically come to mean a period of time or a generation, as we

---

[1] מַשְׂכִּיּוֹת, literally wall pictures or figured or pictured walls · hence, some say, our *Mosaic.* Referred to in Koran, sura liii. 19, 20.

find it in that wonderfully poetical, rhythmical couplet at Eccles. i. 4; but its earlier meaning yet lingers in דאר, which signifies a circle, as at Joshua xvii. 11 : דּוּר אֲבוּת is literally circle of the fathers or ancestors. Now was this graves, or could it have been graves? To our idea it is more likely a circle of stones, since we find Jeremiah so clear on the Jews of his time, " saying to a stone, Thou art my father," etc.

Indeed, I cannot help entertaining an idea that the לֶחֶם אֲנָשִׁים (food of the men) means something very different from what the lexicographers and commentators would fain have it bear. For why, if it was a custom for friends and relatives to send food to mourners, should the prophet Ezekiel have so inveighed against it (see Ezek. xxiv. 17 and 22), any more than against simple, natural mourning for the dead? I conceive that the mourning for the dead here was the feasts to ancestors, and the לֶחֶם אֲנָשִׁים the food offered to them—a portion of it eaten by the mourners. The word לֶחֶם is often used for feast, as it was in the allied Chaldean; and here, then, we should have the prohibition from eating the feasts of men or of the dead, as distinguished from feasts to pure nature-gods, against which Ezekiel might well take up his parable. So here again we have the worship of ancestors lurking under another term, utterly unsuspected because of the dodges and devices of Hebrew professors and self-interested clergymen—self-interested so far as their very profession urges them to try to make out the whole Hebrew business far better than it was. And just here let me parenthetically inquire why it

was that the Manna of the Wilderness was called
לֶחֶם אַבְרִים, food of the strong.

Some very significant traces of original purpose
and tendency remain to the end in the Hebrew.
" Among the Hebrews the conception that Jehovah
eats the flesh of bulls and drinks the blood of goats,
against which the author of Psalm l. protests so
strongly, was never eliminated from the ancient
technical language of the priestly ritual, in which the
sacrifices are called לֶחֶם אֱלֹהִים, the *food of the deity*"[1]
—that is, the food of the ancestors. It is Elohim, not
Jahwé, mark, and Elohim was often used for elders,
for judges, and for ancestors. It is Elohim that is
used by the Witch of Endor when she says she sees
" gods "—that is, " ancestors," old men—coming up.

In truth, there is a most distinct reminiscence of
offerings to ancestors in the whole circle of Hebrew
offerings—they are all edible; they are all the choicest
and most perfect of things edible. The very express
warnings against offering these same things to
ancestors, as most evidently was the tendency of
the Jews, is almost proof presumptive of their real
origin.

In fact, in the very use of נֶפֶשׁ without מֵת, as at
Lev. xxi. 1, for the dead—that is, the departed soul
or ancestor—you have one of the most remarkable
testimonies language could supply in support of our
position ; and the use of נֶפֶשׁ in that sense is absolutely
convincing there, that departed ancestors are meant.
If מֵת had been in any way used, then doubt might
have arisen ; but the verse is as absolute as though
no context on the same matter followed, with detailed

[1] " Religion of the Semites," p. 224.

law, which, by-the-bye, is there an absolute repetition of Lev. xix. 27, 28, where also לְנֶפֶשׁ is used for the dead. At Deut. xiv. 1, we have these laws repeated in short summary, only dead there is מֵת, which is proof clear of what Deuteronomy is—an attempt to disguise the real nature of what both pre-Mosaic Hebraism and Mosaism were and had been—the initiation through discerning priests of a process which has been going on ever since to transfigure Hebraism (*see* note at p. 42). In this use of the word נֶפֶשׁ we, no doubt, have the cause for its coming in later time, through being used for the dead, to mean body or corpse as well as life and soul, the Deuteronomist studiously helping this by trying to identify the sense of it with that of מֵת. And in a certain sense the earlier Hebrews were through this more advanced towards a doctrine of immortality of the soul than were their descendants, who claimed revelation, and yet made such laws against worship of the dead. Hence, in our idea, the perversion of the use of נֶפֶשׁ to mean dead body as well as soul.

The severe penalty of death for cursing father and mother (Lev. xx. 9) is unintelligible utterly, unless as a reminiscence of the worship of ancestors, where the cursing of father and mother would amount not only to blasphemy, but to possible weakening of the stability of the state through undermining its religion. In the Mosaic legislation we have characteristically enough, " Honour thy father and thy mother, that thy days may be long in the land," instead of "that thou thyself in turn may become a worshipped ancestor." Sir Henry Maine, very maladroitly, actually tells us to

compare this with the Chinese law and promise of
reward. He did not look at that matter long enough
or philosophically enough.

Over and above all this, the worship of ancestors
lies implicit in the whole legislation, and especially
in the sacrifices and the sacramental eating involved
in them. There can be no doubt of it. The tabu
on animals, which was carried up into the Mosaic
legislation, was simply due to the sacredness of the
animal to the clan which worshipped it as embodying
the spirit of the ancestor. These were ceremonially
unclean—that is, were forbidden for ordinary eating
and became clean by consecration; in other words,
were to be eaten only sacramentally or sacrificially,
a process by which it was believed that the eaters
were brought into closer relation with the spirit or
soul of the dead ancestor—a kind of god-eating, and
nothing else—nothing else. טָמֵא means this kind of
ceremonial uncleanness—no more than this. Much
as Judaism advanced, it never got rid in the least
of this element; the process remained essentially
the same, only the object was in a superficial way
changed. It was not *directly* with the ancestors the
people in sacrificial eating were brought into contact,
but with Jahwé the God, though Jahwé in the minds
of most remained very mixed ; and in the time of
Ezekiel the old ancestral worship, in the form of
offering to the old animal totems, was actually carried
on by the heads of the house of Israel in secret in
a " chamber of imagery," which was entered through
a hole in the wall, and where "clouds of incense went
up." And need you wonder when in the holy place,
beside other holy things, was that serpent, the totem

of the tribe of Levi, worshipped there, and clouds of incense went up to it there also.

Mr. Addis discusses this point in his " Hexateuch " (ii. p. 92), where he says :

" There is the strongest evidence that the Semitic clans abstained from the flesh of certain animals because they looked upon them as especially holy, and, indeed, *as their own ancestors* (italics are mine). . . . The Semites, as they advanced in civilisation, instead of speaking of the animal as a god, regarded it as sacred to the deity ; *but the primitive idea shines through the later gloss.* Consequently, when the Hebrew clans grew together into a nation, the sacred animals of all the clans would be forbidden food, and the primitive reason of the prohibition would fade from the memory. While, however, sacred animals were tabooed as a rule, they were, on the very ground of their sanctity, eaten on special occasions sacramentally, *i.e.*, to unite the worshipper with the dæmon which inhabited the animal—that is, the spirit of the ancestor."

And then let the worthy and learned friends of Sir Henry Maine turn up their Bibles—Lord Shand especially, as a well-trained Bible-reading Scot, should be ready—at Isaiah xliv. 12—18, where they will read :

" The carpenter stretcheth out his rule : he marketh it out with a line ; he fitteth it with planes, and he marketh it out with the compass, and maketh it *after the figure of a man, that it may remain in the house* —he maketh a god, and worshippeth it." Let them read the whole passage, and then answer me : Does Isaiah there refer to teraphim or to something else— to images of ancestors, or to images of gods of another kind? Even if so, the case is one of worse and worse for Sir Henry Maine, since then they had in their houses images of ancestors that even the prophets did not much, if at all, rebuke, and images, figures of men, of another kind, which they sometimes did rebuke. And Christians say this is the rock from which they were hewn. No wonder we have John Kensits, etc., etc., etc.

Another very important if indirect proof of worship of ancestors among the Hebrews is very strangely found in the weight attached to the having a son; and this, be it noted, not *in the first place* in earlier times for the sake of inheritance, or for preserving the father's name, but, as Sir R. Burton has well said in "The Jew, the Gipsy, and El Islam": "The son is expected to liberate his father and mother from Sheol."[1] The very process of liberation here, as well as elsewhere, is simply a survival of one part of the observance of early worship of ancestors. This was simply a modification of one form of offering to the *manes*, before Sheol had really any place in Hebrew thought, and had no meaning other than death, as at various passages of the Bible it may now be found. "The throes of death," at more than one place, are the "pains of Sheol."[2]

The very word Ba'al, בעל, in spite of all the theological dust thrown up about it, there can be no doubt means, not originally Lord, Master, but begetter, father; and to that very word is largely due the whole confusion among Semites of father-

[1] P. 47.

[2] It was with the early Hebrew tribes just as it was with the Hindus: "Without sacrifice for the dead, performed by a son, the soul of a father could never be liberated from that part of Hell called *Put.*" (See Duncker, vol. iv. p. 230.)

hood with other relations—the father or *presumed*
begetter all through this tribal life being dominant,
so that not alone in the famous case Sir Henry Maine
deals with as though it were special to that people,
of the wife really in law becoming the *daughter* of her
husband ; it was so with the Semites generally, and
with the Hebrews in particular. Certain forms of
phraseology preserved this fact to the last, just as
certain forms of law have done it among certain
other peoples. Professor Robertson Smith dwelt at
more than one place upon the וֹלד, and its philosophy, and, connecting it with this בַּעַל, and
cognate terms, reached precisely the same result.
This use of the word בַּעַל, as actually a synonym
of this descended worship, continues so late at least
as the date of the prophet Nahum ; for the phrase
occurs as representing really ancestral worship in the
very second verse of his prophecy. It is found in
innumerable cases elsewhere, too many to cite here ;
and, while in this sense the very prophets unconsciously or half-consciously were denouncing Moloch
—a later form of the Syrian or Phœnician Ba'al—
they were serving him as Ba'al in many ways—Ba'al
as the great begetter, father, ancestor. With a slight
modification, to bring this out the better, read : " Go
not to the Gilgal, for there is Ba'al's chapel, there is
Ba'al's court," meaning there were sacrifices, human
sacrifices, to the begetters, ancestors—sacrifices, in
fact, to the *manes*. The whole worship of the ox,
indeed, led to and allied itself with the worship of
Ba'al, and Moloch in Phœnicia and elsewhere was
represented with an ox's head.

The more research is carried back the more do we

see that on all sides influences were carried from Chaldea—from Turanian Chaldea, in which worship of ancestors was a consolidated faith, that came to underlie all that followed—that alike to Hebrew Semites and to Egyptians it commended itself, and maintained itself under all the amalgam of later elaborated customs that formed what they called religion. From this point of view, some of the most remarkable results are derived from the discovery of the tomb of Menes, the first Pharaoh. Its construction and orientation, no less than absence of paintings on the walls, are distinctly after the ancient Chaldean and not the later Egyptian style —a point of the utmost significance as to origin or influence, more especially along with traces of burning. The building is not only a tomb, it is a storehouse and dwelling-place. Adjoining the outer wall are a series of sixteen chambers, forming a gallery round the outer chambers. These, on being explored, were found to be filled with all kinds of provisions, furniture, etc., for the deceased. So here as elsewhere we find the reminiscence of offerings of food, etc., to the departed—to ancestors, of whom the king, by his paternal relations to the people, becomes a sort of idealised type. Here, doubtless, were the nation's offerings, as well as those of family, friends, and ministers—a national memorial to one who in a sense stood as representative to them of the ancestors of all.

" The bond which kept together the families of an early Hebrew tribe was its common religion—the worship of its reputed ancestor. Every Hebrew family, like every old Roman and Greek family, was held firmly together by the worship of its ancestors; the hearth was the altar, the head of the family the priest. At a man's death his nearest male relative inherited the property, and at the same time the duty of carrying on the cult. If there were no sons, one of the slaves took up the office. The chief of the tribe was, of course, the priest of the cult. The names borne by some of the tribes, *i.e.*, Caleb, 'a dog,' show that the earliest form of the Israelite religion was fetishism or totemism."[1] The scene described by Ezekiel of the heads of the houses of Israel in his time in their chambers of imagery, simply reverted to this practice.

Now, the presence of this religion is most marked; it is omnipresent, either by actual practices still persisted in, or by protests against certain forms of it. What then could have led Sir Henry Maine to the most unnecessary, stupid, and ignorant *ipse dixit* that there are but two references to it in the Hebrew Scriptures, when, like his own Hindu books, they are literally full of it?

And even when the name of Ba'al comes to be shadowed with discredit, what have we in Hosea (ii. 16, 17)? The confession that, with the Hebrews for a long period, that is, even up to the time of Hosea (reigns of Jotham, Uzziah, and Hezekiah), Jahwé had been identified with Ba'al—nothing less than this, and called Baali — my lord, begetter, ancestor; and even now it was to be nothing but a mere change of name, for Ishi, while it means husband, like Ba'al, *may* also mean father, precisely the same confusion arising in it and through it of the relations

---

[1] Oxford, pp. 83, 84.

of husband and father as in Ba'al. There can be no mistake about it. Read : "And it shall be at that day, saith the Lord, that thou shalt call me Ishi [my husband], and shalt no more call me Baali [my lord]. For I will take away the names of Baalim out of her mouth, and they shall no more be remembered by their name."

With all this lying clear before the eye of the student, does it not seem a very bold, unnecessary, and ignorant statement, that of the wise and learned Sir Henry Maine, that there are very *few traces of ancestor-worship in the Hebrew ?*

And how funny it is to read this from a powerful pen in reviewing Mr. Lang's new edition of " Myth, Ritual, and Religion " :

" Historically, we find ancestor-worship more prominent among the Aryans, human sacrifices among the Semites, whilst among the most ancestor-worshipping people the world has ever known —the Chinese—the latter practice is non-existent."[1] There are clear traces in survival of human sacrifices among Chinese as among the Aryans. As to the Sanskrit, there is the Purushamedha, etc., etc. ; and ancestor-worship, as proved here, is pervasive among Semites, among Hebrews.

Mr. Crooke (at p. 113 of " Popular Religion and Folklore of Northern India ") gives a whole list of remote aboriginal tribes that worship ancestors ; and in these cases, he says, Hindu influence is generally out of the question. Several of them in days not so very old practised human sacrifice. The " Athenæum " writer's notion aids him to what

[1] "Athenæum," June 10th, 1899.

seems a nice, neat, effective distinction, but the facts
are very sadly against him.

At p. 57, "Early Law and Custom," Sir Henry
writes:

"Ancestors, as divine beings to be worshipped,
are referred to in the Vedas, and stand rather
obscurely under the name of Pitris in the background among the Hindu gods, but every day in
the dwelling of a Hindu the *Shradda* is offered to
father, grandfather, and great-grandfather, and the
offering is made with special observances on particular days and on particular occasions." This
might, with but the change of a few words, be
modified at every point to meet the Hebrew:

"Ancestors, as divine beings to be worshipped,
are referred to *often*, in fact, throughout the
Hebrew Scriptures, and stand by no means obscurely,
under the names נְחֻשְׁתָּן, תְּרָפִים, etc., etc., in the
background of Els, Elohi, Elohim, Jahwé, Ba'al;
but every day in the dwellings of the Hebrews the
teraphim were brought out, oiled or anointed, and
offerings made to father, grandfather, great-grandfather, with special observances on particular days
and on particular occasions."

What a fine point Maine would have made of this
had he but known it, instead of the very, very poor
point he has made !

In Hebrew as in Roman development you find
many points which touch each other, and touch each
other very much to strike light, as flint and iron do.
But Sir Henry Maine missed all that, and the many
enlightening and suggestive links that lay between,
because he knew no Hebrew, yet dealt constantly

with themes to which some degree of this knowledge was essential for the most superficial comparative purposes; and that he *could* have written that there were very few—only two—references to ancestor-worship in the Hębrew, is the most salient and damnatory proof of it.

IX.

When Sir Henry Maine writes: "Any contact with it [worship of ancestors] which may be found in Christianity or Mohammedanism is due to accidental causes" ("Early Law and Custom," p. 212), he is very, very far astray indeed in respect to Mohammedanism, as we shall soon see; but even as regards Christianity, some very able critics and anthropologists—Dr. E. B. Tylor among them—find in the reverence for saints, and the necessity for relics in sacred buildings, still felt and acknowledged by large sections of Christendom, nothing but a modified survival of worship of ancestors; and the worship of the Virgin Mary, with these thinkers, is nothing but a phase of this old worship crossed by a revival of the early idea of mother-right, as is not unnatural, seeing that it especially flourished among the Teutons, with whom, as Professor Karl Pearson has shown, *Mütterrecht* was strong, and who were the first to accept Christianity in any broad and truly national or racial sense, and indelibly stamped their mark on it.

Nor let this be regarded as wholly without parallel or analogous proceeding. The "worship of ancestors" or of the dead has always tended towards a sort of canonisation or saint-making, if in all cases

it is not followed up to the roots and so named.
Sir Halliday Macartney, in an interview published
in the " London Review," June, 1898, told that the
Chinese Emperor, in addition to other honours con-
ferred on him, " had ennobled his ancestors for three
generations." This ennoblement of the dead is in
every respect a religious act, and is an ensaintment,
nothing less; it is simply Chinese canonisation.
Ming, the founder of the Ming Dynasty, not so
very long ago, would no doubt have ennobled his
ancestors if he had had record of them, which he
had not, and therefore had no " tablets " of ancestors,
he having been a foundling and a herd-boy, and,
quite in the spirit of essential Chinese religion, he
inaugurated a new phase of the worship, and
appointed certain days on which unknown ancestors,
" ancestors who had no tablets," were to be
worshipped, and this was called *Siuh-ku,* " Pitying
the Unfortunate." Christian sainthood is nothing
but an elevated form of this same phase of ancestor-
worship.

But as regards the Arabs, worship of ancestors
among the early Arabs was absolutely universal, and
Mohammed struggled in vain to cast it out. True,
he, in a sense, got rid of the image of Abraham,
which up to that time had been the chief object
in their temple; but they only transferred their
reverence to the ancestral stone—the black stone—
against which he could do no more than give a law
prohibiting the circling of it *naked* (see sura ix.),
and this circling of stones naked was nothing but a
pronounced phase of ancestral worship : indeed, all
upright stone-worship was only an indirect ancestor-

worship. The stone dedicated to each Hebrew tribe, for example, was the emblem of an ancestor, and symbolising that part which was most sacred. And with a people whose female ancestor bore such a mythological name as Hagar (Flight), and whose male ancestors were Abraham and Ishmael, worship of ancestors is declared in the very names, and is not accidental in its traces in Mohammedanism even now.

And certainly it does not look confirmatory of Sir Henry's wholly unqualified dictum to read that "the Muslims of Egypt to this day provide food and even furniture for their dead, as did their forefathers, after 1,300 years of Islam."

Further yet, one great and dominating series of facts. In the whole idea of bloody sacrifice (for which the "unbloody" was everywhere and always but a substitute) there lies implicit a suggestion, and a very direct suggestion, of offerings to ancestors. What else can mean the Arabian meat-offering to Ocaisir? The reader can find reference to it in Robertson Smith's "Religion of the Semites," p. 223, if he does not care to go as far as Goldziher's "Culte des ancêtres chez les Arabes." No inquirer nowadays of the least scientific turn can doubt it. Even Robertson Smith is compelled to say: "The table of the shewbread has its closest parallel in the *lectisternia* of ancient heathenism, when a table laden with meats was set beside the idol."[1] The idol! Well, yes; it was not seldom an erect stone or shapeless block, supposed to contain at least a spirit that could appreciate the spirit of the bread offered,

---

[1] "Religion of the Semites," p. 225.

and appropriate it; so that it had organs of appropriation—refined organs, yet like ours, in so far that it enjoyed what we can enjoy—nothing short of an ancestral spirit.' Robertson Smith, without thought in that place of its bearing here, refers to a peculiar case, as he thinks, of a true sacrificial feast, that is made of the first-fruits of rice, which is called " eating the soul of the rice," so that, as he says, the rice is viewed as a living creature, and in such a case, he argues, "the rice may be regarded as really an animate victim." So it is universally, indeed, through the whole realm of substituted sacrifices, and this because none of the human ancestors, so far as we yet do know, were vegetarians! But ancestors at bottom they all were, and Hebrew sacrifices, more than anything else, prove it. And Sir H. Maine did not see far here.

Moreover, it is notorious that the heathen Arabs cut their hair and wounded themselves for the dead

---

¹ In the *lectisternia* the food was placed before images of the gods *reclining on couches*—the ordinary offerings of this sort were made almost daily both in Greece and Rome. What could possibly be the reason of making the gods recline on couches to partake of these offerings, precisely like human beings? This could hardly have been honouring to gods conceived as really distinct separate existences, loftily throned, with a fixed residence in heaven, or in the sky, or among the clouds, or on high mountains; yet the gods of both Greece and Rome were so conceived, and yet they were also conceived to come and eat or imbibe their share of the feast, reclining on couches, in these *lectisternia* of Greece and Rome. The Jahwé of the Hebrews was in like manner, as Robertson Smith suggests, presumed to come in exactly the same way to the shewbread as he came down to eat of the sacrificial meals with his priests and people. And, by the way, let me note here that I should be very glad to hear from Mr. Andrew Lang how he explains this very peculiar point on his main theory put forth in the very ingenious " Making of Religion."

precisely like the Hebrews, and more, they went a
step further—they laid the hair as an offering on the
tomb of the ancestor, and to this day one of the last
acts of the pilgrims to Mecca is to cut off the hair
and lay it in a certain place; and, wherever we find
hair offered, or wool as a substitute for hair, there is,
in our idea, some reference to this. The *rationale*
of these observances, at all events, as more or less
practised by all Semites, and by many tribes beside,
is the belief that by cutting their flesh they establish
a connection between themselves and the spirits of
the dead, just as the mutilators of themselves fancied
they thus established a relation between themselves
and Astarte; and if the Hebrews did not actually
mutilate themselves before the altars of Jahwé, they
never ceased to practise the accompanying rite—
touching themselves and then the altar, or *vice versâ*,
with the blood or the fat—the altar being presumed
to hold the spirit of the god, or (originally?) ancestor.
This is indeed the basis of all ancient savage and
half-savage oaths or vows, and its *rationale* and
process are seen as clearly in the Hebrews as anywhere; for there the spirit of the altar is taken to
witness by touching of blood, and the ancestral
stones to witness of covenant by being smeared with
blood or with oil, which, as Robertson Smith shows,
is simply fat—another part of the god's share of
the sacrifice.

The whole idea of incense everywhere, indeed, is
based on the ancestral principle; for all over the
East it was a part of hospitality to spread incense
for a guest, precisely as in worship originally for an
ancestor: what was enjoyed by the guest would, it

was believed, be enjoyed by the ancestral spirit.
Welhausen, again, has conclusively proved that the
Arabs at set times poured libations on graves with
ceremonies of worship,[1] and in a modified way they do
it now, and erect stones of a distinct phallic character
over graves, precisely the same as the early Hebrews
did (this being with them the original of libations to
the god) ; and these broadly corresponded with the
χοαι of the Greeks.

But here we can command proof more relative still.
Though Mohammed expressly forbade his followers
to mark their skins with scars, proving that it was
before his legislation a habit to do so, many Arab
tribes indulge in it. All the Mohammedan explanations of the practice, even at the Holy Mecca, are
utterly beside the mark and misleading. Burton thus
describes one form of it :

" In most families male children, when forty days
old, are taken to the Ka'abah, prayed over and carried
home, where the barber draws with a razor three
parallel gashes down the fleshy portion of each cheek,
from the anterior angles of the eyes almost to the
corners of the mouth. I am tempted to assign to it
a high antiquity, and cannot but attribute a pagan
origin to the custom still prevailing, in spite of all
the interdictions of the Olema."[2]

It is clear what Burton means, that these marks
are consecrations to the *manes*, corresponding with
what takes place both among adults and children of
many other tribes and races : Sawahils, Somalis,
Barabarabs, and some of the Abyssinians. Long

---

[1] " Skizzen und Vorarbeiten," iii. p. 161.
[2] " Pilgrimage," ii. p. 234.

before Mohammed this observance was practised, and is nothing but a reminiscence of worship of ancestors. The act is called " Tashrit," or gashing. Take the above, in connection with this :

" The Prophet, who doubtless had heard of those pagan mournings where an effeminate and unlimited display of woe was *often terminated by licentious excesses,* like the Christians' half-heathen ' wakes,' forbad aught beyond a decent demonstration of grief. And his strong good sense enabled him to see through the vanity of professional mourners." [1]

Mohammed's words were directed against adult mutilation and " mourning for the dead " in the sense of arranged observances often leading to " licentious excesses," let it be remarked, as practised in many places, but the " gashing " of children was not directly condemned, therefore it has been largely maintained.

And there is yet more—far more. In names and place-names existing now and used every day there is proof abundant that, in spite of laws and orders and Olemas, the Arabs to-day are ancestor-worshippers ; that, under all their reformed observance, the old habit remains and works. If Sir Henry Maine had only lived to read with care my old friend Professor E. H. Palmer's vocabulary of the Arabic names and words supplied to him by the active workers for the Palestine Exploration Fund, he would very soon have found good cause to change his mind and to delete that stupid and ignorant remark of his about any traces of ancestor-worship in Mohammedanism being merely accidental, or otherwise than engrained

[1] " Pilgrimage to Al-Madinah," p. 24.

in language—living language—to testify against him.
What does the word *Mâshûk* mean? Let any admirer
of Sir Henry's turn there to that, and tell me. But
do not let him answer till he has gone a little further
and read under شيخ داود (Sheik Dâûd) as follows :
"Sheikh, elder, is used for a *saint*" (mark that,
please) "or a saint's *tomb*" (mark that yet more,
please). "Dâûd is the Arabic form of the name
David (beloved). . . . The name David itself is
identical with Mâshûk in signification."

The saint and the saint's tomb both alike are
honoured there still : the very stones are with them
sheiks, elders, old ones, saints. Like the Jews of his
day, as Jeremiah had it, "saying to a stone, Thou
art my father." What more would you have here from
me ? The Arabs are like the Jews in this.

Were it worth while, we should go further and fare
yet better. But it isn't worth while. The ensaintment under Mohammedism is, of course, irregular,
very irregular, compared with Chinese ensaintment ;
but it is there—the testimony to ancestor-worship
essential and engrained, witnessed in grave and
monument even now, as well as in word and name
and place-name. And how, I ask of Sir Mount-
stuart Grant-Duff, and Lord Shand, in especial—
they being Scots, Church-going, Bible-reading Scots,
is this : How else could the word sheikh have, in
so many instances, come to mean really "saint" or
manes, as found not only in literature, but in names
and place-names, as in Jebel, Sheikh, and Dâûd ?[1]

---

[1] Yes; and the man who, along with Colonel Conder, then a
Lieutenant of Royal Engineers, collected these Arabic words and
names was Lord Kitchener, then, too, a Lieutenant of Royal

Hassan and Hussein, sons of Ali, as the great
Metawileh and Shiah saints, are in fact nothing but

Engineers—part of a great and memorable work which he did in
Palestine through a series of years. When I read in the newspapers
his tale of the more than a hundred "poems" sent to him within a
short period after his return from Khartoum, I could not help, as I
had just then been re-working over that valuable volume arranged
in order by Prof. Palmer, setting down these lines by way of modest
supplement to " the Hundred " :

> "Good Kitchener, how fain I'd sent to you
> Another to that ' Hundred,' yet your due ;
> For I am sure, none of that ' Hundred ' spoke
> Of your great work in Palestinian yoke :
> This very day I've, joyful, looked anew
> O'er book our Palmer set in order true,
> Of Arab words and names part found by you,
> And got from it more joy than I could gain
> By following you o'er sandy Soudan plain—
> Though there a victory indeed you won,
> Yet was it not in Palestine begun ?—
> Where hint you gained of moral ever true :
> By battle-force the utmost you can do
> Is incomplete, till Peace, great Peace, hath crowned
> The victory with useful tribute found,—
> To raise and gladden by the gift of good
> And knowledge, till, all savagery subdued,
> Your name is praised as teacher, saviour too—
> Far grander than the warrior's tribute due !
> By making sweeter dark-skinned people's lot—
> Remembered when your battles are forgot ;
> Then, truly joined with Gordon, you shall stand—
> A saviour, teacher of that sunbeat land,
> Light-bringer to the dark—the true man's goal,—
> For while that speaks for brain, this speaks for soul.
> Oh, happy 'tis, that when a man walks free
> To loftier purpose, then all ranks can see—
> Acknowledge him true hero, seek to aid,
> Till fruits of victory are nobler made.
> And earlier work for education's cause
> A root from which the latest substance draws ;
> The earlier, later in your life made one—
> In ' Happy Warrior's ' peaceful benison."

tribal ancestors, in a slightly new guise, possible only
to a people who had once very openly and consciously
professed and practised that religion. In view of all
this, is there nothing in the fact that several tribes
of Arabs used the following as their form of oath:
I swear by the blood streams around Andh, and *by
the stones set up beside Suair*"?

More, much more, we might add; but surely that
is enough to show that Sir Henry Maine was far, far
out when he said any contact with worship of ancestors
in Mohammedanism was purely accidental—as if,
indeed, there was or could be anything accidental in
such a case.

X.—*The Matriarchate.*

Sir Henry Maine very cleverly and studiously
avoids thoroughly tackling this vast question though
he cannot help glancing at it. But, as is the way
with him, he puts it aside with an air of authority,
not of philosophic doubt, but of philosophic certainty,
which only, however, too painfully betrays his doubt
or his lack of power to enter on and face it.
"*Originally*," he says, "it cannot be doubted, the
ancestor was a male." Oh, cannot be doubted?
Much, much is it doubted now. Not to speak of
the work of Germans like Preller and von Hartmann;
in our own country we have thinkers like Professor
Karl Pearson and Professor Rhys Davids who,
indeed, have much doubted it; and the more they
think, and the further they go, they can but doubt
it the more. With Professor E. B. Tylor, the
strange and puzzling phenomena of the Couvade
are only, and can only, be accounted for by its

H. O

marking the passage from the maternal to the paternal form of rule. Mr. Hewitt finds it clear and definite under the modified patriarchal rule of India. On the Pacific Coast of North America, among the tribes of Kwakiutl Indians, as we have seen already, we have the remarkable phenomenon in all its stages — Matriarchate, Patriarchate, and in process of passing from first to second—a very remarkable living disproof of what Sir Henry Maine has said; and there are a few others.

With regard to India, the whole effect of the remaining matriarchate institutions that prevailed among the Turanian and Dravidian tribes, was to percolate into and modify the customs and ideas of the Aryan intruders, who, in this respect, could not subdue, but only receive. We read:

" The village community in India was originally matriarchate, and it still bears traces of it in foundation Dravidian. It is to these people and their maternal ancestors, the Dravidian Sons of the Tree, that we must look for the origin of the Indian village." [1]

And again:

" Wherever we find these communistic villages, we find also the village religion based on tree worship, and the first villages must thus have been organised by a people to whom trees were the homes of the gods. The earliest villages were those founded by the Dravidian races who called themselves the Sons of the Tree, and are now represented by the Marya or tree (marom) Gonds and their Indian cognates, some of whom, like the Southern races of Australia,

---

[1] Hewitt, i. pp. 45, 57, and ii. p. 120.

still use the 'boomerang.' These people made the
village, and not the family, their national unit; and
made it a rule that the mothers and fathers of
children born in their village should never belong
to the same village (endogamy and exogamy thus
combined and systematically adhered to), and that
the children should be brought up by their mothers
and maternal uncles without the intervention of the
father, and should be regarded as the children of
the village and state in which they were born. Thus
each village was ruled by the mothers and maternal
uncles of the children born in it, and it was this
system of government which they took with them
to Europe, where they became the Amazonian races
of Asia Minor and Greece. It was these matriarchate
tribes who were the ancestors on the mother's side
of the Dolicho-cephalic Basques and the cognate
melanchroia or dark-skinned races who were the
agriculturists of the neolithic age.[1]

The sister's son is still the family priest among
many of these Turanian and Indian tribes.

Mr. Growse, in his valuable and interesting
Memoir of a District, tells how, at the festival held
at Bar-sāna in Mathura on the 22nd Feb. 1877, the
women of Bar-sāna, the wives of the Gosain priests
of the temple of Larli-ji, meaning "the beloved
one," were attacked by the men of Nand-gānw, who
were armed with round leather shields and stags'
horns, while the ladies defended themselves with
long heavy male bamboos. The combat was next
day repeated in a reversed form on the village of
Nand-gānw, when the Bar-sāna men attacked the

[1] Hewitt, i. p. 103.

wives of the Gosains of the Nand-gānw temple, but the battle here was fought round the yellow pennon of the men of the yellow races, and *was more like a phallic orgy than a fight.* A similar combat formed part of the ceremonies of the Holi festival of Bathen, in the north of the Mathura District, held in 1877, on the 2nd of March, some days after those of Bar-sāna and Nand-gānw.

Mr. Hewitt, commenting on this passage, says:

" We see in all these ceremonies a complete reproduction of the seasonal dances of matriarchal times, when the young women of one village met the men of another at the dancing place, under the shade of the mother grove of one of the villages, in the same way as is still customary among the Ho Kols; and we find the Ho custom of prolonging the festal period by celebrating the Magh festival in different places in the several villages of each tribe or confederacy reproduced in the dates fixed for the Holi festival in the Mathura villages."

Khand [Khond = Gond] society, Mr. Hewitt says, is constituted on a patriarchal basis, but this rests on matriarchal foundations existing before the Khand, whose name means the swordsmen, conquered Orissa. They altered the original matriarchate customs, which made the village the unit, to meet theirs which placed the family as the groundwork of the tribe. Hence they divided the Goches or villages into *Khambas* or joint-families.[1]

And this is Mr. Hewitt's grand result:

" These two forms of matriarchal and patriarchal marriage flourished side by side in India; the

[1] i. p. 154.

matriarchal system being generally retained in South Western India—the country of the Nairs who still maintain customs which are nearly identical with those of the original forest tribes, while the patriarchal system of the Mundas is that on which the Bengal marriage systems are founded.   But it was the matriarchal races who originally gave life to the social organism, and they were not only a cultivating but a maritime race who developed in India the early system of navigation which they had first learned in the Equatorial Islands." [1]

Thus it will be seen how far, very far, Sir Henry Maine was astray; how far he was from possessing the divining power that would have enabled him to detect beneath the varying surface of Indian institutions the relics of one old type which was almost uniform and has given a colour to all the different developments, because still lying, like a hidden backbone, beneath them all.   Mr. Hewitt was for many years commissioner in the Mathura district, and patiently studied institutions there, his knowledge thus derived falling happily into range in his wide scheme of "Ruling Prehistoric Races."   His research only serves still further to convict Sir Henry Maine of being too much the formal lawyer to be the philosophic discerning ethnologist and comparative student of peoples, their customs and religious ceremonies and celebrations.

When Sir Henry Maine so ominously fails to perceive the substratum thus seen to lie beneath the varying surface of Indian life and custom, we need not expect that he would have forecasted

[1] i. p. 57.

results of inquiry into the prevailing customs of, say, Australians, or told us what a passage like this points to :

" Among the Australian natives children of either sex always take the mother's family name, while a man may not marry a woman of his own family name. Ties of blood relationship are thus nothing to the bond of family."[1]

"Originally, it cannot be doubted, the ancestor was a male." That is enough: with all the phenomena, or survivals or traces of ceremony and observance lying open for Sir Henry Maine to see, as for Mr. Hewitt ; yet, like one who walked from Dan to Beersheba, and found it all barren, the gifted Sir Henry Maine could but write, " Originally, it *cannot* be doubted, the ancestor was a male ! "

*   *   *   *   *

Or it may be that some of the most worthy and very learned gentlemen who, at the meeting of the Indian section of the Society of Arts, in March, 1898, were so profuse in their praises, so unqualified in their eulogies of Sir Henry Maine—not only as a jurist, an administrator, legislator, codifier of Indian law, but as thinker, writer, anthropologist, will be able to justify him here—to prove that I am wrong, wrong all along the line—that I am an erring critic of a truly great man and great thinker, I shall be glad ; and if Sir Mount-Stuart E. Grant Duff, withdrawing himself from his close and elaborate studies of epitaphs of all times, and later reminiscences and light fantastic anecdotes, or Lord Shand

---

[1] Calvert's "Monograph on Natives of Western Australia," p. 45.

(my old friend of shrievalty of Kincardine days and even earlier, whom he in his many, many important calls may well have now forgotten), or Sir Frederick Pollock, or Sir Courtenay Ilbert, or Mr. Fred. Harrison, or Sir Alfred Lyall, or Mr. Lee-Warner, or Mr. Tupper himself, or Mr. Lawrence Gomme, or Sir Richard Stracher, or Sir Trueman Wood even— one or other of them will convince me of this I shall be indebted to them and ever grateful to them, deeply grateful, as fully restoring to me an earlier youthful admiration. I will sit corrected and humbly beg them to forgive me for having even glanced at what I had come to think streaks of clay half hidden in the feet of their idol, whose head was no doubt all gold and ever shone golden to the sunlight.

IV.—SOME OF SIR JOHN LUBBOCK'S BLUNDERS.

I HAVE read and studied the works of Sir John Lubbock, and have often wondered whether he blunders as much—rounds off his figures as boldly—in matters I do not understand as in matters that I think humbly I do understand. Among ants and bees I do suppose he is happy, as figures do not want to be quite so much rounded off there. But in anthropology, on which he is set down or set up as a great authority, I confess I find him rounding off his figures in quite a wonderful way. In this place I shall deal with but two points, and the first shall be his long series of stupid blunders about freedom of action on the part of savage or tribal men as regards women taken in war.

I. Sir John not only fancied the tribal men could do as each individually liked, but based a long series of arguments on the assumption. He was taken to task about it, and stuck bravely to his point, showing, if not courage, then certainly ingenuity. Let me recall the whole matter; it will be found amusing, as amusing as a game of hunt-the slipper, which again it considerably resembles.

Sir John, in dealing with MacLennan's theory of marriage by capture, as arising from exogamy, declares that he goes for **the very reverse.** " MacLennan," he says, " considers that marriage by capture followed and arose **from that** remarkable custom, namely, of marrying always out of the tribe, for which he has **proposed the** appropriate name of exogamy. **On the contrary,** I believe that exogamy arose from marriage **by** capture, not marriage by capture from **exogamy, that** *capture, and* **capture** *alone, could give a* **man the** *right to monopolise a* **woman** *to the exclusion* **of his fellow-** *clansmen ;* **and that** hence, even after all necessity for actual capture had long ceased, the symbol remained, capture having by long habit come to be received as a necessary preliminary **to** marriage." (The italics, of course, are mine.)

How knowing **and clever these** neat-looking sentences seem, **if you don't know any** better. **It is** indeed **pretty bold theorising; perhaps if Sir John** had been **more cautious he would have been wiser.** Want **of caution and** discretion **has not** always **been so** transparently his **fault in more** practical matters.

Further careful researches in the customs of many tribes—Red Indians, Australian, and other tribes— **make** it clear that MacLennan was so far **in** error about the laws of marriage by capture and of exogamy as related to them. This error led him **to a wrong** generalisation. **The** institution of the tribe, **indeed, is** primarily for the regulation of marriage as **a matter** between groups and **groups,** or more properly between clans and clans. **The clan** issues from the communal family,[1] and **certain marks of** the origin remain with

[1] See **Major** Powell's Intro. **to Bureau of Ethnology** Report, Washington, **1881-2,** R. xxxvi.

it. Limited marriage, or the right of temporary sexual association, is still communal among the Australian tribes, for example, but this is a more primitive observance still surviving among conditions of more complexity. Within the clan no relations of kinship are recognised save of fathers and mothers, elder brothers and younger brothers, elder sisters and younger sisters. In this fact lies the reasons for marriage outside the clan. The clan is held responsible to the tribe for the conduct of its members. All controversies within the clan are settled by the clan ; but controversies between members of different clans are settled by the tribe. And as marriage is absolutely, from considerations of kinship, a matter between clan and clan, it is and has always been, a subject for decision and control of the tribe. Major Powell thus makes his main points clear :

" Every savage man is exogamous with relation to the class or clan to which he may belong—he must not marry within it ; and he is to a certain extent endogamous in relation to the tribe to which he belongs, that is, he married within that tribe ; but in all cases, if his marriage is the result of legal appointment, he is greatly restricted in his marriage rights, and the selection must be made within some limited group. Exogamy and endogamy as thus defined are integral parts of the same law ; and the tribes of mankind cannot be classed in two great groups—the one practising endogamy and the other exogamy.[1]

Wife-capture is not from an alien tribe, but from a group within the tribe. When women are taken in war from alien tribes they must be adopted into some

[1] Bureau of Ethnology, 1881-2, p. lxiii.

clan within the capturing tribe in order that they may become wives of the men of the tribe. When this is done the captured women become by legal appointments the wives of men in the group having marital rights in the clan which has adopted them.

There is no point on which Messrs. Fison and Howitt, who have more closely on the spot studied the customs of Australian natives than has been done anywhere by any one else, are more decided than on this. They write :

" The individual has no rights as distinct from the group to which he belongs ; and, moreover, it is directly contradicted by evidence which can be tested at the present day. . . . They maintain the tribal right against the individual with regard even to war-captives as strictly as they maintain it with respect to any other women."

Messrs. Spencer and Gillen, speaking for the Central Australian natives, decisively say :

" Anything that looks like marriage by capture is rare, and it is clear that the customs do not seem to indicate that they owe their origin to anything like the recognition of the right of the captor as captor." " Natives of Central Australia," p. 105.

This point has been specially and fully discussed by Mr. C. Staniland Wake at p. 248 " Marriage and Kinship," and certainly Sir John Lubbock gained nothing by his ingenious endeavours to put himself right. Mr. Howitt's deliverance in addition to that of Messrs. Spencer and Gillen, that in Australia at least individual marriage did not arise by the monopoly of female captives " is, with these other evidences, surely enough.

The necessary process of adoption of women war-captives into some clan within the capturing tribe shows this far-wandering on the part of Sir John Lubbock, who, great anthropologist as he is, never dreamt of it, though it lies close before him in his Bible, as we shall immediately show. In assuming individual freedom with regard to the monopolising of such women, he talked utter and unmitigated nonsense. Their admittance by adoption into a clan would very largely limit the numbers that could possibly lay claim, and that claim would be regulated by a wholly different code from claims of individual prowess, etc. The whole business of the seizing of the maidens of Shiloh for the remnant of Benjamin (which Sir John Lubbock must surely have read of in his family Bible !) was thus on all fours with the primary savage practice, and also (what is more) so was the making of the thing right with Shiloh by the heads of the tribes afterwards.

Sir Alfred Lyall (at p. 163 "Asiatic Studies)" has made clear the rationale of this practice by reference to the custom of the Meenas of the Punjaub, by which a woman from a separate tribe is "solemnly put through a form of adoption into one circle of affinity, in order that she may be lawfully married into another " ; and he believes that " this fiction looks very like a survival of a custom that may once have been universal among all clans at a more elastic stage of their growth, for it enables the circles of affinity within a tribe to increase and multiply their number without a break, while at the same time it satisfies the conditions of lawful marriage."

Now, it was not to be expected that Sir John

Lubbock should know detailed facts which have since then been brought to our notice, but the vice of his method remains the same. He takes up MacLennan's error, and proceeds, in the most cocksure, dogmatic and unjustifiable way to argue on it. And even so, Sir John's poor argument was already in so far met by MacLennan's clear statement that in any movement for wife-capture, the tribe, and not the individual was, strictly speaking, engaged, and that the whole rights of the individual would be limited by the necessities of the tribe—individual action, in the sense Sir John means, was utterly non-existent, and there were amply sufficient facts in existence then to prove it, as MacLennan said. There were hundreds of cases to dwell on : " Some classes of Andrians and nobles in Madagascar must not marry out of their own tribe." Among the Garos of India a man cannot take to wife a girl of his own *maháro* (clan), but must select from one of the maháres with whom his family have from time immemorial allied themselves. This survival of tribal law is clearer among the Burmans than perhaps anywhere else, and more stringently applied ; for among them a man may not marry a woman of the same surname as himself. Sir R. Burton has given many cases among wild tribes of Arabs.

But Sir John, in his Bible, might have found this matter well illustrated, and in such a way as to give him pause about capture in war enabling, and alone enabling, a man to monopolise a woman, to use his own exquisite and enchanting phrase.

" When thou goest forth to war against thine

enemies, and Jahvé hath delivered them into thine hands, and thou hast taken them captive,

"And seest among the captives a beautiful woman, and hast a desire unto her, that thou shouldst have her unto thy wife ;

" Then thou shalt bring her home to thine house, and she shall shave her head, and also pare (or dress) her nails.

"And she shall put the raiment of her captivity from off her, and shall remain in thine house and bewail her father and mother *a full month* ; and *after that* thou shalt go in unto her and be her husband, and she shall be thy wife." (Deut. xxi. 10—13.)

Clearly, therefore, in the Mosaic law, certain very strict rules and ceremonials had to be complied with before a war-captive could be taken as wife,—that is, the captor was not free to " monopolise a woman "— to use these exquisite and enchanting words, or in other words, to do as he chose ; and I should say this law was a survival of the purely tribal law expounded by Messrs. Fison and Howitt and Messrs. Spencer and Gillen for Australia, and by Major Powell for America, etc., and commented on so well by Mr. Staniland Wake and others. A captive woman, according to Deuteronomy, could not be appropriated to one man without strict preparatory observances and rites of alliance—rites which implied special sacrifice and offering, and by conformity to these the tribe or nation was at every step recognised or satisfied as against the individual will or desire. Both Sir John Lubbock and the enterprising Westermarck have fallen into no end of error through their assumptions of individual freedom in certain directions which did not exist, and never could have existed under tribal rule. Another man, who should have known better, has blundered beyond expression on this very matter. Mr. Goldwin Smith, in his chapter on Judaism in his " Guesses at the Riddle," sets these facts forward, among others, as instances of fine consideration and humanity—which really were not much in their way —when even the " women that had lain by man " were so thoroughly out of it. But just glance at two things : (1) the Hebrews were polygamists, and they remained to the end distinctly tribal ; (2) this was a case of marrying admitting into the tribe really in the first place. Now, we have found innumerable instances, in purely savage history, of what appears at once far more consideration than this toward the women taken in war, and more definite and extended regulations. Thus, the Gallas of South Africa do not sell their daughters, but if a young man wishes to marry he offers to one of his companions "to exchange sisters." If he should have no sister then he takes the first opportunity to join a war-party, with the idea of capturing a female prisoner whom he may adopt as a sister, and thus be enabled "to exchange sisters." This captive is treated with the utmost kindness and consideration—the full ceremonies of admission into the tribe requiring some weeks ; and all must be done according to the rules laid down, and to the satisfaction of headman and priest.[1] The war-captive with the Jews, too,

[1] A most peculiar ethnographical point arises about these very Gallas, putting mere geographical associations completely aside, if they are accepted. Dr. Munro, in his " Prehistoric Problems," not only includes properly in the order, Homo Caucasicus, fair and dark Europeans, Semites, Persians and Hindus, but also Copts, Berbers,

fared better than some women at home, or else this passage is sadly out of joint.

"They" [the Hebrews] "were, indeed, forbidden to commit adultery and fornication; but these were thought to concern only women of their own nation, their law not extending to foreigners; and we find accordingly that public stews were openly tolerated among them; and women residing there taken under the protection of the government, as appears from the two harlots that contended about a child and were heard in open court by Solomon."[1] In some points presenting close analogy with our own case; ruling classes getting three times the economic rents for brothels that they get for other houses.

So that what would appear at first view a piece of fine consideration is merely a survival of the most stringent tribal law: and just as the not seething a kid in its mother's milk was due to ancient lustration of the land with this milk—most probably a substitute

and even such still darker African tribes as the Somalis *and the Gallas*. Even in Central Africa, we elsewhere read, there are tribes, the Gallas especially, whose customs and traditions clearly point to Egypt, Syria, and other regions. Desmoulins gives an account ("Histoire Naturelle des Races humaines," p. 168) of a fair-haired race established in one of the hottest regions of India. By avoiding inter-marriage with the dark tribes round it, he says, it has preserved its original peculiarities during the long space of six hundred years. This is the Afghan tribe of the Rohillas, settled on the south of the Ganges since the accession of the Patan dynasty to the throne of Delhi in the 13th century. Dr. Shaw, in his travels, p. 120, describes inhabitants of mountainous regions of Auress, in Algiers, as being fair and ruddy, and their hair of a deep yellow. All this is of the utmost importance with regard to study of custom and tradition; and the necessity for a classification differing from that dictated, however indirectly, by old-fashioned notions of geographical belts or circles.

[1] Potter ii. p. 234.

for animal and then for human blood—so here we have simply a modified ancient tribal observance, practised by them in common with hundreds of other races.

We have a further illustration of the law referred to in Madagascar. If a free man wish to marry a slave-woman he must previously redeem her, and so make her his equal in social position—the same applying to the war-captive = slave—that is, he had to do the equivalent of admitting to the tribe.

So we see how far astray all these writers, with Sir John Lubbock at their head, have wandered, and found—mares'-nests.

II. Sir John Lubbock, in his "Origin of Civiliza-tion" (p. 158), gives an engraving from Lafitau's "Mœurs des Sauvages," representing a savage dance. He remarks very baldly—so baldly that it is a most notable instance of not rounding the figures—that the plate "represents a sacred dance as practised by the natives of Virginia. It is very interesting to see here a circle of upright stones, which, except that they are rudely carved at the upper end into the form of a head, exactly resemble our so-called Druidical temples." Will it be believed that this great anthropological authority does not in the least understand the plate he introduces to us? He omits, at all events, to note *the* important points about it : (1) that some of the figures carry branches in their hands, and that others have the topped rod or sceptre—undoubtedly a phallic emblem—one has a series of separate leafy branches for a kind of headdress, or rather upper body dress, from the

H.   P

waist to above the head, and that otherwise they are really naked;[1] while (2) yet a third set of figures carry in their hand either a wooden or stone disc with a handle, and on this disc is clearly engraved a crescent, so placed as to symbolise or actually to present a pair of horns. If they had but added a full moon or disc within the crescent or pair of horns, we should have had in Virginia an exact reproduction of the Phœnician or Carthaginian figure on sacred stones—the full moon within the horns of an ox; and (3) most important and significant of all, three figures, with arms entwined over each other's shoulders, dance in the centre within an oval figure—clearly the *Yoni*—it is most certainly boat or ark-shaped. Here, then, you have three figures—the central one of which, largest and nearest to the observer, by embracing, so to speak, of arms unites the other two.

Even in "The Dictionary of the Bible" we read, under "Idolatry," this of the religion of the old Semitic races as a deification of the powers of nature :

"These powers were considered either as distinct or independent, or as manifestations of one supreme and all-ruling being. In most instances the two ideas were co-existent. The Deity, following human analogy, was conceived as male and female—the one representing the active, the other the passive principle of nature. . . . The transference of the attributes of the one to the other resulted in their

---

[1] The Israelites were naked when they danced round the golden calf—in the Potraj Festival of Southern India, women walked naked to the temple, clad in boughs of trees—sacred trees—alone.

mystical union or conjunction in the hermaphrodite, as the Persian Mithra or Phœnician Ba'al, or the two combined to form a third, which symbolised the essential unity of both."

This is precisely what we have in this Virginian trio within the *yoni*, the third figure and larger uniting the other two by arms round their necks. This, from one point of view, is the Eternal Trinity, which, combined and re-combined, fluctuates between a *tertium quid* as here, or the son, who as he is begotten begins to supersede one or other or even both of the parents, precisely as in the idea of the flame begotten of the two fire-sticks consuming them. The Son in the Christian creed in certain systems holds his ground, but under Catholicism it is for good reasons impinged on by the Virgin.

Room, abundant room, there surely was to say something here of the marvellous migration of symbols, or to present some feasible explanation of such observance—an exact reproduction, not so much of Druidical temples, *pace* the great anthropologist, Sir John Lubbock, as of Phœnician, Syrian, and even Jewish dances ; only in place of the mere mark of the *yoni*, as here, there was in these cases an ark or some more or less boat-shaped repository of the sacred emblems which, we know, was precisely a *yoni* symbol. What a field of comparison and speculation was opened here! Those savage figures, save for adornments of leaves and sprigs or sprays or small branches of sacred trees, are naked; but so were the Israelites, as said already, when Moses, coming down from the Mount, found them dancing like these natives of Virginia round the golden calf, and David made himself naked even when dancing round the ark on its return, perhaps with palm or willow and citron in his hands (topped rods or sceptres, Phallic emblems, too), much to Michal's disgust, but much also to her after undoing in one particular line.

V. MR. GOLDWIN SMITH AND HUMANITY IN JEWRY.

MR. GOLDWIN SMITH, in the same passage, as I have dealt with in former chapter, refers also to the law laid down not to fell trees or stop up wells, etc., in a conquered city, and founds on it a testimony to fine humanity in Jewry. But what does the valiant Professor say to Elisha's prophecy directing, most plainly directing, Jehoshaphat against the Moabites " to fell every good tree, and stop every well, and destroy all good land with stones " ? If living prophecy was better than a dead law, how stands it with regard to Hebrew humanity here ? Or is it all true that the higher criticism has laid down, *pace* Professor Sayce, that the Mosaic law was not in existence till much after the time that Elisha—nice man !—prophesied, or is said to have prophesied, with the help of music, too—music, whether sweet or not ! This is a point on which I should much like a little talk with Professor Sayce, remembering well a long conversation I had with Professor Robertson Smith some time before his death on this very subject.

But, bating that, perhaps the most learned and thoughtful Professor Sayce will kindly answer me this one question : " If the Mosaic laws were written, or any part of them written, in the time of Moses, and accepted by a people largely literary even then, what about this Elisha—nice man !—prophesying like this when these laws could not but have been in that case well known to him—unless (1) there is some mistake or doubt about that, and the invention of these laws at a late period was the biggest attempt ever made to whitewash a cruel, murderous, and hateful set of tribes ; or (2) unless Elisha was an ignoramus beyond all other Jews of that time, or all the times from the day of Moses down to our own. I wait patiently for Professor Sayce's answer. Truly, Mr. Joseph Jacobs and Mr. Israel Abrahams are right—right as any trivet was ever right—Jewish music was very advanced, and by the most unexpected cause had reached its advancement, even though Jewish genius does not, and never did secure its best results in its own special environment.

But what does Mr. Goldwin Smith say to the *consideration* of this law in the light of Elisha's prophecy in illustration of it ?

VI. MR. GRANT ALLEN AND JAHVÉ.

ONE of the most remarkable and ominous things to me in recent literature is the fact of men writing ambitious and professedly expert scientific and exhaustive books on topics that are most intimately connected with Hebrew development, and evolution of ideas of God, and ideas very closely connected, without, as appears, the slightest knowledge of Hebrew or Arabic, not to speak of Chaldean or cuneiform or Sanskrit. They may generalise and write popularly; but they are not fully equipt, or even half-equipt for the business they have taken in hand. The two gentlemen I here particularly think of are Mr. Andrew Lang and Mr. Grant Allen. Both write too much with an air of omniscience, but from lack of Hebrew, Arabic, etc., have gone astray, and very sadly astray in more respects than one—Mr. Lang indeed talking utter nonsense about it being "highly probable" that the Hebrew "passings through the fire" were mere harmless rites, though it is very significant that Mr. Lang fell down from the "highly probable" to the lower and more cautious "possible," the very first chance that he had to modify and correct in his "Modern Mythology," as may be seen at p. 58. It was funny to find Mr. Lang, in the "Contemporary Review," dealing with such delightful off-hand and knowing *naïveté* with Mr. Grant Allen, when he was as regards an essential condition in nescience so absolutely in the same boat with him! We have already dealt with Mr. Lang as he deserves, meanwhile let us direct attention to one particular manifestation of the risk such men run, when they will set themselves tasks like these without even a smattering of Hebrew or other oriental tongue—without ordinary mastery of one of the most essential instruments.

Mr. Grant Allen, at pp. 192–4 of his " Evolution of the Idea of God," has much to say of Jahvé. He gives long passages in which he uniformly renders the word " God " in the English Authorised Version and the Revised also, as though no other term than Jahvé is ever used in those parts of Genesis dealing with the patriarchs and other portions of the Pentateuch. But in doing this he " finds himself out " in the most decisive manner. If his enemy had prayed that Mr. Grant Allen should write a book—a big book—with the design of finding matter against him, that enemy's prayer has certainly been answered.

One of our great complaints against the translators of Authorised and Revised Versions is that the words El, Eloah, Elohim, Adonai, El Shaddai, and Jahvé, and, in many cases, Ba'al even, are all translated God, Lord, the Lord God, God Almighty, whereas we should, for many reasons, like them given exactly as they are in the Hebrew. The translators have been so in love with this style, and have so indulged it that they have given ground for the most transparent misconceptions and misleading notions. They even translate the בְּנֵי־אֱלֹהִים

of Job as sons of God. Satan, in one sense, *was* a son of God, but he is not so declared in Job. Elohim there clearly stood for mere nature—that which hinders and opposes spirit, or may do so. If Dr. Driver had but worked out his distinction between Elohim as creative and nature maintaining force or forces, and Jahvé as spiritual, moral, soul-enduing force with reference more especially to this and to the Psalms, etc., we should have thanked him. The בְּנֵי־אֱלֹהִים are clearly sons of the opposers or adverse ones, mere hinderers as subtle forces of nature, and the only translator we are aware of who has been bold enough to get consistency in the way we suggest is the almost forgotten young lady, Miss Elizabeth Smith, who, in the closing years of last century, produced a masterly version of the Book of Job, while she was quite a girl.[1]

But now look at Mr. Grant Allen, and how he stumbles over Jahvé. He writes thus at pp. 192-4 :

"Jahvé appeared to Abraham in Haran and promised to make of him 'a great nation.' Later on, Abraham complains of the want of an heir, saying to Jahvé, 'thou hast given me no seed.' Then Jahvé brought him forth abroad, and said, 'look now toward heaven and tell the stars ; so shall thy seed be.' Over and over again we get similar promises of fruitfulness made to Abraham. 'I will multiply thee exceedingly ;' 'thou shalt be a *father* of many nations ; ' 'I will make thee exceedingly fruitful ;' 'kings shall come out of thee ;' 'for a father of many nations have I made thee.' So too

---

[1] We are glad to see that the Dictionary of National Biography has given her due place.

of Sarah, 'she shall be a mother of nations; kings of people shall be of her.' And of Ishmael, 'I have blessed him, and will make him fruitful, and will multiply him exceedingly; twelve princes shall he beget, and I will make him a great nation.' Time after time these blessings recur for Abraham, Isaac, and all his family: 'I will multiply thy seed as the stars of the heaven, and as the sand upon the sea-shore, and thy seed shall possess the gate of his enemies.' From the beginning to the end of Hebrew legend we find a similar characteristic of the ethnical God amply vindicated. When Sarah is old and well stricken in years, Jahvé visits her and she conceives Isaac. Then Isaac in turn 'entreated Jahvé for his wife, because she was barren, and Jahvé was entreated of him, and Rebekah his wife conceived.' Again, 'when Jahvé saw that Leah was hated, he opened her womb; but Rachel was barren.' Once more, of the birth of Samson we are told that Manoah's wife 'was barren and bare not;' but 'the angel of Jahvé appeared unto the woman and said unto her, Behold, now thou art barren and bearest not; but thou shalt conceive and bear a son.' And of Hannah we are told, even more significantly, that Jahvé had 'shut up her womb.' Jahvé remembered Hannah, and she bare Samuel, and after that 'Jahvé visited Hannah.'" Strangely enough, though it is said to have been the angel of Jahvé that visited Hannah, she herself says it was a "man of Elohim."

So on and on Mr. Grant Allen goes.

It will, perhaps, be a surprise to Mr. Grant Allen to learn that he has no justification whatever for thus using the name Jahvé in all these cases, without any

note or explanation.   It looks as though he had pro-
ceeded in dense and total ignorance of that which we
submit he ought to have known before proceeding to
write as he has done of the Hebrew Jahvé and some
other things Hebrew.   He does not seem to know
how near in some cases Jahvistic and Elohistic
writings lie to each other in that mosaic which we
call the Books of Moses or the Mosaic Books.   Just
look at this, as the shortest way of showing broadly
and effectively what we mean :

It is not Jahvé but Elohim that talks with Abraham
after Abraham has fallen on his face at xvii. 3, and it
is Elohim that changes his name and vows to be an
Elohim to him for ever, and to be the Elohim of his
seed for ever.   At verse 9 it is written : " And Elohim
said unto Abraham, Thou shalt keep my covenant," etc.
It is Elohim, not Jahvé, oddly enough, that com-
mands circumcision, which it has become a common-
place to say is the seal of entrance into the covenant
of Jahvé.   It is Elohim that speaks all through the
last part of chapter xvii., so that it is not Jahvé, as
Mr. Grant Allen puts it, but Elohim that says Sarah
shall be a mother of nations, and of Ishmael that
" twelve princes shall he beget, and I will make him a
great nation."   If Jahvé visits Sarah, so certainly does
Elohim, as proved by more than one text.   It is Elohim
that destroys the cities of the plain, and it is Elohim
that then remembers Abraham.   It is not Jahvé but
Elohim that comes to Abimelech in a dream by night
(xx. 3), and Abimelech, the Philistine, mark, calls this
deity Lord.   When Abraham speaks of the fear of God
as not in this place (xx. 11) it is the fear of Elohim.
In the next verse but one it is Elohim that caused

Abraham to wander "from my father's house," and at verse 17 it is Elohim to whom Abraham prays; yet strangely, very strangely, and very awkwardly for Mr. Grant Allen, it is Jahvé that *closes up the wombs of the house of Abimelech because of Sarah*, Abraham's wife. It is Elohim and not Jahvé that causes Sarah to laugh, at xxi. 6. It is Elohim and not Jahvé that tells Abraham (verse 12) to do unto Hagar as Sarah desires. It is Elohim that hears the voice of Ishmael, and it is the angel of Elohim that calls to Hagar out of heaven (verse 17). Abimelech tells Abraham that " Elohim is with thee in all that thou doest "(verse 22), and it is by Elohim that they (the Philistines, mark you) make Abraham swear. It is Elohim, not Jahvé, that tempts Abraham (xxii. 1) and directs him to offer up Isaac. Both to Isaac and Jacob the being who reveals himself says that he is the Elohim of Abraham. Though it was Jahvé that was in this place (xxviii. 16, 17), yet it is the House of Elohim בֵּית אֱלֹהִים. At verse 20, it is, "If Jahvé Elohim will be with me, then shall Jahvé be my Elohim," and the stone which he erected should be house of Elohim בֵּית אֱלֹהִים.

The words for " God the God of Israel" are El-Elohe Israel at xxxiii. 20. Jacob has used the very word Elohim for gods (teraphim, images) at xxxi. 32.[1] It was the face of El, not Jahvé, which Jacob saw at Peniel.

It is Elohim and not Jahvé that hearkens unto Leah at xxx. 17, so that she bears unto Jacob the

---

[1] If Elohim is frequently used for **Teraphim**—confessedly on all **hands**, images of ancestors—may we not **have here** the legitimate connecting link, linguistically speaking, **for the** naming often of **elders** (old men) judges, ancestors—Elohim, as we find, for instance, **in the answers** of the " Witch of Endor "?

fifth son ; and it is Elohim whom Leah thanks in next verse for giving her her hire, and, after the birth of the next, for giving her a good dowry.

It is Elohim, not Jahvé, that tells Jacob to go up to Bethel in 1st verse of chapter xxxv. It is to Elohim that Jacob builds the altar at Luz, xxxv. 7. It was Elohim that appeared unto Jacob again xxxv. 9. It is Elohim that says at verse 11, I am El Shaddai. It is not to Jahvé but to Elohim that Samson is to be dedicated a Nazarite, and most puzzling of all Jahvé sends "a man of Elohim" to Hannah.

In Deuteronomy throughout the phrase translated "the Lord God" is Jahvé Elohim—a peculiar hybrid indeed. Jahvé and Elohim are used almost alternatively in the account of Balaam, whereas Chemosh was his god. Elohim it is whom he meets and who speaks to him, and the spirit which comes on him at Numbers xxiv. 2 is not that of Jahvé, but רוּחַ אֱלֹהִים. It is Elohim who speaks at first to Balaam and continues up to the point in Authorised Version, when it is said "the Lord refuseth to give me leave to go with you," when it is יְהוָה, and this is translated "Lord" at verse 13. It is Jahvé Elohi beyond whose word Balaam cannot go, which is translated the Lord my God. It is Elohim that comes unto Balaam at verse 20. The Hebrew at Numbers xxiii. 8 and xxiv. 6 is יְהוָה, but there it is used for god *in the merely general sense*, the sense in which we are sometimes told Elohim should be understood, though from the instances now given we have found it used in as special and definite ways as Jahvé itself.

What does Mr. Grant Allen say to all this in connection with his assertion elsewhere that in the eighth

century, B.C., there was a great change in the view
of Jahvé? "To Amos and to the true [? first] Isaiah
Jahvé dwells in the sky above, and is Jahvé of hosts—
leader among the shining armies of heaven, the King
of the star world." Was the "Jahvé, God of heaven "
of Gen. xxiv. 3, a different being from "Jahvé of
hosts"? or were they the same? An answer will oblige.

Besides, has Mr. Grant Allen really faced the fact
that, according to the deliverance of Elohim to Moses
(Exod. vi. 3) : "And I appeared unto Abraham, unto
Isaac, and unto Jacob, by [the name of] El Shaddai,
but by my name Jahvé was I not known to them,"
—a deliverance which, if true and genuine, is contradicted by all of Genesis where Elohim and Adonai
and Jahvé are used? And if that deliverance is held
to be true and genuine, Mr. Grant Allen is doubly
wrong in giving it, despite such an authority, that
Jahvé at all spoke to Abraham, Isaac, and Jacob.
Or does he hold that here "there is nothing in a
name"? There is, at all events, such a thing as
scientific and critical exactitude. We venture to
press the question : Was Jahvé a mere name which
stood exactly for the same bundle of traits or attributes
as El Shaddai had for long ages covered, or was he
in such respects different so as to justify our positing
in him a step or steps in the evolution of the idea of
God, or was he not? We should much like to have
Mr. Grant Allen's definitive and clear answer to this ;
and then, either way, we shall have a few more
questions to ask him. If Jahvé merely carried forward
under another name the attributes and personality of
El Shaddai and Elohim, how can it be said that
"nothing is known of El Shaddai, who is vague and

shadowy, like all the local Hebrew gods before Jahvé;"
and does Mr. Grant Allen here find development or
evolution, or does he not? We cannot infer anything
else from some of his words than that he holds they
really remained the same; while he is all for evolution, and yet holds by fixed qualities and even
quantities (!) under different names. His whole
method justifies us in attributing to him the opinion
that names don't matter. Goethe declared in Faust
that they were but cloud and smoke shrouding the
glow of heaven; but here we are not poetical and
dramatic, but critical and philosophic — quite a
different temper, demanding for its true interpretation a very different method. If Jahvé was merely
a new name for an old god—for former Hebrew god
or gods who were so very vague and shadowy, while
Jahvé is something else, how does Mr. Grant Allen
account for and justify the great change? The
question of where he came from is not then of the
importance it would otherwise be—whether from
Midian and Jethro, or from Syria or Phœnicia!

Mr. Grant Allen boldly writes:

" No local Hebrew god, save Jahvé [so Jahvé was
only a local Hebrew god too, though not vague and
shadowy!] has left a name that can now be discerned
with any approach to certainty " (p. 189).

Now, pray, what does Mr. Grant Allen here mean
by a name and a local Hebrew God? What are
El, Elim, Eloah, Elohi, Elohim, Ba'al and Shaddai,
not to speak of קְהֹשְׁתָּן to which incense was offered
up at least till the time of Hezekiah, and the
people worshipped it? The same thing done to an
image anywhere else, even in a grave-yard or over

a tomb, we think Mr. Grant Allen will admit would entitle it to be called a local god. Were they then, we ask him, all or either of them local Hebrew gods (we shall not throw in the teraphim, though they were frequently called *Elohim*, nor the images in "the chambers of imagery" which the heads of the houses of Israel "bowed down to and a cloud of incense went up")? Jacob became Israel, who was the El to whom he became prince—what really lies in the assertion embodied in אֵלִיָּהוּ? Were El and Jah, two distinct beings before, as implied and asserted in that name, or were they one before as well as after, or two after as well as before? Was Jahvé absolutely the same as Shaddai; and, if so, how did it come that precisely as in the case of some other early gods, Shaddai became שֵׁדִים? These are not unnatural or unnecessary questions either, as bearing on the evolution of the Idea of God. If, as Mr. Grant Allen dogmatically asserts, "The only people who evolved a fine monotheism were the Jews"—excluding wholly even the Arabs—then it is desirable that something more than Mr. Grant Allen has yet said should be said as to why, down even to the latest lyrical Hebrew efforts, Elohim was as freely used as Jahvé. At 1 Kings xix. 8, Horeb is called הַר הָאֱלֹהִי, and Elohim is used in an exactly analogous way in Psalm lxxxii. Why, after so pronounced a development in Jahvé, according to Mr. Grant Allen, did the Hebrews use almost indiscriminately older terms for god as alternatives for Jahvé? With Mr. Grant Allen Jahvé becomes Elohim quite to suit his ease and convenience, but that doesn't quite suit us.

Nor let it for a moment be supposed that this is
merely a trifling formal affair—on which no principle
or point of importance depends. On it indeed hangs
a point of tremendous importance in the scientific
study of the Evolution of the Idea of God. The
moment we clearly recognise an Elohistic and
Jahvistic record, and distinguish between them, we
are met by this question, why does the Elohim so
persistently alternate with the Jahvé in that fashion
—why does the suggestion of the polytheistic origin
and confirmed polytheistic tendency of the Jewish
people constantly crop up even in the very latest
writings of the Hebrew singers and prophets? We
shall soon find that the Elohistic leads us away in a
wholly different direction from that in which Jahvé
leads us—insisting on a wholly different origin.

Von Bohlen indeed maintained that the whole
import of this Elohistic writing proved that it really
was of foreign origin, not Hebrew; that it was con-
structed from the traditions of foreign people, and
that it thus retained the foreign polytheistic forms
and especially the Chaldee ideas, and had nothing
at all to do with the Hebrew people in its origin.
Bleek, Ewald and others would fain have got rid of
this idea ; and the former wrote rather cavalierly of
Von Bohlen ; but, though Bleek and Ewald were
great scholars, neither of them had what Von Bohlen,
like Renan, had—quick and fine intuitions ; and there
is no doubt now that Von Bohlen was right—right
as any trivet ever was—since day by day discovery
is now revealing to us how much in the Accadian and
Chaldean goes to support the position he took in
tracing the Elohistic idea or tradition or element to

Accad or Chaldea. So much indeed is this the case that scholars who may not in the least have Von Bohlen's position in mind, nowadays, with more exact knowledge—result of exploration and research, of one accord take the exact stand that he did. Here are some words from a living American critic :

"Traditions of nomadic days were treasured in the memory and transmitted from generation to generation until they were finally woven with later material and coloured with later conceptions, to form the wonderful texture of a record which has become sanctified in the eyes of the best part of the human race. It may have been during this long period of its wandering infancy that the Hebrew people stored in their tenacious memory the Chaldean legends of the origin of the world, the creation of man, the garden of the Tigris and Euphrates, which was the cradle of mankind, the destruction of all living things by a flood of waters, and of the surviving family that repeopled the earth. Their reckoning of time and even the consecration of one day in seven to rest, which long after became a matter of such scrupulous observance, they derived from the ancient empire which they regarded with so much awe and so much aversion, and out of the tale of Ur-Chasdim they created their own ancestor."[1]

Is it then, seeing that results like this hang on the distinction between Elohistic and Jahvistic, too much to demand that a man writing on the " Evolution of the Idea of God," should not go upon the easy, but ignorant, unsatisfactory and perilous method of simply translating the words God and Lord where

[1] Fiske, "The Hebrew Scriptures," pp. 12, 13.

they occur in our Authorised Version into Jahvé? Mr. Grant Allen, we cannot but conclude from his own pages, has done this ; and in so far, his book—his big book—is a sad fiasco—behind the day—unscientific, loose and valueless, so far, at all events, as it aims at dealing with things Hebrew, if not, more broadly, things Semitic.

Gesenius would even go for the origin of the very name Hebrews back to times when they were still in Chaldea. "As an appellative it," עִבְרִי, "might mean, *those beyond*, *people of the country on the other side* (with reference to the land beyond the Euphrates), from עֵבֶר *land on the other side*, and the derivative syllable י—. It might then be appropriated to the colony, which under Abraham migrated from the regions east of the Euphrates into the land of Canaan (Gen. xiv. 13) ; though the Hebrew genealogy explains it, as a patronymic, by *sons* (posterity) *of Eber* (Gen. x. 21, and Num. xxiv. 24)." [1]

If this is so, Gesenius might well have applied the same reasoning to Elohim ; and what we recommend to Mr. Grant Allen is to give four years as far as possible exclusively to Hebrew, and then apply Gesenius's arguments here indicated to the Elohim and the Elohistic elements. That will keep him in good fettle—as a prime gymnastic training for his next big book—as big as " The Evolution of the Idea of God," if not even bigger.

Professor F. Hommel, one of the most thoughtful and cautious of critics, standing so to say between the new Wellhausen and old Dillmann and Robertson, while he cannot deny the clear existence of Elohistic

[1] Gram. p. 9.

and Jahvistic elements, is reduced to the necessity
of declaring the two elements to be so inextricably
fused together as to make it impossible thoroughly to
separate them, the text having undergone revision
and modification by so many, many hands.[1] But it
will at once be admitted that such a set of facts,
however much they may suggest caution in dealing
with minor questions and difficulty in settling them,
cannot do away with the necessity, when the facts
are once recognised, of an effort to compass some
broad and general separation, and this the more
that the very work on which Professor Hommel is,
in "Ancient Hebrew Tradition," more especially
engaged, is that which should from Von Bohlen's
point of view present itself to him as one of the
very problems for which his exhaustive Akkadian
and Chaldean studies—more particularly on names
and their compounds—have specifically prepared him,
at all events to say, and say with some approach to
absoluteness and exactness, how far he has found
hint of the Elohistic element more especially tracing
itself from Akkadian sources, or whether it certainly
does not trace from there. This once definitely
declared, Professor Hommel would be free to develop
other points, perhaps more or less in the direction
of Mr. Margoliouth's article in "The Contemporary
Review" for October, 1898. But the difficulty will
not be got rid of by declaring it insuperable and
barred practically, which is precisely what nowadays
it cannot and ought not to be.

Another very peculiar point arises here, as any
studious Hebraist could have told Mr. Grant Allen.

[1] "Ancient Hebrew Tradition," p. 12.

It is the Elohist that is fond of mentioning sacred
pillars, and of telling how the patriarchs were so
addicted to pouring libations over these pillars and
sacred stones. Now, how does this bear ? Exactly
in the direction indicated above. It is another
element in the cumulative proof that we must trace
the Elohim, etc., etc., from the half-Turanian Accads,
a matter on which Mr. Grant Allen, who is such an
expert in the cuneiform that he has told us one or
two surprising little things in his own fascinating
manner, in his remarkable little essay on "' Left to
Right' or ' Right to Left,'" which if it does not give the
title to one of his severely scientific volumes, should
of right (or of left) have done so. Mr. H. Baynes, in
his "Idea of God," traces the El, Elohim clearly
enough. But when he comes to Jahvé it is very
different indeed ; he is on less firm ground there,
and wisely leaves it ; and though Mr. Andrew Lang
has made a little clever byplay round the Jahvé
name in those deep and ingenious " Sign of the
Ship " [sometimes all too Jonah's ship-like] notes in
" Longman's," he has not added much light, though
" more light, more light," is the cry, as with Goethe.
And with regard to כְּחָשֻׁן it is very suggestive in this
connection that an anthropologist of repute connects
the serpent in the oddest manner with the discovery
and the working of metals—a discovery and a practice
which, though undoubtedly Turanian in origin, are
both expressed and perpetuated by the fact that a
metal serpent should have had the place it had
in the Hebrew temple up almost to the very last !
Mr. Gladstone himself had some peculiar thoughts
and doubts about that 'ere serpent, but he did not

extend his survey far enough, not even to Accad
there unfortunately, any more than he did in his
" Ancient Ideas of a Future State," the more's the
pity. But here is what he cautiously says about
that serpent :

" The serpent is manifestly a literal and ordinary
serpent, though it must be remembered that primitive
peoples are apt to regard animals, and especially
noxious animals like the snake, as demoniacal." So
they do, but with reasons more relative than Mr,
Gladstone there glanced at.

Mr. Gladstone, however, was right, only right,
when at the outset of his " Impregnable Rock " he
writes :

" It is a curious question, how far one ignorant
like myself of Hebrew . . . is entitled to attempt
representations concerning it." With Mr. Gladstone
indeed the lack too often made itself felt, but in this
case it is clear that it was at least a little painfully
realised by him, whereas in the cases of some of our
adventurous younger spirits, it is never in the least
realised, and thus, alas ! they only the more thoroughly
suffer by it.

But here, patent before you is the most remarkable
fact that, though along with a good deal else, you
have coming clear along this Chaldean, or more
properly Accadian (*i.e.*, Turanian) line, the influence
that gave to Hebrewism the most spiritual idea it
had of godhead, so that Professor Cheyne, in dealing
with the Accadian hymns and contrasting them with
the Hebrew psalms, can only say that here assuredly
is proof that before God had educated men on the
banks of the Jordan, He had educated them on the

banks of the Euphrates, adding that in his idea the psalms of David stood to the Accadian hymns precisely as the Christian hymns stand to the psalms of David.

And then, since we are dealing thus with Elohim and Jahvé, would it be too much to ask Mr. Grant Allen how it comes that in a writing—Ecclesiastes, namely—which by good authorities is held to be of late date, the word throughout and without exception for the Supreme Being is not Jahvé but Elohim, and Elohim in cases where not the general but the specific and determinate is clearly indicated? A writer on the evolution of the Idea of God, if he deals at all with the Hebrew development, is bound to notice this frankly, even if he cannot account for it satisfactorily. According to Mr. Grant Allen, Jahvé so completely superseded Elohim — their deriving from different sources is almost implied in such supercession—that Jahvé may be uniformly used instead of Elohim wherever Elohim occurs, and yet in what is professedly a late writing Jahvé does not at all occur, but only Elohim. Mr. Grant Allen should yet tell us whether (1) he accepts the writing for what it professes to be, or whether (2) he regards it as so early as to date from pre-Jahvé days, and (3) whether Jahvé could justifiably, from his theoretical point of view, be used uniformly for Elohim there, as he has freely done with parts of the Pentateuch.

If Mr. Baring-Gould will kindly turn to Psalm cxxxviii. he will read, "I will praise thee with my whole heart: before the *gods* will I sing praise unto thee." The word for "gods" here is Elohim, which shows that while Jahvé was worshipped, other gods

(Elohim) were believed in, even at that late date. Does this make for Mr. Baring-Gould's idea of strict Hebrew monotheism, or does it not? I shall be glad to hear from him on this point, and also from Dr. Fairbairn, of Oxford. Does Elohim there mean gods, ancestors, old men, judges, or what does it mean? A clear and explicit answer will oblige.

It would have been of the utmost importance to Mr. Grant Allen, in view of one of his own arguments, had he been able to distinguish here. More than one good authority has, on the grounds we have indicated, held that the Elohist has on the whole more elevated ideas of the godhead than the Jahvist—that he was less of an anthropomorphist, etc., etc. Even in a book which Mr. Grant Allen might well have had before him, he would have found a concensus of opinion on this head, with very decisive pronouncement on his own part by the able Hebraist and thoughtful scholarly author, who is of that mind and gives ample ground for it. I refer to Mr. Addis's valuable work on the "Hexateuch and its Documents," vol. i., p. lv. (David Nutt). Mr. Addis dwells on the fondness of the Jahvist for making Jahvé appear in dreams, etc., and from this he draws his own conclusions, which I am surprised beyond measure Mr. A. Lang did not use, and use to effect in his "Making of Religion" when dealing with dreams directly. As for Mr. Grant Allen, he should have well considered before he committed himself to certain things. And though we have said that he would have found these facts in favour of one of his arguments, he most certainly would not have found them in favour of another of these arguments, so that now let him lean which

way he will, his book for all true inquirers is cut in
two.   For if the Elohist, who preserves the traditions
and the terms of the earlier polytheistic writers
(including Accadian), had nevertheless attained to
higher and purer and less crudely anthropomorphic
ideas of the godhead, how does Mr. Grant Allen
explain the decadence apparent in the too materialised
Jahvé on the ground either of evolution or of development?   The Rev. Mr. Baring-Gould has gone, alas!
too directly and indiscriminatively on this tack too,
especially in a certain very eloquent passage of his
great book, " Religious Development."   Perhaps he
would kindly help Mr. Grant Allen to clear up the
matter for us, and to distinguish decisively between
Jahvistic and Elohistic, which he certainly has not
yet done, so far at least as we know.   Our final word
on Mr. Grant Allen meanwhile is that either he must
get rid of some facts or his dialectic must become
more refined than we have yet found any proof of it
being in " The Evolution of the Idea of God."

   And as we suppose the wonderful well-grounded
book sells still, and sells largely, we see how out of
ideas, whether of evolution of the Idea of God or other,
the money flows into some lucky hands, and English
scholarship, and English thought, and deepest English
research are thus endowed and magnified ; and all the
world over the praises of such writers are sounded as
finders, seers, revealers, makers—men of fancy, invention, creators, beginners of new systems and of new
worlds of truth, morality, and thoroughness indeed !

   And as a last word, let me say that nothing has
recently given me a more hearty laugh than Mr.
Andrew Lang on Mr. Grant Allen's " Evolution of

the Idea of God," in the "Contemporary Review."
Mr. Lang made a small hit or two about Australians,
for example, not using the bow and arrow, and therefore Mr. Grant Allen was wrong in ignorantly quoting
a stupid remark that these Australians cut off the
thumb or forefinger of the right hand of a defeated
enemy, in order that he might not again use the bow.
That, however, was a small and quite an incidental
matter.   But to put things square about a confirmed
and ignorant and shameful confusion as regards
Jahvé and Elohim was not a small matter, but
radical so far as a large section of Mr. Grant Allen's
book went.   But Mr. Lang there knew no more than
his author.   Author and critic were alike in their
nescience there, which just shows the depths to
which learning and science have fallen in England:
Arcades ambo they of English ignorance, conceit,
pretence and the self-assertion to which literary men
can show themselves capable in thus vying, vying
outright, with the politicians and the "statesmen,"
—so they all hang together—great men and great
thinkers *in England;* but—nowhere else.

NOTE.—In this Chapter we have followed Mr. Grant Allen in his
spelling of Jahvé, and adapted ours to it. *Koholeth* mentions God
some twenty-seven times, but it is always under the name of Elohim,
which, as one orthodox critic says, to remove any suspicions that
might arise, "belonged to him" (that is, God or Jahvé), "as the
Creator"—exactly the idea of one of Dr. Driver's fine distinctions,
This is another point for Mr. Grant Allen to consider and to reconcile
with some bold assertions of his.

VII.—MR. ADDIS AND THE HEXATEUCH.

. MR. ADDIS certainly set out with a splendid idea
in his "Hexateuch." The first volume was published
several years ago, and the second only last year.
His idea was by different kinds of type, italics,
Roman, black, large and small type, to show precisely and at once to the eye the various portions
attributed to different authors : in idea and plan he
thus anticipated the Chromo Bible. He shows himself
very advanced and liberal, not allowing preconceived
notions or accepted ideas to weigh too much with
him. In cases of doubtful translation he has been
bold to put down the *literal* rendering, and in no
case is this more conspicuous than in the rendering
of Deut. xxiii. 18, where he translates קדשה consecrated whore, as it ought to be, both the Authorised
translators and the Revisers having rather *shied* clearly
presenting to the reader's mind what is most distinctly meant there—that the Hebrews, like many
other races, consecrated whoredom in order to aid
the revenues of the temple. That this is a fact,
an undoubted fact, is proved by many things, this
passage for one, where קדשה is translated in both
versions whore merely, whereas the word for common unconsecrated whore is זוֹנָה. That reason
remained for the legal protest is well proved by what

we find in some of the later prophets and records, which tell that there were houses of consecrated male and female prostitutes close to the temple, and that a certain later king did his level best to get rid of them.

On all such points as these we find Mr. Addis remarkably honest and thoroughgoing, determined unduly to strain no point in unreasoning favour of these Jewish records.

Now and then we have to confess, however, that we come on statements which just a *wee* stagger us, statements made, we conceive, in the interests of a certain conservative sentiment that is fain to make out Judaism something better than it was, that may the more fitly join on to Christianity. Here is a specimen from note at page 53 :—

"*The Hebrews had no inclination to abandon the worship of Jahvé, their national god, nor did they associate other gods with him in any arbitrary way.* But when Judah, under Ahaz, became a vassal kingdom to Assyria, the Assyrian deities had, according to common Hebrew notions, a claim to recognition by the inhabitants of Judah ; they had become, in a sense, the gods of the land. Similarly, at an earlier period, Ahab built a temple for the Tyrian Baal, because there was an alliance between northern Israel and Tyre. Jahvé, therefore, and Baal were the gods who watched over the treaty, and the Israelites had relation to both. But, of course, this mixture of religion was a breach of the Mosaic principle, which prescribed, not indeed monotheism, *i.e.*, belief in one god, but monolatry, *i.e.*, worship of one god only. . . . Such a deity as Jahvé differed from the nature gods of the other nations."

Now, even though we had settled in our minds, as clearly as Mr. Addis apparently has, what was "the worship of Jahvé," we are yet so inclined to go with Mr. Montefiore where, in the Hibbert Lectures, he goes on the idea that not only did the people, but the priests in large numbers, really mix up Jahvé and Baal, that in their minds the two were practically inseparable, and with Prof. Robertson Smith, who deliberately held that human sacrifices were actually made to Jahvé, that we cannot but regard the last part of Mr. Addis's sentence as eating up the first. They did not, he says, associate other gods with Jahvé in an arbitrary way, and suggests that, if the low and ignorant did so, the men at the top were all serene— all right as a trivet! What are we, then, to say of Solomon, who thought it was all right to build in Jerusalem a temple to the god of his Moabite wife, if only he brought the earth from Moab on which to build it? The same remark applies to some of the sentences of note at page 41. If Jahvé was essentially opposed to graven images, according to the "Mosaic" legislation, what of נְחֻשְׁתָּן in the temple, what of the teraphim (images of ancestors) with which no one found fault if the ceremonies of the temple were but attended to? what of that image from Nob that David consulted and swore by? what of the ephod and the lots by which divinations were made? What of the rods that represented tribes, and of the stones in circles that represented tribes also, if not something yet more definite? What of the מִטַּף יהוה, and, what is more, the מִטַּף אֱלֹהִים?

Mr. Addis, at Vol. II., page 262, has a note which we humbly think hardly goes far enough to be wholly consistent. Speaking of the "bells and pomegranates" on the high priest's robe, he allows that the bells were charms against demons who guarded holy places, and were so used to frighten them away. No probable reason, he adds, has been given for the use of the pomegranates there. But the reason, we think, was not so very far to seek. The pomegranate, because of its many seeds, was, over a large part of the East, one of the symbols of increase. As such, it was put into Astarte's hand in her greatest celebrations. The worst evil that demons could inflict was barrenness (barrenness of the earth, of animals, and of women), as indeed we find it in the Persian, where Armaiti, the genius of earth, is specifically armed against it, and in the Hindu, where rice is often used as a charm in precisely the same way, and pearls, as being like rice, and cowries are hung round the necks and arms of deities and of some of their priests. The ladies of ancient Accad put some fish-scales in their breasts as a charm against the Evil-eye, and as a tribute to Ea-Han or Oannes, fish-god, god of fertility; and even now the ladies of Germany and some parts of Scandinavia put, as the Custom-house officers through losses have come to know, some fish-scales in their purses for luck!

The charm against barrenness was never forgotten or neglected by Eastern peoples—the worst curse of the Evil-eye was barrenness. The bells were general in force against demons; the pomegranates were special as against the special demon curse of barrenness. Bells, as charms against demons, were used in the Christian church, and as such were christened

and consecrated; and if this is so, we only see that
Mosaism did not in all cases denounce heathen and
ethnic conceptions and symbols, but took them up,
included them, and nurst them in its own way. The
bells sounded on the high priest's robe, and the
pomegranates shone in witness of life and generation; if they had not done so he would have died
symbolically—in his successors = " *lest he die!*"

It is very significant to find Moor, in his " Hindu
Pantheon," telling that, among other essential furniture in the *Lingapuja* of Hindu women in the "Deval"
or domestic temples, there is a bell (*gaut'ha*) which
is rung at certain times to scare away evil spirits.
Certain flowers and seeded fruits are also there
(instead of the pomegranates), and a cup *novady*,
with water to sprinkle these flowers, etc. Pomegranates, too, as every one will remember, held a
large place in certain lines of decoration in the great
Solomon's temple. Bells are sounded now at certain
parts of the Roman Catholic ritual, and they mean
practically the same as pomegranates and incense
and lights—the warding off of evil spirits.

Mr. Addis, following Robertson Smith, fully recognises this principle at work in another case—that of
the charms or amulets referred to at Deut. vi. 8,
where the very words of Jahvé are to become such
—" Thou shalt bind them for a sign," etc., etc., on
which he thus remarks: " The author knew that the
superstitious use of amulets was dear to the Israelite.
Instead of trying to root it out, he skilfully provides
the devout Israelite with amulets, which were at the
same time badges of the monotheistic creed." And
this is just precisely what Mohammed did, what the

Buddhist leaders did, what the sages of China and
Burmah did. But a question arises as to tendency,
and the popular lack of discrimination in all such
matters. Amulets of this sort! Can Mr. Addis tell
in how far their use aided the persistency in other
amulets — the שַׂהֲרֹנִים which Isaiah, at chapter iii.,
so severely rebukes, and which we find were exactly
the same as those which Gideon took off the
Midianitish camels and Midianitish men—שַׂהֲרֹנִים or
"little moons," as Prof. Cheyne translates them—
not in his text, however, where he gives "crescents,"
but, oddly enough, in an explanatory note. "The
one is taken and the other left," truly; but the
pomegranate on the priest's robe represents the
exact expression of the same principle: Judaism
may by a slight degree have elevated it, as it did
many other things heathen; but it is there, because
it had been in so many places before, as a charm
against barrenness, a point in which Mr. Grant
Allen, who, in his "Evolution of the Idea of God,"
finds Jahvé so pre-eminently a god of *fruitfulness*, and
hater of barrenness, will most assuredly agree, though
it is very odd that just there it is Elohim that does
the wonders in helping fruitfulness, and Jahvé that
stops up certain wombs on account of Sarah.

Mr. Addis's note to שְׂעִירִים [= he-goats, satyrs] at
Lev. xvii. 7, we confess, does a little surprise us.
He translates it " satyrs," and explains it as " hairy
beings," " demons of goat-like form." The people,
he thinks, could not rid themselves of the idea that
there was something supernatural about them " (page
337, note).

The שְׂעִירִים or he-goats—the Hebrew root means

hairy or bearded, and by derivation is, in fact, applied
to barley as bearded—wherever we find them, are to
be regarded as having originally typified the male
and fructifying principle of nature. At 2 Chron.
xi. 15, they are closely linked with calves, and there
they are translated in the Authorised Version "devils."
Our belief is that, as typifying fertility, they had
become ensigns, perhaps totems, of certain tribes.
The word "satyrs," which Mr. Addis adopts, does
not seem to us to be much better than the perversion
"devils," and, in fact, is silly and meaningless when
closely linked with calves. The Revisers, it would
appear, were of our mind, but were not bold enough
to proceed thoroughly on it, and temporised and
compromised, with the results that we shall make
clear by this table :—

	HEBREW.	AUTHORISED.	REVISED.
Lev. xvii. 7	לשעירים	Devils	He-goats; margin "or satyrs"; devils got rid of; satyrs half ditto.
Deut. xxxii. 17	לשדים	Devils	Demons.
2 Chron. xi. 15	לשעירים	Devils [linked with calves]	He-goats; margin "or satyrs"; devils got rid of; satyrs half ditto.
Psalm cvi. 37	לשדים	Devils	Demons.
Isaiah xiii. 21	לשעירים	Satyrs	Satyrs; margin, " or he-goats "; satyrs half got rid of.
,, xxxiv 14	ושעיר	Satyr	Satyr; margin, "or he-goat "; satyr half got rid of.

And so, despite Mr. Addis' sticking to the "satyrs,"
the Revisers show a *slow* progress towards disposing

of them *in Mr. Addis' sense.* Hosea is particularly hard on the calves, if not on the he-goats, and at xiii. 2 he writes: "They say of them, Let the sacrificers of men kiss the calves;" thus associating the calves with human sacrifice—a point which English critics have sometimes dealt with openly and honestly—to the effect that they sacrificed men, and kissed or worshipped calves, when the procedure should just have been reversed.

With regard to the Urim and Thummim, which Mr. Addis finds so obscure, we are more than surprised that he does not quote Dean Plumptre and Sir R. Burton's very bold derivation of Thummim from the Arabic *Tammim.*

We are a little surprised too that Mr. Addis should be so firm in his idea of the obscurity of the etymology of Torah. תּוֹרָה surely originally means oral instruction—a guiding round or pointing out, as, of course, the early teachers were peripatetic, as later the prophets were not only inclined to wander round, but to be ecstatic and dance even naked when prophesying. When we have the word in such relations as תּוֹרַח הָעֹלָה—the law of the burnt offering, it specially includes the direction of moving round and sprinkling, etc.; so that here we have actually a kind of suggestion of the wheel of the law. דּוּר, as applied to a town, had the same meaning as *urbs* in relation to *orbis*—a circle that could be gone round, and the word came to mean a circle, a revolution of time, a generation. The same thing exactly applies to the allied word שׁוּר, which has undergone precisely the same process; meaning at first merely going round about, it then came to signify a traf-

ficker, and finally came especially to mean looking
round, turning round to gaze at or make note of.
The very same thing applies to the Arabic word
Sura, by which the chapters of the Koran are originally designated. תּוֹרָה is from the root יָרָה, to
cast about, lay a foundation, to make a circle, and
cannot, surely, be wholly viewed apart from the תּוּר
to go round about or to surround; and in the later
speech this came to mean trafficker, because not only
are they always going round, but are the great news
bringers—in a way, oral instructors. It has been
said by Carlyle that the true pulpit is now the press;
here we have it in the combination of journalist or
news-bringer and teacher, implicit in a notorious
Hebrew word, as recognised in the days of the
Judges. More than this; various words in other
languages for going round have come, in precisely
the same way, to mean traders, merchants. The
Roman *lustro*, indeed, in that direction witnesses a
very happy perversion illustrative here, for it came
to mean actually a going round, and colloquially it
was used for a vagabond, because he was constantly
going round like a trader—most often only another
kind of vagabond. How funny it is, in view of this,
to come on such a sentence as this from Sir Richard
Burton, in one of the very first notes to " The Pilgrimage to Al-Madinah and Mecca": " The vagrant,
the merchant, and the philosopher, among Orientals,
are frequently united in the same person." The
word Torah thus, by glancing at its affinities, has
direct reference to going about, pointing out, in-
structing, measuring, laying foundations.

And speaking of Robertson Smith, the frequent

references to him and citations from him here suffice
to prove what a power he was in this sphere—how
keen in thought, how clear in style, with grasp,
power of uniting under one light things that might
appear disparate, along with the rare gift of suggestion, and making the old and distant leap into light
by imaginative association with the near and familiar.
He had just got into full possession of his kingdom
when he was called hence; but he remains on this
very account all the more inspiring, stimulating,
fruitful. No Biblical student, or, for that matter,
anthropological or classical scholar, can now, or in
times to come, afford to pass him by.

With all desire to do Mr. Addis justice, and to
speak appreciatively and sympathetically of his work,
we must say nothing has come nearer to making us
laugh lately in serious scholarship than his remark
in note to Deut. xxvi. 14, where we have reference
to "the giving of food to a dead man." "The
practice of feeding the dead," says he, "has existed
among many nations, probably among all, at an
early stage of their history. This is the only express
mention of it among the Israelites. It is however
implied in Hosea ix. 4"—a very plain implication
indeed—their sacrifices should be to them as *the
bread of mourners*—polluted. And he dogmatically
says that no argument can be raised on Jeremiah
xvi. 7, where the Revisers, to their honour, have
made it plainer as something to base an argument
on. "They shall not cut themselves, nor make
themselves bald for them ; neither shall men break
bread for them in mourning, to comfort them for the
dead." Is that not a clear case of breaking bread

for a dead man to feed him? And what of the
להם אנשים and the real deposit of meaning in the
תרפים? The feeding of the dead is inseparably
associated with the cutting of the person, rounding
the hair, etc., which is legislated against strictly in
Leviticus and Deuteronomy, and making baldness
between the brows. Why, the very shewbread has
significance only in this way, as Robertson Smith
most clearly demonstrates.

We have noticed a few misprints in spite of the
evident care with which the sheets have been read.
One of them is so significant of the easy way in
which the eye can be deceived even by very famili-
arity with English letters as compared with those of
any other language, that we must crave space to
point it out. It is at page 41, where "etilim" is
given instead of "elilim" for "no gods." Had the
word here been written אלילים, as it is elsewhere in
the volume, we are certain no such misprint could
have escaped the careful eyes of Mr. Addis and his
"readers."

VIII.—"EATEN WITH HONOUR."

A SOMEWHAT remarkable article from the pen of
Professor Flinders Petrie, titled "Eaten with
Honour," appeared in the "Contemporary Review"
for June, 1897. There is, of course, much of value
in that article, because the Professor has some real
knowledge and observation of his own about Egyptian
matters of some 3,500 B.C.—the time of the early
pyramid-builders—to impart to us. But he is, alas!
a little too easy-going when he surveys mankind
from China to Peru, and generalises thus: "Higher
motives of honour and kindness prevail mostly in
Asia, Australia, and South America, but seem to be
unknown in Polynesia, North America, and *Africa*."
Why, he himself tells us of one—"the little rift
within the lute, the little pitted speck in garnered
fruit"—in the Thlinkets (not Tlinkets) of North
America, who "consumed their bravest," with the
belief, doubtless, that their strength and capability
would pass into the eaters. Things are far more
"mixed" anthropologically than to justify Professor
Flinders Petrie or any other in drawing a *bold* line
across the earth like this. Besides, why did he title

his article " Eaten with Honour," when, according
to him or his German original, Dr. Steinmetz,
exactly one half geographically and on scientific
reckoning is *not* eaten with honour, but the reverse ?
This is his table of classification of motives to
cannibalism :

Honour, kindness, future good, love	20 per cent.
For strength or magic results	19 ,,
As ceremony to acquire position	10 ,,
As a punishment (to eater or eaten ?)	5 ,,
	—54
From hunger or need of food	18 ,,
From preference as food	28 ,,
	—46
	—100

Now, Professor Flinders Petrie is guilty of the
enormity of declaring in his generalised statement
that " Eaten with Honour " seems to be unknown
in Africa, whilst he declares the very opposite of the
Libyans, who, he says, communicated the habit to
the Egyptians. As to Australia, the Professor quotes
from another thus :

" But the men are still eaten, especially chiefs,
and I have heard of cases recently where tough,
skinny old fellows have been faithfully eaten, although
they could not have been very juicy. The reason, I
am told, is that by partaking of the flesh of a person
they inherit the virtues of that person."

And then he actually proceeds to say that, from
all the circumstances, the Egyptian cases were clearly

in motive, etc., similar to this. He writes: "The arranging of the bones into the semblance of the body shows extreme care, which must prevent our looking on this as otherwise than a reverent and honoured burial." And the motives to the cannibalism could not have been different, he urges, from those of the Australians. Well, but what of the pronouncement so absolutely on Africa?

And, then, did Professor Flinders Petrie really think out what is implied in this sentence with strict reference to his classification above: "More than half the dead who are eaten, and in *most* cases when people are killed it is the *aged, sickly, and infirm— the killing of the young and healthy is an aberration unknown in most lands*"? I much fear he did not. He puts down as "From preference as food" twenty-eight, and "From hunger and need of food" eighteen —a very large percentage, almost one-half of the whole; and yet, according to his fine generalisation here, they act—every man-jack of them—altogether unnaturally; they leave, he says, the tender tit-bits —the infants, the young, healthy, and robust, and more especially women—and tackle "the old and tough"—"the old and tough," and the sickly and dying, practically over the whole area! Is that according to human nature and human preference? That is *what I want to know!* Failing Mr. Flinders Petrie, will Mr. Percy W. Bunting tell me what I so much want to know? If Professor Flinders Petrie will exhaustively and satisfactorily answer me this, I shall admit him a fine comparative anthropologist and *thinker*, as well as a clever Egyptologist and skilful excavator and explorer; and if, failing Mr. Petrie,

Mr. Percy Bunting will do it, then I shall declare *him* a fine thinker and noble writer as well as an expert editor and great and most learned lawyer.

There cannot be the least doubt that Canon Greenwell and others interested in the English barrows have shown that, precisely as with the Egyptians, early races in this country stripped the flesh from the bones, and in the process of doing so cut up the body, afterwards arranging and setting the bones together; but when Dr. Flinders Petrie condescends on an individual case he is most especially unlucky.

In addition to his other lapses, he quotes a description from St. Jerome of the Atticotti, a British tribe, as preferring, in Jerome's time, human flesh to that of cattle. But there is always a good deal to be qualified in the reports of saints or missionaries, old or new, about heathens or heathen habits, even if there should be no conscious or intentional mistake in the matter. But it turns out that there is reason —good reason—for believing that St. Jerome was in this case seriously misled by a wrong translation; and if Professor Flinders Petrie wants an authority he will find it in Villaneuva i. p. 245. There is, indeed, a relief in getting any ground for saying and thinking that the Atticottis were not so bad as they have been painted, as Professor Flinders Petrie, even at this late time, has once more painted them; but he must look to Villaneuva, where we fancy he will find set down together the original and the translation.

Professor Flinders Petrie will also find some interesting references to the Atticottis in one of the volumes of Mr. Borlase's "The Dolmens of Ireland,"

which, by-the-bye, does not limit itself to Irish Dolmens, but is in certain chapters finely comparative.
Mr. Borlase amply proves that, though at a certain
stage, like the rest of the world, indeed, they were
eaters of human flesh—it may be originally sacrificially—that long before, long, long before the time
of St. Jerome they had abandoned it, and that St.
Jerome's evidence is not to be relied on in that case,
as Professor Flinders Petrie has unluckily, with the
full consent and aid of Mr. Percy Bunting, relied
upon it. I think, too, Professor Rhys has something
to say about the Atticotti in "Celtic Britain."

IX.—PROFESSOR RHYS DAVIDS AND GODDESSES.

In a very thoughtful passage of Professor **Rhys** Davids's "Buddhism" (a series of **lectures** delivered in America), **we** find a suggestion that goddesses are invariably the oldest recorded gods, and that they were invariably worshipped by women, who **at** certain times had women-leaders. He writes:

"A much more solid basis seems to support **the** argument that as the oldest recorded gods are **goddesses, and as man** makes **god in his own image, the** *original*" (italics **are ours**) "**deities must have arisen at a** time when **women** were the leaders, **as in** other **things, so** also **in** theology. They **were born of women,** for it was women who conceived **them. And we** must make room in our theory at least as much **for the awe** inspired by **the** Mother-Earth, and by the mysteries **of** the stars, **as** for the worship of ancestors. We have to explain **how** it was that the oldest divinities were almost, if **not** quite, exclusively **feminine.** We **have to explain** why the moon was worshipped before **the sun, and** certain stars before them all." [1]

But **here** the Professor **surely** proceeds all too **closely on the** idea that in **all** languages Moon is

[1] pp. 11-12.

feminine, which it is not, and is not, indeed, in the language from which ours descends. And beyond this we have instances where the Earth is the father, and Corn is the mother, as is, for one, the case with the Pawnee Indians; and, more important than all, चन्द्रमष (çandramas) the moon in Sanskrit is masculine, as Mond is both in old German and modern German, as indeed the moon is in all the Teutonic tongues.[1] This needs to be accounted for before we can accept the Professor's theory absolutely, though no doubt the mother-age accounts for much, yet something inevitably went before it even. And though we did find that in anything like a universal sense moon worship preceded sun or other worship, that would not, in some cases at all events, in the least make for the Professor's view of early gods being goddesses, unless we set aside, and pretty boldly too, the witness of language, or proved that it had, in all the opposing cases, in most substantial respects changed as regards the sex of certain objects of nature.

This has a closer bearing on some related theories of things connected with the origins of religion and mythology than might be supposed. The crucial point of difference between Professor Max Müller and Mr. Andrew Lang lies here: The former says that early men could not help themselves, and applied terms implying sex to inanimate objects of nature, and came to call them male and female because they had applied such terms—hence mythology, a disease of language. Mr. A. Lang, again, declares that

[1] Mr. Nesfield points out that *çandramas*, as well as Indus and Somas, are masculine.—"Caste System," p. 72.

early men first regarded these inanimate objects as male and female, and then came to apply to them names indicating sex because they had already perceived something in them which suggested it. But since a very considerable section of the human family are, as their language proves, in direct opposition to the rest about the sex of the moon, which was one of the earliest objects of worship and imaginative exercise, there must be something very confusing and indefinite in the signs on which Mr. A. Lang says the early men founded their ideas of sex in inanimate objects, since even with moon, one of the earliest objects worshipped, some said it was male and some said it was female. This fact, in the last result, suggests some lacunæ in the schemes alike of Professor Rhys Davids and Mr. A. Lang, which it is most desirable they should satisfactorily fill up further.

X.—MR. MARGOLIOUTH'S INGENIOUS ENDEAVOUR.

I HAVE been much interested in an ingenious endeavour of the Rev. Mr. Margoliouth's to identify the Jahweh of the Hebrew with the Chaldean Gods Ea and Sin, made in the "Contemporary Review" of October, 1898. The reverend gentleman does not seem to feel the least embarrassment at the thought of any lessening of the old claim to direct revelation in the case of the Hebrew scriptures; nay, having accepted the all-powerful facts of likeness between the Accadian and Hebrew accounts of creation, garden of Eden, temptation, deluge, etc., etc., he actually thinks that this is in favour of the Hebrew as being in the line of a long continued development. Nothing less than this. Only it needs to be asked of Mr. Margoliouth and the editor of the "Contemporary," whether they still, even in the vaguest way, hold by the idea of special revelation, or have abandoned it altogether? There is, in our idea, hardly a safe middle resting place for them.

Mr. Margoliouth's ingenuity cannot be doubted; but he must excuse our saying that he only goes where it suits him and selects only what seems to make in his favour. In so wide a field this is easy; but the cause of truth and real scholarship is to be advanced only by looking **round, and all** around impartially and fearlessly. **Mr. Margoliouth** looks very ingenious; his theory **is very** new, **as he claims it is**; but to be **all "new"** is sometimes **to be doubtful, and we shall just use a little** space **to point** out one or **two things and ask** Mr. Margoliouth **a few questions.**

And first of all we have **to say, in** mere honesty, **Mr.** Margoliouth, in **the** words of witty **Artemus, should have** "pursood **the** subject furder" before writing **as he** has done. The two triads of leading Shumiro-Accadian gods were these : Anu or Ana Heaven, the father of all the gods; Ea, at once god of the sky **and** of the **sea;** and Bel, son of El, the active creator and orderer of things, lord of cosmos and vitality. **The** second triad consisted of the **moon,** the sun, **and** the **power of** the atmosphere ; **Sin,** Shamash **and Raman [or Rimmon, as Mr. Margoliouth wrongly writes** it, with **some chance** of confusion with **the** Syrian Rimmon רִמּוֹן **the Pomegranate** god (**2 Kings** v. 18), quite a different **conception].** All these were but Semitic transla-**tions of** the older Turanian Shumiro-Accadian names. **Thus Sin** was Uru-ki or Nannar, which last word the professor links with sin as though it were a mere Hebrew variant) ; Shamash was **Ud or** Barbak, and Raman [1] **was Im or** Mermer.

Merodach **again is** only a kind of Hebrew modifica-tion of the Turanian Amar-utaki (brightness of the sun), and **he is** the only begotten of Ea—sky there as well **as sea—and Dam-Kina,** earth, and his office is

---

[1] **Raman,** by the way, was not god of tempests, in the specific **way Dr. M.** would make his Rimmon : he was the god of rain, and **dew, and** moisture—only of tempest as associated with these.

to act as mediator between Ea, or Anu, and man.
He it is who listens to the supplications and prayers
of those who suffer or are burdened with sin and
penitent; bears up to Ea or Anu, who is too high
and exalted for them to approach, the report of their
penitence, their longing, and their needs; and then
secures for them by his mediation deliverance from
evils and from enemies; from the powers of witchcraft, from the burden of their own sins. He is, so
far as we yet know, the precursor and prototype of
all the mediators between gods and men, that human
races everywhere have essayed to create for their
own redemption. In order to gain apparent aid to
his own theory Mr. Margoliouth sacrifices this lovely
idea, which is the highest reach towards the central
idea of Christianity that any form of heathenism has
shown. So much do men pay for setting out with
preconceived ideas and fancies which they make
their scholarship, like Issachar, an ass couching
down between two burdens, to support. Only as Mr.
Margoliouth seems to hold a sort of brief for Judaism
this attitude of fairness would not only have spoilt
his theory, but shown the barrenness of the land made
by Judaism even, when, according to him, it adopted
and took over, rejecting, shamelessly—turning out
the best ideas, which it could not appreciate or
accept, and so transforming all into a vast filthy *caput
mortuum*. The great gods—shadows far removed,
dim presences uplifted to heaven—have always and
everywhere given place to something nearer more
human, as in Krishna and, with reverence be it
spoken, Jesus Christ. And invariably the mediator
becomes really, if not formally and nominally, the

great, efficient, active god; the well realised and
sought for—as Lord Amberley, in a passage he gives,
illustrates it by the Roman Catholic form of Christian
reverence by the money paid in offerings to the gods.
In this case while God the Father got only a few
pence or nothing at all, Jesus Christ got at the
average rate of say £1, and the Virgin Mary as much
as £1 10s., which says something by the way of the
return upon us, even in these latest forms of the
very earliest—the idea, after all, of female divine
rule, and its accompaniment and source really, the
reign of mother-right ; for there, in practical result,
estimated in money, the true measure of devotion in
these days of ours, the Virgin Mary stood above her
son and far, far above the distant, heaven-dwelling
Father—who, in fact, reckoned by money contributions to him, was nowhere—received at most a few
pence and often "*nothing at all.*" The first in the
hierarchy, here as elsewhere, is not by any means
first in real influence and power, as reckoned by the
money-amount of devotion of the worshippers. They
are not first in real influence as judged by another
test. Professor F. Hommel, in his " Ancient Hebrew
Tradition," a large part of which is devoted to tracing
out Hebrew connections by names, from early monuments, proves that even in compounded names, the
deities of the nominal first rank are less recognised
than those which nominally belong to lower or
secondary triads.

Mr. St. Chad Boscawen, in his " The Bible and
the Monuments," has systematically presented by
parallel passages a most convincing array of proofs
of the very large indebtedness of the Jews to Accad,

H.   S

all over the field of their legendary lore—the Creation, the Fall of Man, the Serpent, the Temptation, the promise of a redeemer in Merodach (*Amar-utaki*), who would defeat the tempter and restore the fallen.

> The asuan (fruit) they ate, they broke in two ;
> Its stalk they destroyed :
> The sweet juices which injure the body :
> Great is their sin. Themselves they exalted—
> *To Merodach their Redeemer, he appointed their fate.*

We cannot therefore understand Mr. Margoliouth when he writes :

" It was, in fact, not before the city of Babylon had risen to supreme importance in ancient Chaldea that Merodach (the God of the rising Sun) became the chief deity on the banks of the Euphrates."

Amarutaki, the mediator (Brightness of the Sun), was in fact, if not theoretically or formally, the chief god of Shumir and Accad, ages before the date when Mr. Margoliouth, to suit his thesis, would first erect him into eminence.

According to the tradition, it was Samash the Sun-god that made the flood, and at the time of this flood, there was a Sippara city of the Sun-god, and it was there that the traditional Xisuthrus built his boat in view of the flood foretold to him, and all the records, documents, and precious things were stored in this city of Sippara, the city of the Sun-god.

Von Bohlen gave some very good grounds for thinking that " the introduction of Jahweh was as late as David and Solomon "—grounds, some of which have not yet, to our mind, been completely discredited. But this is clear on the face of the

record, El Shaddai was known to Abraham and to
the Patriarchs, and Elohim succeeded him ; Jahweh
came on at a much later date ; "by my name of
Jahweh was I not known to them." Now, how does
Mr. Margoliouth account for this great and lengthened
blank, if Jahweh is but the development of Ea-Sin,
which should have been in some sense continuous,
surely, and not intermittent to meet his needs, for
intermittency spells, in all such sense, more or less of
doubt ? Or are we dealing with sets of empty names
merely, each and all of which are tied to a set of
attributes, which only vary by a little more or a little
less of separate traits and powers, as indeed lies
implied in too much, say, of Mr. Grant Allen's
" Evolution of the Idea of God " ?—more's the pity !
And if we have thus but a mere set of names, with
no real and sufficing distinction, you raise the uncom-
fortable question whether any comparative science of
religion is possible at all, and whether, in endeavouring
to compare and classify and distinguish gods and
gods' names, we are not over large areas simply
threshing straw, or indulging in a sort of intellectual
or unconscious thimble-rig? There is no use in
Mr. Margoliouth or any one else trying to creep away
from this ; either way a dilemma waits on him. If
Jahweh and Elohim and El and Eloah and El Shaddai
are merely names for the same being, and any line of
identity or continuity proved for the one suffices for
the other, there is no good over that area in any
attempt at comparative analysis of them whatever ;
and if again, they are not, where does Mr. Margoliouth
find the point of connection between Jahweh and
Ea-Sin during that long period, when it is clear

Jahweh was not known to the Jews? Mr. Margoliouth wants first of all to make this absolutely clear; he needs—greatly needs—to justify himself with regard to these former gods of the Hebrews, and in no half and half way. Till he has done so, he but walks round and round a scaffolding and tries to argue himself, and to lead others into the belief, that there is a building, the foundations of which are not yet truly laid.

Then, a further point. If Jahweh is but a continuation of Sin, the moon-god of Akkad, why is it that in Hebrew לְבָנָה moon (that is, the white one) is feminine; and not only this, but all the related adjectival forms? If Lebanon—white or Moon-Mountain—had been associated with Jahweh as his mountain and dwelling place, then we could have so far understood it; but Sinai, even though it seems *outwardly* to connect Jahweh with Sin, has no real and inevitable relationship to him; any other mountain would do equally well for Jahweh, for his people it was by the way a mere point of passage; but why, and let Mr. Margoliouth answer it frankly, is לְבָנָה in Hebrew feminine, in view of derivation from moon and moon-god masculine?

Mr. Hormuzd Rassam's remarkable discovery at Aboo Hubba in 1880 does not quite bear out in all respects Mr. Margoliouth's view. Mr. Rassam sank a shaft and alighted on an old temple, in the centre of which, before the altar, was a stone tablet, the inscription on which clearly told that the temple had been dedicated to the Sun-god, reading thus: " Statue of the Sun-god, great lord, dwelling in the house of light, which is in Sippara." These inscriptions were so

ancient that the characters were linear rather than cuneiform ; and from other tablets and inscriptions found
there—among them cylinders of Nabonidus (the Babylonian King overthrown by Cyrus), who repaired this
temple—it was proved that this was the temple of
the Sun-god, erected by Naram-Sin (mark the *Sin*
compounded in the name there, which proves that
even then the Moon-god, Sin, under that name, was
in the front rank of gods), son of the famous Sarguna
of Accad, the first Semitic King of Babylonia, who,
he said, lived 3,000 years before his time ; so that the
date of the building of this temple to the Sun-god
was at the very least 3750 B.C. This disproves two
things, assumed, as we may say, by Mr. Margoliouth :
(1) that the worship of the Sun-god was late, and (2)
that Moon-god worship, in any direct sense at a specific
period, was superseded by it ; Naram-*Sin* itself fully
attesting that—and going to prove that sun worship
and moon worship went along harmoniously together
in Accad at the very early date of 3750 B.C., under
the first and second of the Semitic kings ; if not sub-
stantially long, long before them, for we hear of no
sudden revolution in religious ideas and customs, the
Semitic and Turanian elements having gradually
united, fused, producing what we know as the
Accadian system—the leading Semitic ideas over-
coming the pure Shamanism and demon worship—
witchcraft, etc., so far as to provide the most effective
forces against them. How long must the Sun-god
have been worshipped before Naram-Sin thus erected
a great temple at Sippara ? that is one of the questions which it is needful for Mr. Margoliouth to realise
and to answer, and answer plain, as a much demanded

supplement and rider to his very, very original, but also rather too facile article in the "Contemporary Review." The process of answering that question, we take it, will be the best exposure of his own vague and most groundless theory about Sun-god and Moon-god in Accad.

Professor Hommel, to refer to him again for a moment, writes : " Thus we find at a very early date such names *Narâm-Sin* = Beloved of Sin, or the Moon-god, and *Sin-bani* = Sin creates,"[1] while the chief temples were still devoted to the Sun-god.

Goldziher, indeed, holds and gives some ingenious arguments and curious facts in support of his view, that moon-worship is older than the solar-worship; but that, as a mere general statement of early condition, is one thing; it is quite another to try to affix any such mark or distinction within the period of definite monumental or tablet record.

Another very peculiar point of difficulty arises here, touching at several sides a very great question. The moon as well as the Moon-god, Sin, in the Accadian and early Chaldean, is masculine, so that, even though we did find here that the moon was the earliest object worshipped, so far as clear records will aid us, it nevertheless yields no support to Professor Rhys Davids's view that moon-worship implies the worship of the feminine,[2] or that " the oldest divinities were almost, if not quite, exclusively feminine." If, over

---

[1] "Ancient Hebrew Tradition," p. 62.

[2] See "Buddhism, Lectures delivered in America."—"We have to explain how it was that the oldest divinities were almost, if not quite, exclusively feminine. We have to explain why the moon was worshipped before the sun, and certain stars before either, and the mother earth before them all."

the wide field to which the Shumiro-Accadian points
us, the moon was at earliest times worshipped as
feminine, thus illustrating—according to Professor
Rhys Davids—a very primitive law of mother-right ;
by what wonderful process of change of sex in language did it come about, that, precisely at the point
where we meet with clear record by monument and
tablet of earliest Accad, we find the moon worshipped
not as feminine but as masculine ? Had the moon
and Moon-god there been feminine, Mr. Margoliouth
would have found it far more difficult than he does
to identify Ea with Sin, and Sin, not forgetting Sinai
and its sound and significance, with Aa, Ya, Yahweh, as
he does so cleverly, and yet finds Hebrew monotheism
only magnified by the identity and derivation, etc., etc.

Another question still : If Sin, the Moon-god of
Accad, is but a member of a divine triad and nexus
or plexus of triads, and if for his complete character
association with the sun-god is essential, is it possible
so to detach him more or less arbitrarily from his
place and associations as to transform him into a
solitary, and what is more, an unsexed and unwifed
god in Palestine ?

One of the most essential marks of these Accadian
gods is their constant association with goddesses.
Not only do the lists of the triads, etc., prove this, it
is proved by the constant conjunction of goddesses
with gods in those wonderful hymns, which, as
Professor Cheyne, of Oxford, cannot but confess,
stand to the psalms of David as the psalms of
David stand to the Christian hymns, only with this
difference—and a vast, vast difference it is, scientifi-
cally and comparatively, at all events—that, while

the Accadian hymns never lose sight of the goddess, the psalms of David never allow her presence, or, in the most remote way, suggest or countenance her, the hymns of the long period, at least, of patristic and Latin Christianity, do, in what is certainly a little more than a half-and-half way, fall back on the old goddess in the worship of the Virgin Mary—Ocean Queen and Queen of Heaven—a point on which, if we take Dr. Newman's famous sermon on the Virgin Mary, one great portion of the strength of the Roman Catholic Church lies as working on and answering to the longings of human nature—mother-hood being the eternal and inevitable other side of fatherhood. Well, now, is the relation of god and goddess in the Accadian essential to the conception or is it not? If it is, you cannot, at your own sweet, ingenious will, draw away your god and leave his goddess inert behind you as if she were *non est.* You must accept her too as an essential element in the conception. If it is not, then truly, you may do, as Artemus says, "You pays your money and you takes your choice." But a question, a plain question, here again arises for Mr. Margoliouth to answer, and answer plain: If Sin, the Moon-God, was not solitary and unwifed, but social, a part of a system and with a wife, how could he become the Hebrew Jahweh, most solitary and unwifed, without true mark of sex or of fatherhood—the mere master, ruler and tyrant, as even the eloquent and learned divine, Dr. Fairbairn, finds him, and finds in this his grand guarantee of monotheism? And if Sin becomes Jahweh, thus, what room for evolution, not to speak of revelation, in the said Hebrew Jahweh?

One question further:—Could the chief god of a people most firmly believing in the divinity of pairs and refusing to recognise singles or solitary in this connection, have become, under any possible scheme of development and acceptance of elements from without, the pre-eminently single or solitary god? Could a married man—a man who had entered into the deep experiences of such relationship—ever cast off so entirely his part as to become a bachelor and sworn solitary and sexless tyrant?   The question is not extravagant, but comes as near to analogy as experiences human and divine can do.   The "divinity of pairs" is always pointing us in one direction, and that of singles or solitaries in another.   Certainly Mr. Hewitt finds it so, and presents many arguments and instances in support of his view.   Here is one: "In West Prussia, which, like East Prussia, was once the country of the Lithuanians who worship the sun-god Rā, the last sheaf is called the Corn-baby (our Northumberland kernababy).   Thus, the original daughter of the earth-mother and the Meridian pole, the parents of the corn-growing races of Asia Minor, was the seed-grain, the corn-mother of the future year.   That the myth in this form was conceived by a Turanian race, speaking an agglutinative language, and believing in the *divinity of pairs*, is shown by the worship in Java of the first and last sheaf." [1]

If, then, the identification of Jahweh with Ea and Sin (the Chaldean moon-god) is so complete and satisfactory as Mr. Margoliouth thinks, and so completely justifies, as it were, the special and peculiar

[1] i. p. xxxi.

attributes of Jahweh, how did it come that, as
Jahwehism was more and more developed under
prophets and prophecy, they so earnestly sought
to detach it from what Mr. Margoliouth not only
regards as its basis, but the essential and inalien-
able something which, as Goldziher would say,
kept it from passing truly into the solar plane, to
which at some points, at all events, it naturally
seemed to tend? I should like to hear Mr. Margoliouth's full explanation of this. Does he maintain
still in Jahwehism a clear connection with moon
worship, long derived, after Jahweh, through his
prophets, denounced all these new moons and new
moon celebrations; or does he regard these as
merely secondary and opposed to the true spirit of
Jahwehism? If he is inclined to trace a progress in
Jahwehism from a lower to a more transcendental
form, towards that pure monotheism of which he
speaks, like too many others, just a little too
fluently, does he regard the denouncing of the new
moons and new-moon feasts as an essential part of
this progress, or does he not? And when he has
given me an answer to these questions, clear and
explicit, it is not impossible that I may have another
question or two for him to answer with equal
explicitness. For, if these prophets of Jahweh
were right in saying for Jahweh, "I hate your
feasts and your new moons," how does he justify
the habit of Jews to-day, as he himself so
eloquently tells?

"The Jews of the present day, indeed, observe a
religious rite which very strongly reminds one of
the moon-cult from which their wonderfully pure

monotheistic religion *originally* sprang. [What did it spring from then, *not originally?*] At an early date after the appearing of the new moon, or as soon as the renewed crescent is visible with sufficient clearness, the Hebrew prayer-book enjoins on the Israelites to assemble for a religious service *in the open* [italics are mine], and the ritual which is then observed amounts, *to say the least of it* [italics mine again], to a devout and joyous salutation of the new-born luminary of night. The benedictions, psalms, prayers and versicles recited are, of course, such as could give no direct offence to the higher and purer religious consciousness of Mosaic and transcendental Judaism (!), but the mythological significance of the rite in question is none the less clear and unmistakeable. . . . He who at the proper time," so goes the saying, "pronounces the benediction on the new moon is one who welcomes the very presence of the Shechinah, or divine glory."

"The Shechinah, or divine glory" in the new moon —that is nothing new—that, truly, is not in the least special to the Jews. I will undertake to find it so with scores on scores of tribes in North, South, East, and West, for Mr. Margoliouth's benefit, if he wants them; and with all of them besides, significantly enough, a call to assemble for religious services in *the open*, and, in not a few cases, to an orgy, with sexual promiscuity afterwards, as it is to be feared—greatly feared—was really the case with the Jews—at all events, Plutarch plainly spoke of this being "a bacchanalian festival" in his time, and he surely knew well what these words *bacchanalian festival* meant.

"Direct offence to the higher and purer religious consciousness of Mosaic and transcendental Judaism!" How could that be? When the element of moon-worship, according to him, pertained to its very essence. Without it, surely, Judaism, at the moment of its change, could not have become what it was; and it became something else than it had been. If "their wonderfully pure monotheistic religion *originally* sprang from the moon-cult" and for ages remained identified with it, did it not necessarily entirely change its character and become something else the moment it was detached from it? But, as a matter of fact, it is not detached even now, though Mr. Margoliouth would go for "the merely mythological significance" of an element which is now practically operative in observance and conduct with the presumption of utmost edification.

Now, this much established and admitted—moon-worship still a force for presumed edification in Judaism—to which ideal are the present-day Jews devoted in these persistent celebrations of the new-moon—to the ideal of the days before the later Hebrew prophets, who, speaking for Jahveh, denounced them as hateful to him, or not? There are only two ways—either they hold by the one ideal or by the other. I call on Mr. Margoliouth to say which it is, and to say it definitely.

XI.—MISS KINGSLEY AND FETISH.

I HAVE tried hard and earnestly to get some kind of consistent, intelligible view out of Miss Kingsley's chapters on *Fetish* in her new book, "**West African Studies**," and at last confess myself utterly baffled—always clear and clever where she deals with facts there observed, here she is confused and confusing.

Fetish either means some definite form of spirit recognition in *material shape,* **or it** does not. **If it does** the **first,** then, **it is needful to** draw **a** definite if broad **circle round it, and then say " there it is—** that **is,** *Fetish* "—all **outside it is something else : and if it does** the second, then the danger is great **of** confusing fetish with superstition generally, with witchcraft absolutely, with spirit recognition in all forms whatever. This is merely to confuse, to level up all terms to one, and empty them one and all **of** specific meaning. Miss Kingsley, **in** my idea, has so far done this. She identifies *fetish* with *ju ju,* **which** she **says is a toy, a** doll ; and then she proceeds **to present many instances of the** " gods of fetish, who," mark you, " do **not require a material** object to manifest themselves **in."** Now, **look at that.** There is fetish *and* there **are** gods of fetish. **Are** they one **and the same,** or what, or has Miss Kingsley done **there a bit of** verbal juggling or thimble-rigging ?

If they are the same, why speak of fetish and gods of *fetish ?* Language is against Miss Kingsley there ; a god and that of which he is a god are two distinct things, and no clever process of verbal juggling can make them *one.* The Philistines and the god of the Philistines are two things : Baelzebub, the god of Flies, and the flies are two distinct things : so the gods of fetish are, on the same analogy, different from the fetishes. And this about Baelzebub is not in the least affected by learned theories about gods being anointed with oil and so attracting flies more in some places than others, etc., etc.

Tando is the high god of Ashantee. Is he a fetish, or a god of fetishes—or what is he ?

Fetish carries with it immediately the idea of some material, in which a spirit is supposed to reside. One great speculator on religions and races of men holds that the fetish strictly is that chosen by and pertains to the individual. Each man can have his own fetish, which would thus be something allied to the personal totems chosen by individuals in other tribes, though because of the sympathetic and imitative powers in men, they tend to run in groups each choosing a material like the others for fetish, whilst all spirits apprehended as detached from special fixed presence and locality thus are something different. That distinction would at least aid us a certain way to clearness. But, when we hear that the Mburri of the Mpongwe comes in the form of a man, Nkala as a crab, and great nzambi Mpungu only as pestilence or tempest ; then, it is clear, these are not, under the distinction given above, *fetishes,* but something else. It does not help matters a bit to tell us that fetish is

not truly pantheistic—in fact, such remarks are misleading, and can only gain credit from the thoughtless.
Pantheism is the most highly abstract of modes of
thinking, and abstraction is not characteristic of
savage thought, where perceptions of distinction are
not finely manifest. When Miss Kingsley quotes
certain civilized philosophic verses she is far out.
" The African has a great over-god, and below him
lesser spirits, including man " [no, not man, but the
assumed spirit of man], " but the African has not a
god-man." Here is proof of the want of power of
abstraction of which I spoke, cited as though it tended
wholly the other way about. Besides, is this over-
god of the African a fetish, or a god of fetish, or
what strictly is he? or does he really remain fixed
in properly abstract quality, as we are led to suppose,
that in their conceptions assumed human spirits with
them do? " The class of spirits that are human souls
always remain human souls;" and this, according
to Miss Kingsley, explains the non-worship of
ancestors over large spaces she is concerned with.
Good Heavens! of all I have yet read and heard,
it is the conception of human spirits remaining
always human spirits that is the *fons et origo* of
worship of ancestors: the human spirit, without the
impedimenta of bodily organ like ours, able to move
about and penetrate where a body could not, but
still—pure human spirit alike in vice and hatred, in
possible joy and sympathy and help—this is the root-
idea alike of Burmese Nats, and of all other worshipped
ancestors in India, China, etc., etc.

Miss Kingsley speaks of the African thus : " You
will see him," she writes, " before starting out to

fight or hunt rubbing medicine into his weapons to
strengthen the spirits within them, talking to them
the while," etc., etc. Are these spirits fetish, are
they human spirits, or what ? An answer will oblige
—a definite and clear answer.

We are told there are fourteen classes of spirits in
fetish, but, alas ! we are not favoured with a clear
list of them. Others, we are told, reduce them to
six. In Miss Kingsley's fourteen are all spirits known
and recognised by these Africans included as spirits
in fetish, and is the over-god included too, and the
human spirits always fixed as human spirits ? She
says what is given to human spirits are gifts, not
sacrifices, and would fain on this raise a very large
and important distinction. Now in all languages I
know, gift [= offering, which is just gift] and sacrifice,
offering of food, the words originally are the same ;
מִנְחָה ın the Hebrew itself, is gift originally ; and
more discussion has taken place over this than
perhaps over any other word, more hair-splitting
and ingenuity to try to bring it definitely to cover
the same area as the זֶבַח. Precisely, the same
in the Roman—in all languages ; there is no distinction of the kind Miss Kingsley would set up—
none. Why, Mr. Addis in his " Hexateuch " (Nutt)
most elaborately shows that what supports the idea of
some special something in Jewish sacrifices are mere
glosses, and that the earlier and truer conception
shines through all, through all that these were gifts of
food, etc., for the Manes, and that Jahwé to the last
in the minds of the masses remained strangely mixed
up with them. Professor Robertson Smith practically
said the very same about the Hebrew Shewbread—

hat it was *ipso facto*, identical with the *lectisternia* of heathenism, at which the gods were persuaded to come and lie on couches and eat their spiritual share of it.

The distinction between gift and sacrifice raised by Miss Kingsley is thus unscientific and even ignorant; and certainly is crassly misleading. Gifts offered to ancestors are—in my idea, supported by a wide survey indeed—the origin of all offering and sacrifice, and as I read Miss Kingsley's chapters, so far as facts crop up in them, I find they all make in one way—completely different from what she means and fancies; and that quite unconsciously she supports her friend, Mr. Batty of Cape Coast, "in indicating nothing but a stage in the worship of ancestors": much more than she as yet perceives will she find this to be "fear of the ancestor-ghost hunting members of its own family," because setting aside notions of incarnation with Nki and Ewe in certain parts, there is a class of human ghosts called the well-disposed ones, which are ancestors undoubtedly; and it has, moreover, to be pointed out that the fact of being well disposed does not in one iota in itself prove the existence of ancestors worshipped, but rather the fact of being ill-disposed does this—the demon quality in the ancestor being that which is most present to the mind of the worshipper on earth. Hence Grimm says that there is no devil in the religion of early or savage peoples; their gods (ancestors) are their devils! "Human spirits always remain human spirits"; and in nothing is this more marked than in readiness to avenge any neglect, indifference, or failure to conciliate. But I cannot follow or understand Miss Kingsley here.

A friend of mine, Mr. E. T. Head—one of the

H.   T engineers engaged on the Tarkwa Railway, just returned home on furlough—tells me that the Fantees are most faithful in observing the feast of the full moon; they bring firearms and discharge them with all the noise they can, they beat tum-tums, have songs and dances, and utter prayers and petitions for fruitfulness and fortune, one of their names for the moon really being fortune or luck;[1] the whole proceedings being clearly acts of worship. If the Fantees celebrate the full moon and worship it, I should like to know from Miss Kingsley whether the full moon is fetish or what it is?

Mr. Head also described to me the ceremonial at burial with the Fantees, among whom he was and whose customs he had good opportunities of observing. When a person dies, the fact is announced by loud beating of drums, etc., etc., the friends and relatives gather, a goat or kid is killed, and its blood sprinkled over the coffin or covering, and the flesh of it is cut up into small fragments; a portion being given to each one present, who either plants it in the ground or preserves it for luck. With reference to this, I should like to ask Miss Kingsley whether there is no clear trace of worship of ancestors here, and whether this is a portion of fetish worship properly?

Not a little else that Mr. Head told me alike of the Fantees and other races with which he was brought into contact, so far as I can see, conflicts with Miss Kingsley's deliverances, but these, meanwhile, will suffice.

[1] Had I known this fact when I wrote the note at p. 15, I would have added this there, as a most extraordinary instance of similarity of idea and practice at distant points.

XII.—PROFESSOR RHYS ON CÆSAR AND THE CELTIC BRITONS.

CÆSAR describes the Celts of England as painting themselves with woad, as clothed in skins, and as wearing moustaches, but no beards, and he says that they practised polyandry—fraternal polyandry. A number of brothers lived together, having one wife in common. Professor Rhys will not admit that this is possible. He thinks Cæsar was either misled by the fact of a number of brothers sharing one home under the *patria potestas;* or else that he had heard reports about some people of an earlier race in remote corners, and applied it to the Britons.

" So far from this having been the custom of the Celts of Britain, it is not certain that it can have been to any great extent that of any Aryan people whatsoever." [1]

As regards some Aryan peoples in respect to this and to some other things we have already dealt with them, and may elsewhere have some more to say soon.

Professor Rhys would also have it that the painting with woad was only an occasional thing—when going to war or to some great ceremony. I was disappointed that I could find in Professor Rhys's index or books no reference whatever to infanticide or to human

[1] Rhys, " Celtic Britain," p. 55.

T 2

sacrifice. Does the Professor maintain that the British Celts were entirely innocent here where savage races almost without exception were guilty, showed no trace of certain of the other phenomena which almost always go along with infanticide— certain forms of promiscuity, nigh to polyandry? Grimm confesses to some habits of early Teutonic tribes which hardly bear out Professor Rhys's idea in last clause of sentence quoted above—a peculiar kind of marital communism or legalised promiscuity, and we have traces of the same thing in India among Hindus, and certainly there are some passages in the Mahabarata that lean that way and to utmost sexual grossness. Again, what does his philological argument from *caws* (cheese), as derived from the Latin caseis, avail him? If derived from the Latin, it could not have been in existence before the Romans, and the legitimate argument from that would be that they had not the thing, else a word with no suspicion of Roman alliance or derivation would have been found for it. Is there such an ancient word?

XIII.—LANG AND "JAHVÉ."

MR. ANDREW LANG is, despite modest, over modest asseverations to the contrary, one of the greatest Hebraists that ever lived, and naturally concerns himself with themes that are related to Hebrew and Oriental tongues. Thus, in a recent "Longman's Magazine," he sets down the result of the most sober and extensive researches in conflicting derivations of the Jahvé name thus :—

"When the Teutonic judges of the Old Testament wander into anthropology, as they often do, then one knows where to have them. The people, of course, *does* not know where to have them, and is likely to swallow their statements about 'Animism' and 'Fetishism,' and so on. For instance, they dispute as to Jehovah's name being :—

            Indo-Germanic.
            { Assyrian.
            { Babylonian.
            Egyptian.
            Kenite.
        Canaanite.

Is it the Indo-Germanic root, *div'* ;
        or Armenian, *Astvat ;*
        or Babylonian, Ia-h ;
                    { *Ioh* (Moon God !)
        or Egyptian {   or
                    { *Nuk-pu-Nuk* (translated) ;

Or, is the name of Hebrew origin? The people *have* a right to know. But nobody knows."

[Mr. L. might condescend to look after singular and plural verbs. Here, like a freeman, he has it both ways.]

Really, now, the *naïveté* of Mr. Lang putting Nuk-pu-Nuk just there overcomes me, as though he were like a child again. Nuk-pu-Nuk, translated, gives in Hebrew the well-known אֶהְיֶה אֲשֶׁר אֶהְיֶה, " I am that I am"—quite a different thing, tracing to different roots altogether from Jahvé.

And there is more than this arises in such attempt to identify Nuk-pu-Nuk and Jahvé. It was Elohim and not Jahvé that told Moses at Exod. iii. 14, " I am that I am" = Ehjeh asher Ehjeh, and that told Moses to say unto Israel, " I am " hath sent me unto you. Mr. Andrew Lang in his keen desire to let people know " where he has them "—the German critics—rather goes astray himself in not distinguishing where he might easily have distinguished between Jahvistic and Elohistic, and so have aided to let the people know a little. But what confusion of ideas is here. Mr. Lang, like Mr. Grant Allen, seems to think that wherever God or Lord appears in the Authorised Version the original is Jahvé. But it is not, it is often Elohim and Eloah, El Shaddai and even Baal. He might do better, in our idea, in tracing derivations FROM Jahvé than in tracing origins of it.

And yet wait a wee, wait a wee. One thing he omits, significantly omits, to trace the Ea, Io, Ia, Ya, Iao, Yao, Iah or Yah, and Yahu, and to identify this Yahu with the *Yahoo* of Dean Swift. Dean Swift was a scholar, and knew more than appears.

Nor does **Mr. Lang** trace out the relation of Jahvé and Yakhvè, which would have brought him by a single round slant back to the same point. Mr. Grant Allen might also put his mind into this matter, for he too has found Jahvé, yes, *found* Jahvé, where he has certainly no right to find him, and in company with **Mr.** Andrew Lang might do a lot to find him elsewhere: perhaps in Io, Ea, El, etc., who knows?

Nor is the **Yahu =** Yahoo, after all, quite so improbable or impossible. We know what has come of the *baga*, *buga*—god—of certain **tongues.** From its being, as Jahvé was, associated so closely with fear, it came at last to be used as a sound to frighten babies with—the mother-tongue, **like** mother-right, triumphant—hence *bug*-bear, *buga*boo, *bogie*, *bug*, and by combination of two, *humbug*. When the little ragged-school **Sunday scholar** in Edinburgh told his teacher, **on being asked,** "What was the Pestilence that walketh **in darkness?**" that it "maun be the bugs 'cause they **aye** come out at nicht!" he was a bit of an unconscious or farseeing evolutionist, and his mythological critical example is to be recommended to **Mr.** Andrew Lang and Mr. Grant Allen—*arcades ambo* on their going backward **instead of** forward.

In the Hebrew **there is no neuter.** All things animate or inanimate—sun, sky, **moon,** stars, earth, wisdom, **wit,** thought, emotion — are all either masculine or **feminine, and with** regard to the great inanimate presences **of nature they** are feminine mostly. The **Hebrew thus should,** above all languages, carry **down in its** naming **of such** objects the deposit from **a time when,** as Mr. **Andrew** Lang says, the **people thought they** saw **sex in** these things, and

gave them names accordingly. And indeed, in a
certain way, the thing would not work out badly
at all in his favour here—only in the last results he
must take the penalties as well as the prizes. For,
you see, Mr. Andrew Lang must go the whole hog,
and not profess to go the whole hog and cunningly
turn back halfway just when it suits him. In this
Hebrew there was literally nothing without sex,
without life, without individuality, the mountains,
without any stretch of metaphor, with the Hebrews,
clapped hands; the sun, a strong man, each day
ran his race and rejoiced in it too; the sea rose up
and raged; the stars in their courses fought; and
so on. It was favourable to poetry of a certain
kind; but to some other things it was not favourable.
But since the great inanimate objects of nature were
feminine, how did it ever come, on Mr. Lang's
theory, that they found and gave supreme place to
a god like Jahvé, who had in him nothing of
feminine, a non-begetting but wholly male monster?
According to all analogy, the Hebrews should have
had a feminine god, with a whole pantheon of
feminine gods around her.

In respect of no neuter Hebrew is typical of all
the Semitic tongues. None of them have any
neuter. Now, in Arabic, you see clearly that they
went for the feminine—had three tremendous female
gods—and the worship was entirely consistent with
their femininity. Professor Rhys Davids certainly
has it all in his favour here as bearing out that idea
in his Buddhism (American lectures), that the earlier
gods were all feminine. And even after Mohammed
the clear traces of this earlier worship of female

deities remained, remained in a thousand forms, remains even to-day. But the Jews, with precisely the same predisposition in the naming of the great objects of nature feminine, according to their Scriptures, show no tendency of the sort. We have no female god named or acknowledged : we have no recognition, in truth, of the great fact Mr. Lang swears by, that early men saw sex in the great objects of nature and named them accordingly. How do Mr. A. Lang and Professor Rhys Davids account for this—account for the very surprising difference between Hebrews and Arabs, as we find them here—account for the very astonishing difference between the confession of their Scriptures on this head? Yet in Hebrew אֱלֹהִים is used, literally used for a goddess at 1 Kings xi. 5. How do these two gentlemen account for that? Definite and clear answers will much oblige, no humbug—עשתרת.

NOTE.—Since this volume was printed, it is with the utmost regret that I have heard of Mr. Grant Allen's death. But so far as I have dealt with him, it is on *principles*, just as I have dealt with Sir Henry Maine, and strictly there is no personality there. The books remain, and are still to be judged as substantive contributions, or what the writers aimed at being such, to science and to literature. Mr. Grant Allen was utterly a stranger to me—the one letter I did venture to address to him about some points in what he wrote on the cuneiform I am sorry to say that he never answered, or, if he did, his answer never reached me. I have on these accounts the less reserve in letting this essay go exactly as I wrote it, in the full belief that it would be read by him. His friends and admirers may do him the service of defending his book and him, and I shall be very glad to see their efforts : his book, in my idea, introduces a bad example, and assuredly in some things this example of his should not be commended or followed.

INDEX.

THE END.

BRADBURY, AGNEW, & CO. LD., PRINTERS, LONDON AND TONBRIDGE.

BY THE SAME AUTHOR.

JUST PUBLISHED.

WITH ILLUSTRATIONS.

"OUR COMMON CUCKOOS, OTHER CUCKOOS AND PARASITICAL BIRDS."

Price 6s.

DR. JAPP has for years past devoted time to Ornithological Study, and here the results of his observations on the habits of Cuckoos are presented.

As the Author does not **find** himself altogether in favour **of the** views of Mr. Darwin and **Mr.** Romanes, this book cannot **fail to** interest students, while the popular way in which it is written **will appeal** to all lovers of nature and bird life.

CONTENTS.

PART I.—STRANGE POINTS IN LIFE HISTORY OF *CUCULUS CANORUS:* OUR COMMON CUCKOO.

PART II.—FURTHER STRANGE TRAITS AND SOME DEFINITE RESULTS.

PART III.—MR. DARWIN AND MR. ROMANES DEALT WITH.

PART IV.—EVIDENCE FROM ALL PARTS OF THE WORLD.—THE FACTS WHOLLY AGAINST MR. DARWIN AND HIS FOLLOWERS.

PART V.—STRANGE FACTS ABOUT CALLS AND YOUNG BIRDS OF *CUCULUS CANORUS.*

---

*Publisher—*THOMAS BURLEIGH, 17, Cecil Court, W.C.

AT ALL LIBRARIES.

"HER PART."

A NOVEL OF REAL LIFE.

BY

A. N. MOUNT ROSE.

8vo. 6s.

OPINIONS OF THE PRESS.

" A pleasant story of village life."—*Academy*.

" An interesting and distinctly promising work."—*Observer*.

" The scenes of the story mostly lie in the village of Derlington, and the rustic gossip and scandal of a place where each makes it his business to know the business of his neighbours, is very well done. It is a book with much promise in it."—*Lloyd's Weekly Newspaper*, October 15th, 1899.

" The story opens well with some excellent rustics, and maintains a level of more than average excellence."—*Outlook*, October 7th, 1899.

" A story of considerable merit. . . . The scene is laid for most part in the village of Derlington, in which Mrs. Winyard, with her young son, resides during her supposed widowhood, and the humours of village life are very happily hit off, the talk of the inhabitants being given in. dialect. Some of the minor characters are strongly drawn, especially Helen Rayner, who rejects Peter Gray, the Grocer's assistant, but finally marries him. Then a music-loving vicar and his sister are also very capably pourtrayed, and, by the way, there are some capital songs in the volume."—*Scotsman*, October 9th, 1899.

" Miss MOUNT ROSE has the root of the matter in her, and shows a gift for lyrical expression. As a new writer, she claims consideration, and her book is so good that it deserves to find appreciative readers."—*Sheffield Telegraph*.

" Bears marks of considerable care in the writing, and a good deal of thought has been given to the characters."—*Manchester Guardian*.

THOMAS BURLEIGH, 17, Cecil Court, W.C.

www.ingramcontent.com/pod-product-compliance
Lightning Source LLC
Chambersburg PA
CBHW020930120726
47905CB00008B/2461